ADVANCE PRAISE

"Sherye writes about a subject that I've witnessed firsthand in my time as a Juvenile Drug Court Coordinator. I came across many youths, like DeSean, who were at the wrong place at the wrong time and needed someone to see their potential. I love how Sherye captures his story and shares truth in such a poignant way for believers to see the power we hold in knowing when to stand for others who genuinely need Christ's mercy. We should never underestimate the power of a second chance."

—**Katie L. Trundt, Esq.**
Former Madison County Juvenile Drug Court Coordinator
Birmingham, Alabama

"Once again, Sherye Green has written a book that is so easy to read. Once you finish the story, you feel you know each character personally! In getting to know these characters and their situations, it reminds me that God, in His infinite wisdom, takes care of each of us! As a former Youth Court Counselor, I was particularly interested in reading about godly people stepping up to assist children in need. What a blessing!!!! Even though we have to go through dark valleys in our lives, God often allows us to go through them so we will appreciate the mountaintops!"

—**Kathy Mumbower**
Former Youth Court Counselor
Clinton, Mississippi

Through a Dark Valley

Sherye S. Green

an imprint of Sunbury Press, Inc.
Mechanicsburg, PA USA

an imprint of Sunbury Press, Inc.
Mechanicsburg, PA USA

For information about special discounts for bulk purchases, please contact Sunbury Press Orders Dept. at (855) 338-8359 or orders@sunburypress.com.

To request one of our authors for speaking engagements or book signings, please contact Sunbury Press Publicity Dept. at publicity@sunburypress.com.

Scripture quotations marked (GNT) are from the Good News Translation in Today's English Version, Second Edition Copyright © 1992 by American Bible Society. Used by permission.

Scripture taken from the International Children's Bible®. Copyright © 1986, 1988, 1999 by Thomas Nelson. Used by permission. All rights reserved.

Scripture quotations taken from the (NASB®) New American Standard Bible®, Copyright © 1960, 1971, 1977, 1995 by The Lockman Foundation. Used by permission. All rights reserved. lockman.org.

Scripture quotations taken from the (NASB®) New American Standard Bible®, Copyright © 1960, 1971, 1977, 1995, 2020 by The Lockman Foundation. Used by permission. All rights reserved. lockman.org.

Scripture quotations marked (NLT) are taken from the Holy Bible, New Living Translation, copyright ©1996, 2004, 2015 by Tyndale House Foundation. Used by permission of Tyndale House Publishers, Carol Stream, Illinois 60188. All rights reserved.

Scripture quotations marked MSG are taken from The Message, copyright © 1993, 2002, 2018 by Eugene H. Peterson. Used by permission of NavPress. All rights reserved. Represented by Tyndale House Publishers.

FIRST SCRIPTORIA PRESS EDITION: May 2024

Set in Adobe Garamond Pro | Interior design by Crystal Devine | Cover by Lawrence Knorr | Edited by Sarah Peachey.

Publisher's Cataloging-in-Publication Data
Names: Green, Sherye S., author.
Title: Through a dark valley / Sherye S. Green.
Description: First trade paperback edition. | Mechanicsburg, PA : Scriptoria Press, 2024.
Summary: *Through a Dark Valley*, Book Two in The Timothy House Chronicles, continues the story of Abbie Richardson and Keith Haliday—two individuals who have suffered incredible losses. They are discovering that hope can spring anew despite deep sorrow and heartache. Abbie and Keith, navigating a developing romance with each other, will battle dark forces that threaten Timothy House, the school on whose faculty they serve. *Through a Dark Valley* is a testimony that God's love and life-changing power can redeem even the most difficult circumstances.
Identifiers: ISBN : 978-1-62006-536-5 (softcover).
Subjects: FICTION / Christian / General | FICTION / Christian / Contemporary | FICTION / Religion.

Designed in the USA
0 1 1 2 3 5 8 13 21 34 55

For the Love of Books!

This book is dedicated with tremendous admiration and respect
to those who serve to protect the lives of children
and ensure their safety.
May your hearts be fearless,
your devotion unwavering,
your principles uncompromising,
and your endeavors triumphant
as you battle great forces of darkness.
May God equip and empower you for every good work
and grant you success.

Even if I walk through a very dark valley,
I will not be afraid because you are with me.
Your rod and your shepherd's staff comfort me.

—Psalm 23:4 (ICB)

CHAPTER

1

In order for evil to go unnoticed, it only need stay below the radar. Blend into the crowd. Fade into the woodwork. This little corner of northeastern Tennessee, particularly the little town of Robbinsonville, seemed the perfect place where Durrell "C.J." Dykes could blend in. His job as an auto mechanic put him in contact with a wide variety of individuals. His sporadic attendance at Great Harvest Church gave him a leg-up on building a reputation as a Bible-toting Sunday man. His workstation at Howard's Tire and Auto offered him countless hiding places for his drug of choice—methamphetamine.

Now age twenty-two, C.J., short for Cool Juice, had the wiles of a jackal and the cunning of a fox. A high school dropout by age sixteen, C.J. had come from a long line of others taking the same path. In fact, he had endured the educational system of a small Illinois town longer than any of his kin. Resistance to the establishment, a disdain for authority in general, and a belief that too much education only ruined your natural smarts were cherished values in the Dykes family.

Wheat-colored, naturally curly hair cascaded down onto his shoulders, often causing him to shake it out of his dark brown eyes, eyes that had only become more hardened as years passed. C.J. was of average height, broad-shouldered, and stocky and was friendly with a weight bench if the rippled muscles under his grease-stained T-shirt were any indication. His square hands looked like two medium-sized hams, his blunt fingers often darkened with grease and motor oil. The young man was pleasing in appearance, with a square jaw and ruddy complexion that helped him maintain a lie about being younger than he actually was.

He was just plain enough, though, to be easily forgotten. C.J. thought that happened to be one of his most advantageous physical qualities. He looked like a hundred other guys.

Since dropping out of high school almost seven years ago, C.J. had managed to stay one step ahead of the law. So far, those he knew in Robbinsonville were none the wiser. He'd perfected a method of rolling down the windows, cranking up the fan, and turning down the thermostat on the air conditioner while driving drunk. He'd done it too many times to count, all without being stopped by the police.

Two years ago, though, he'd had a close call. A highway patrolman approaching at a high rate of speed with lights blazing had just about scared him witless. But on that night, lady luck must have been with him, for the trooper had sped past him into the night, obviously in pursuit of bigger fish. The incident served to add yet another layer of Teflon to C.J.'s coat of armor. He believed himself to be untouchable.

Howard's Tire and Auto was well respected in the Robbinsonville community. Bill Howard, the owner, was a deacon at Great Harvest Church and an involved member of many local civic organizations. His twin daughters were in the eleventh grade at Timothy House. When C.J. had arrived in town eighteen months ago, Bill had been reluctant to hire him. The young man had shown up at the store's front counter one Tuesday, appearing as if out of thin air. Although he had no references, the new hire sailed through his probationary period.

C.J. had an uncanny mechanical nature and lots of experience working with car engines. In the years since high school, he had hotwired at least a dozen cars in Illinois, Tennessee, and the states between, selling vehicles to local chop shops and using the cash to live until necessity forced him to hotwire another. He could not, however, share that tidbit of information with Mr. Bill, what the other employees at the body shop were wont to call the boss.

Robbinsonville was located just ten miles off Interstate 81, a major thoroughfare in this part of the state. Like the hub of a bicycle wheel, the town formed part of a drug dealer's dream circle, connecting easily with other numbers on the dial: Bristol—one o'clock, Johnson City—four o'clock, Jonesborough—five o'clock, Greeneville—seven o'clock, Rogersville—nine o'clock, and Kingsport—twelve o'clock.

C.J. had been patient long enough. The time had come for action.

CHAPTER

2

DeSean Matthews was a needy soul. He was a ship afloat with no harbor, a wave needing a safe beach to crash upon. There was none. Plagued at an early age by a series of mishaps and calamitous circumstances, DeSean had lost anyone who had ever meant anything to him. At seventeen, he had about given up hope of ever finding love and acceptance. Annette Matthews, DeSean's mother, died from a drug overdose when DeSean was four. Her mother, Lurlene Covington, had tried to step in and help her son-in-law's family after her daughter's death. That arrangement, however, didn't last too long.

To put it mildly, DeSean's father, Audie Matthews, and Lurlene hated each other. She was a divorcée, too old to dress the way she did. Needy for male attention, she did not want to be tied down to a four-year-old grandson. The nightlife and sweet-talking men won out. For the next four years, DeSean was left alone for hours at a time. The television quickly became his source of comfort. Oddly enough, television also became his means of learning the English language.

When DeSean was eight, his father, in a fit of rage, threw down a lit cigarette into an oil slick in the parking lot of the neighborhood gas station. Audie hadn't even gotten out of his car. He just slowed to a crawl and tossed the nub of his Camel through the open window of his late model Trans Am. The pumps blew up within a matter of minutes. A customer sitting outside in a car in the parking lot barely escaped alive.

Audie was caught an hour later, going about ninety-two on I-40, heading toward Nashville. An eyewitness at Mason's Grocery, located across the street from the gas station, positively identified him from a lineup. Audie was now serving a twenty-five-year sentence for arson and attempted murder in the Riverbend Maximum Security Institution.

After Audie went to the pen, DeSean, an only child, was taken from his grandmother's custody and herded through several foster homes by the Tennessee Department of Children's Services. Most had been well-meaning do-gooders who had opened their homes with admirable intentions but had never fully allowed their hearts to get involved with the boy. Unable to deal with the complex demands of foster parenting, each family had, one by one, dumped DeSean back onto the lap of child services.

For the last eighteen months, DeSean had been living in the home of Max and Edna Smith, a kind-hearted couple living in Jonesborough, a small town about eight miles southwest of Johnson City. The pair had offered the troubled teen the most stable home environment he had experienced up to this point in his life. DeSean had come to live with the Smiths when he was fifteen, about a month into the first semester of his sophomore year in high school.

Max helped the boy enroll in David Crockett High School, named for Tennessee's legendary hero, Davy Crockett. One of five high schools in Washington County, the school had a decent boys' basketball program. A few weeks after DeSean had arrived at the school, the basketball coach, who lived nearby, drove past the Smith home one afternoon and noticed DeSean out shooting hoops in the driveway. Impressed with the teen's shooting skills, the coach stopped the car, introduced himself, and asked to speak to the young man's family. The next thing DeSean knew, he was sporting a brown and gold jersey as a member of the Pioneer Boys' Basketball team.

DeSean quickly discovered there were several problems with being a high school athlete. First, practice took up all his free time. He didn't have any other plans for his time, but because he'd been alone for so much of his life, the forced camaraderie was a little overwhelming. Most days, DeSean felt awkward and out of sorts with the other guys on the team.

Second, athletes were expected to succeed in the classroom, as well as perform the same on the court. Although possessing a quick mind, DeSean had never had the personal attention of a devoted parent to help him develop good study habits and foster an enthusiasm for learning. Max and Edna arranged to have a church friend, a retired teacher, tutor DeSean twice a week.

Third, athletes not only had to balance the playing field and the classroom, but also had to navigate the mysterious and oftentimes hazardous maze of peer pressure. Although a little rough around the edges, DeSean was generally well mannered and seemed to have been easily accepted into the Crockett High student body. A part of his soul, though, yearned for friends who would not desert him as had his mother, grandmother, and father.

The past year at Crockett High had been difficult and depressing. DeSean heard repeatedly, from both teachers and academic counselors, how challenging the junior year of high school could be. The nine-month period had lived up to its reputation. Despite successes on the basketball court, DeSean had not gained traction in any other area of school life. He felt isolated and much different than his peers. Although he had developed a few relationships, those were shallow at best. Even when with a group of guys his age, DeSean felt like a fifth wheel.

The classroom was a puzzle DeSean had never figured out how to construct. Perhaps because he had been on his own for much of his young life, he was wary of others, especially adults. The teen said little during class periods and rarely asked questions of his teachers. For some unknown reason, DeSean could make better sense of homework assignments or get a handle on the material to be covered on a test, especially in sessions with Miss Karen, the tutor Mr. and Mrs. Smith had hired to work with him. However, by the time he reached the classroom, much of that understanding had escaped him.

DeSean was tired, and his spirit was exhausted. Even though Pioneer was the name of the Crockett High School athletic teams, the term *pioneer* described how he often felt when bushwhacking his way through the deep forests and difficult terrain of personal relationships. The years of being bounced around from family to family had taken its toll on him. He was distrustful and suspicious and had constructed a thick wall of protection around his heart. Max and Edna Smith had certainly done their best to provide a loving home for DeSean, but during these last few years of high school, DeSean felt more disoriented than ever, as if lost in a dark wood with no compass or shovel or flashlight.

From where would his rescue come?

CHAPTER
3

Abbie stopped her SUV in the gravel driveway and sat for a few minutes after turning off the ignition. The three-hour drive from McHenry to Robbinsonville on this Monday morning had taken less time than she had expected. So much had occurred since her last day at Kent Academy sixteen days ago. The surprise going-away party planned by her homeroom class. The luncheon Winnie Jeffers hosted in her home with other Kent Academy colleagues. Arthur Patterson's retirement celebration. The special dinner Lane and Eric Wyatt held in honor of Abbie and Drew, at which Beulah Tanner and Winnie were also in attendance. Abbie had replayed every detail during the drive.

Drew had been home since his graduation from college, and mother and son had spent the past three weeks cleaning out closets, going through the attic, and taking piles of old clothes and unwanted household goods to the Goodwill donation center. As Abbie was still unsure of selling the house, she had decided to rent it to a new staff member at her church.

One Sunday in April, at the end of the morning service, Abbie's pastor, Carter Franklin, introduced her to Stephanie Williams, who was coming on board as a new associate on the music staff. As the two talked that day, Abbie realized her need to have someone live in her home could meet Stephanie's need for a place to live.

Later that afternoon, the young woman came over and was instantly taken with Abbie's home. Like Abbie, she liked spending time outdoors in the garden and seemed especially enthralled with Abbie's patio area and backyard. The two enjoyed a glass of iced tea and a plate of homemade oatmeal cookies in Abbie's den. The more they talked, the more Abbie felt God's confirmation that Stephanie would indeed be the perfect person to rent her home.

A phone call that evening with Dr. Franklin assured Abbie that Stephanie was indeed the person she appeared to be. Her pastor's recommendation sealed the deal. Four days later, a rental contract was drawn up, and the lease was signed for one year.

Keith had called many times in those weeks, and their relationship had deepened in the way one only can when two people discover more of what is hidden within the other's heart and mind. Even so, Abbie still hesitated to let herself feel too much, to invest too much emotion in Keith. Although more than five years had passed since Joe's death and the revelation of his misdeeds came to light, the deep wounds his betrayal carved into her soul sometimes felt like an abyss, too deep and dark and wide for any bridge of love to traverse.

Finally, Abbie arrived in Robbinsonville, and a few minutes later, she was driving through the stone gates of Timothy House. She followed the main drive until it forked to the left toward the student residences on the west side of the campus. Mistletoe Cottage came into view around the next turn.

God, You are up to something good, Abbie thought as she turned off the car and reached for her keys. *I still can't believe I'm really here at Timothy House. Please be with me on this new journey.*

Abbie got out and walked over to the base of the three stone steps that led up to the wide porch of Mistletoe Cottage. How had her dear friend Audry often reminded her? "God may be waiting on you to make the first move, and then He'll show you the rest of the way."

Audry must be smiling down from Heaven, Abbie thought, *to see this new provision from the Lord. Accepting this job was my move. I'm waiting on you, Lord, for the rest of the plan.*

Walking back to her SUV, Abbie pushed the button and lifted the rear hatch. As the electronic door slowly rose, she moved quickly to grab a grocery sack that threatened to tumble out. As she began taking items out, she heard the sound of footsteps behind her. Abbie turned around to find Don Fielding, Keith Haliday, and Josh Hastings heading her way.

"Hey, guys," Abbie said brightly.

A collective "Hello" came from the men.

"We thought we'd help you get settled in," said Keith as he reached into the back of the vehicle and pulled out a crate of books. He shifted the heavy box in his grasp. "This is quite a collection you have here."

Don and Josh likewise grabbed armfuls of assorted suitcases, bags of various sizes, and hanging clothes.

Keith and Josh feigned collapse under the weight of what they were carrying. Immediately, both men smiled and laughed out loud when Abbie met their gaze.

"You bring enough?" Don ribbed cheerfully. "I wouldn't want you to go without."

"Yes, I know I probably packed too much," said Abbie a bit sheepishly. "I wanted to make sure I had all that I needed, especially when making my lesson plans."

Looking toward Keith, Abbie nodded to the heavy box of books nestled securely in his arms. "Those books are some of my most prized possessions," she said seriously. "See that you handle them with care." Her bright smile that followed let him know she was a good sport.

Abbie moved ahead of the three men to hold open the cottage door. As she stepped across the threshold of this stone cottage reminiscent of a Beatrix Potter illustration, Abbie smiled to herself. *This is the start of a new season!*

Once the group had ferried all the belongings inside for the newest member of the Timothy House faculty, Don walked Abbie through her new home. The interior reminded her greatly of Lane and Eric Wyatt's cabin, the Resting Place, which, over the years, they had graciously allowed her to use as a retreat. A worn, river rock chase on the fireplace. Stained, wide-planked heart pine floors. Tall ceilings that added an airy touch to the rooms.

The foursome ended back up in the great room, bright summer sun streaming through the paned windows.

"Why don't we sit down for a minute," Abbie said, gesturing toward two sofas and several wing chairs. "You guys have been working too hard. Let's rest for a bit."

"Don't mind if we do," said Don, lowering his stocky frame into a nearby chair.

Josh settled on one sofa. Abbie and Keith found places on the other.

"Tell me about the history of this cottage, Don," encouraged Abbie. "It's such a beautiful place."

"When Uncle Roger and Aunt Marie bought this property in 1939," Don explained with pride as he settled back into the chair, "most of the buildings were already here." His gaze swept over the room. "Mistletoe Cottage was one of the first buildings built."

"Was there a school already here?" Abbie asked.

"There was, but one of a different kind. All the structures built in 1937 comprised the new campus of a seminary that had been a respected institution in this part of Tennessee for many years, as the school had outgrown its previous location. However, the strain of the Great Depression proved too much for the college, and it closed its doors due to poor enrollment and bankruptcy in 1938."

Abbie listened intently.

"I've probably already told you some of this story about how Timothy House came to be," said Don, "so stop me if I have." He waited for her response.

"I know some of it, but what you've just shared is all new to me. Please continue."

Josh spoke up. "I'm even learning some new chapters of this story."

Keith nodded, waiting for Don to continue. Even though Keith and Josh were familiar with the history of Timothy House, they were always amazed to glean new insights each time their boss, Don, told the cherished story of the school's founding.

"My dear aunt and uncle were never able to have children of their own. Roger's dad, my great-uncle Ted, had started a lumber company in 1910, Stevenson Timber Company. Roger was ten years old that year, and quickly became his dad's little helper. Ted taught Roger all he knew about the timber industry. In the early twentieth century, much of the timber cut in Tennessee was in the western and central regions, near Memphis and Chattanooga. Due to more rugged mountainous conditions, much of the forests of eastern Tennessee remained uncut. This part of the state was a veritable gold mine waiting to be tapped."

Abbie, Keith, and Josh were mesmerized by Don's account.

"Roger's dad died suddenly of a heart attack in 1927 at the age of fifty-two. Roger took over the leadership of the company. Despite the fact that he was only twenty-seven, the expertise and wisdom he gained through all those years of tagging along at his daddy's side would now pay off."

"How sad," Abbie murmured.

"It was sad," agreed Don, "but God, as He always does, turned that tragedy into a blessing. When Roger's daddy died, Stevenson Timber was a million-dollar company, which in 1927 was saying quite a lot, especially here in Tennessee. By the time Roger and Marie decided to purchase this property, Roger had developed the timber company into a multi-million-dollar organization.

"For the next three years after purchasing the land and buildings in 1939, Roger and Marie worked tirelessly in their spare time to refurbish the buildings and develop a plan to begin a school. Although they were never able to have children of their own, my aunt and uncle were fortunate to have grown up in families that provided them with fine educations and many opportunities, including summer camps and trips to many places. Believing that God expects His children to invest and grow the talents He has given to them, Roger and Marie decided to put feet to their faith.

"The New Testament character, Timothy, was Roger's favorite individual in the Bible. That's where the school gets its name. Roger wanted to create an environment in which children could not only learn the ABCs and one-two-threes from teachers committed to academic excellence, but also be challenged to grow in their faith and to learn ways to give back to the world, not just to take from it.

"By 1941, Roger and Marie began in earnest to put together a workable plan for their school. They established the founding principles and wrote down the school's organizational structure. The rest of that year, Roger and Marie began garnering support in the Robbinsonville community, not so much financial, as the lumber company would provide the funds to turn on the lights. Rather, the Stevensons were building relationships through which churches and businesses could partner with the school to develop the hearts and minds of its students. How we run the school today hasn't changed all that much in the past sixty-one years."

Suddenly, Don ended his history lesson. Looking down at his watch, he said, "Gee, I didn't realize I had rambled on for so long."

"Oh, Don," said Abbie. "I could keep listening all day to your story. How fascinating to hear how God has put together all the various facets of the school."

"You are kind to say so," Don replied, "but we need to take a break. I'm sure you and these two fellows need something to eat." He looked over at Keith and Josh. "We all do," the director said, stretching his back slightly as he stood from his chair.

"Sounds like a plan to me," said Keith as he stood up from the couch. "I'd like to hear more of your story at lunch. Wouldn't you like to?" Keith glanced over at Abbie and Josh for affirmation.

"Definitely," said Josh.

Abbie smiled and nodded.

Don gestured in the direction of Covenant Kitchen. "Charmaine has prepared a light lunch for us in celebration of your arrival, Abbie. Let's meet in the dining hall in fifteen minutes."

As the group walked from inside the cottage onto the wide front porch, Abbie thanked them for their help. While the three men headed down the driveway and onto the path that led through the woods, Abbie went back inside the cottage to freshen up.

Once on her way to the dining hall, Abbie reveled in the fact that God was indeed One who gave good gifts to His children.

CHAPTER
4

Summer was in full bloom at Timothy House. The immense hardwoods were adorned with bright, plump green leaves. Large rhododendrons displayed full blooms; some adorned with white blossoms, others a blush color. The short walk from the cottage through the wooded path offered glimpses of brightly colored wildflowers opening here and there, scattered like confetti, as if celebrating the new adventure Abbie was embarking on. As the path opened up into a grassy lawn, Covenant Kitchen stood a few hundred yards beyond. When Abbie came through the dining hall door, she was delighted to find Doris Fielding waiting to greet her.

"Hello, dear girl," said Doris warmly, wrapping Abbie in a tight hug.

"Hey, Doris," said Abbie, stepping back to look into the bright eyes of this woman who had quickly become a trusted friend. "I'm so happy to finally be here."

"We are glad you are!"

The figure of someone standing past Doris caught Abbie's eye. Abbie glanced over to see Evelyn Benson, her new department chair. When their eyes met, the older woman spoke first.

"Welcome to Timothy House, Abbie," Evelyn said, the sincerity of her greeting mirrored in her amber-colored eyes. "We are so glad you're here." She extended a hand toward Abbie, and when Abbie grasped it, Evelyn wrapped her other hand over Abbie's and gave a gentle squeeze.

"Hello, Evelyn," Abbie said, returning the greeting. "Thanks so much!" Nodding toward the three men at their table, she continued, "I arrived earlier this morning to discover a personal moving crew to help me unpack my car."

As if on cue, Don, Keith, and Josh all donned picture-perfect smiles at the mention of their gentlemanly assistance.

"We're a caring community," said Evelyn, nodding toward the trio. "Glad you had help moving in."

Just then, two ladies appeared at their table, their hands laden with plated meals.

"Ladies, shall we?" Don gestured toward the table and then pulled out a chair for his wife. "Lunch has arrived."

The group sat down at the long wooden table. Large fans, hanging from beams far above in the dining hall of Covenant Kitchen, blew a soft, welcoming breeze. Charmaine Jenkins's culinary skills did not disappoint. The head of Covenant Kitchen's dining staff, Charmaine had now been on the Timothy House team for almost fourteen years. Taught the finer points of cooking by her grandmother and mother, ones never recorded in hand-written recipe cards or printed on the pages of cookbooks, Charmaine never failed to delight faculty, staff, or students at any given meal on the Timothy House campus.

For this special luncheon in honor of Abbie's addition to the school's English department, Charmaine and her staff had prepared chicken salad served on croissants, a fresh fruit medley, and a summer corn and avocado salad. Sweet tea, which no one in recent Timothy House history had ever been able to replicate, was the preferred beverage choice by all at the table. The group shared light conversation as they savored their meal. Occasionally, Charmaine would come by the table to see if anyone needed anything, steadily replenishing tea glasses and refilling serving dishes.

"Don," Abbie said after swallowing the last bite of her chicken salad sandwich. "Please finish the rest of your story about how your uncle and aunt founded the school."

As Don began, Charmaine and Lynette Marks, another member of the dining staff, appeared and cleared the plates of those who had finished their lunch.

"Timothy House opened its doors in 1942 with only a faculty and staff of twenty. The first student body had only twenty-five students. You have to remember that this was less than a year after Pearl Harbor was bombed and America had entered World War II. The world was a very different place."

"How many teachers were on the faculty?" Evelyn queried.

"Fourteen, I believe," said Don. "Some of these details have escaped me."

Just at that moment, Charmaine and Lynette reappeared with dessert plates and a platter heaped with lemon squares, dusted with powdered sugar. Keith picked up the stack of plates and, after taking one, passed it around the table. The dessert platter soon made its way from guest to guest. As the conversation continued, the two women ferried cups of steaming hot coffee to the table.

After taking a bite of the lemony confection, Evelyn reached out to touch the arm of Charmaine, who was about to place a small pitcher of cream on the table. "These are delicious, Charmaine! Your talents never cease to amaze me."

Charmaine's face beamed. "Thanks, Evelyn," she said.

Don seconded the compliment. "Best I've ever had, Charmaine."

By now, the kitchen director's face was practically glowing like a lightbulb. "Thanks, Mr. Don."

"I've told you, Charmaine," Don said teasingly, "to call me by my first name. Mister was the name people called my dad."

"I'm working on it, Mr. Don," the reply came as Charmaine disappeared through the kitchen's swinging door.

After a few more bites, Doris turned to her husband, "Oh, dear," she said, "tell them about your first experiences at Timothy House."

Don shared how, in 1953, when he was fourteen, he had begun working summers at Timothy House and helping his uncle and aunt with the physical maintenance of the grounds. Occasionally, he filled in as a referee or player for baseball or basketball games. One of the perks of his employment was a daily afternoon swim in the waters of Shelter Lake. The pride of his family's legacy was evident in Don's every word.

As Abbie listened, she glanced across the table to notice Keith looking at her. She smiled slightly. His eyes smiled back at her, though his mouth had not caught up with the expression. Abbie could feel a blush start to rise on her cheeks. She took a sip of iced tea to cool the sudden rush of emotion and returned her attention to Don's story.

"Remind me when you and Doris came to the school full-time," Josh prompted.

"We came in 1972," shared Don, looking over at his wife adoringly. "We'd only been married seven years. Wilson and Valerie were still very young." Don's voice trailed off as if trying to remember a point he wanted to make.

Doris picked up the conversation where it had ended. "Wilson was only four, and Val was not quite a year old. That was an exciting yet challenging time, wanting so much to love and minister to other people's children yet having two of our own."

"Yes," Don agreed. "There was so much we had to assimilate in that first year. Uncle Roger had come to me a few months before we arrived at Timothy House to tell me that he and Marie wanted to retire. Because they had no children, I was the closest thing he had to a son.

"Doris and I had education degrees and several years of experience. I was in the process of completing my master's degree when Roger made his offer."

"Providence at work," commented Evelyn. "That's one of my favorite themes in the story of this school—God's connecting the dots in the events of people's lives."

"You've got that right," said Don. "Not only does God connect people and circumstances, but He also equips those same people for the work He has planned for them. Even though Doris and I had varied teaching experiences, nothing prepared us for taking over as directors of Timothy House. We were so green."

Don and Doris both chuckled out loud at the same time.

"Bless his heart," continued Don, "Uncle Roger saved my hide. He stayed right by my side during those first years we were here. By the early seventies, the student body had grown to about seventy, depending on the particular semester and group of kids. The world had changed a great deal since 1942, and Doris and I faced serious challenges related to educating teenagers that Roger and Marie could not fathom.

"However, even though circumstances of history change, people rarely do. Roger brought to life the truth of Paul's words from Philippians about God supplying all our needs from the bounty of riches found in Jesus Christ. God has proven time and time again that He *always* provides what is needed. He has been so faithful. He still is. Every day."

Don took one last bite of his lemon square, wiped his mouth with his napkin, and turned his gaze to the school's newest faculty member.

"Know again, Abbie, how pleased we are that you are now part of this school family. I hope this has given you a better understanding of how Timothy House was established and offered a glimpse into what we are still trying to accomplish in the lives of our students. God is going to use you in a mighty way."

Raising her glass of iced tea, Doris chimed in, "Welcome, Abbie! I second Don's greeting."

At this, all the others gathered around the table raised their glasses in Abbie's direction. A collective "Welcome, Abbie" was spoken as glasses clinked together.

Unaccustomed to the direct attention of others and unsure of what to say, Abbie murmured shyly, "Thanks so much. I'm delighted to be here."

From the cheerful faces of those seated around her, all at the table were equally glad Abbie was at Timothy House.

Once Don stood and pushed back his chair, others around the table began to get up.

Before Abbie could stand, Evelyn leaned over from her chair. "I'd love for you to come to my home soon for a visit. We don't live far from school."

"That is so kind, Evelyn," said Abbie.

"I'll be in touch soon to check your calendar."

"Thank you," said Abbie, genuinely touched by the kindness of this new colleague. "I look forward to that."

The group broke up and all made their way to the front porch of Covenant Kitchen. Don and Doris said their goodbyes, as well as Evelyn and Josh. Only Keith and Abbie remained on the wooden steps.

"Could you use some help this afternoon?" Keith asked. Although the question was innocent enough, Keith seemed to want to say more.

Abbie beamed. "That would be great. Would three o'clock work?"

"Sounds like a plan to me." Keith stepped off the bottom step to the ground below. After starting down the path to his office, he turned back toward Abbie and raised a hand in greeting. "See you soon."

"Soon," Abbie said shyly.

As she walked back through the woods to Mistletoe Cottage, Abbie silently prayed. *Dear Lord, thank You for this fresh start to my life. Thank You, especially, for Keith and his friendship. My heart is drawn to him, and I want so much to love him, but I'm scared. He's already had so much pain in his life; I don't want to cause more. Coming here to Timothy House is what I believe You've told me to do. I've taken this tiny first step. Now, I need You to lead me the rest of the way.*

CHAPTER
5

The knock on the front door of the cottage caught Abbie off guard. She was so engrossed in unpacking one of her suitcases that she didn't hear Keith arrive. As she'd only been in this new home—at least new to her—for less than four hours, the sounds of the building were unfamiliar. Luckily, the fact that Abbie walked back through the front room of the cottage prevented her from missing Keith altogether. She could see his tall frame through the front window.

Keith's hand was raised to knock one last time when the door suddenly swung open.

Abbie stood on the other side of it, looking a bit chagrined. "Hi, Keith! Please come in," she said, sweeping her arm forward to welcome him inside. "I'm sorry I didn't hear you at first. This day's been a little overwhelming."

"Don't give it another thought," Keith said, a wry smile on his lips, as he stepped across the threshold. "For a minute, I thought I might have to call the fire department."

Abbie brushed back strands of her dark brown hair behind one ear as Keith followed her into the cottage. Ever since returning from lunch, she had been busy figuring out a plan for unpacking and where best to put her belongings. She motioned for Keith to sit. Abbie plopped down in a wing chair by the window.

"Overwhelmed, are you?" Keith asked. "How can I help?"

"Can you unpack all my suitcases and boxes and put up everything exactly where I need the items to be?" Abbie giggled as she finished this query.

Trying to look serious, Keith replied, "I have many talents, but home organization is not one of them." He smiled broadly at her. "I can, however, help you unpack three boxes. Why don't we get that done this afternoon? Then you won't feel like there's so much to do tomorrow. I've got an appointment late this afternoon with a possible school donor, but until then, I'm all yours."

"Oh, would you?" Abbie looked almost embarrassed to be accepting his help. "I would be so grateful. How about a compromise assistance plan?" she said, looking at him hopefully. "What if we unpacked the two kitchen boxes already in there on the table, and then you could help me move the rest of these boxes into the rooms where they are to go? That way, I'll be ready tomorrow morning to tackle what's left to put away."

Standing up, she pointed toward the kitchen. "I made a pitcher of lemonade. Would you like a glass before we get started?"

"Definitely! How did you know I needed refreshment?" Keith said as he followed her into the kitchen.

After they both had some lemonade to fortify them, they placed their glasses in the sink and turned their attention to the boxes atop the square wooden table in the kitchen. For the next thirty minutes, Abbie and Keith made quick work of the task at hand. One box contained staples of flour and sugar, canned and boxed foods, and an assortment of spices. The second included a small coffee maker, several wooden cooking utensils, a small electric chopper, a hand mixer, and array of colorful dish towels.

They made small talk at first as they opened cabinets and put items away in drawers. The gentle fragrance from a lavender-scented candle filled the air.

"It's so good to see you," ventured Abbie, folding a patterned dish towel. Her green eyes glistened.

Keith stepped close to her and yet kept a tantalizing distance. His voice was low and husky, when he replied, "It's wonderful to see you, too, my dear Abbie."

This was one of the first times Abbie had seen Keith since their visit two months ago on Good Friday in Peter's Chapel. It was the day she had officially accepted the job offer to join the faculty of Timothy House. It was also the same day Keith professed his love for her and told her he would be patient and wait as long as it took for her to feel comfortable about where their relationship might be headed. That day had been a turning point in both their lives.

"It has seemed like a terribly long time since Good Friday," said Keith quietly.

"It has been," murmured Abbie.

Abbie was in uncharted waters. She had worked diligently throughout the past year to rid her soul of the torment her former husband, Joe Richardson, had inflicted upon her. Coming to terms with her anger and distrust of men caused by Joe's actions wasn't an easy task, however, and was something she knew she might still struggle with for the rest of her life.

Stepping back, she moved across the kitchen. "It's hard to believe I'm really here at Timothy House," she said brightly. Not knowing what to say next, Abbie turned and headed out of the kitchen, back to the relative safety offered by the stack of boxes in the great room.

Keith, it seemed, was willing to give her the benefit of the doubt. He picked up the now-empty boxes from the kitchen table and followed behind wordlessly. If Keith felt awkward about mentioning Good Friday, he did an excellent job of hiding it. Nodding toward the remaining boxes stacked in front of the window, Keith said, "Do you know where you want to put these?"

Grateful for a change in the direction of conversation, Abbie replied, "Give me a minute, and I'll sort them out." As Keith lifted each box, Abbie scanned info scrawled on the cardboard with a permanent marker. Soon, each was placed in one of several smaller piles.

"These two go to my bedroom," Abbie said, pointing to two smaller, though heavy, boxes.

As Keith picked them up, he pretended to have pulled his back. "What do you have in these? Concrete?"

She swatted at him as he passed and watched him set them on the floor of the large bedroom just off the great room. His simple, playful teasing had instantly lifted the mood between them.

Next, at her direction, Keith moved a stack of four boxes, also heavy, to the built-in bookshelves on the far side of the great room. "What's in these?" he queried as he again pretended to have difficulty hefting the containers' weight.

"Those are books I've kept in my classroom for years, my personal lending library of sorts. Because I love to read, I've always worked to cultivate that passion within my students. I pray some of the girls living here also might enjoy reading some of my favorites."

Keith picked up a book from the open box and placed it on the shelf. "*Little Women*," he held the book high in the air as he exclaimed in a voice resembling a game announcer, "one of the literary greats of all time. You'll be mesmerized by this story's gripping plot."

Abbie giggled at his antics.

With all the pomp and circumstance of a royal crier, Keith continued bringing up book after book from the cardboard box and making similar proclamations. "*The Hiding Place . . . Anne of Green Gables . . . My Antonia . . . The Borrowers . . . Christy.*"

Even though their arrangement had only been for him to help unpack two boxes in the kitchen and help distribute the other boxes to the rooms where they belonged, Keith seemed caught up in his playacting. Abbie didn't want the moment to end.

As she watched Keith, Abbie felt so conflicted. She desperately wanted to bare her soul to Keith, to tell him all that was on her mind and in her heart. She also knew she was now a house mother for junior-high-aged young women, or soon would be, and knew propriety was to be observed by them at all costs.

Before Abbie knew it, Keith had her entire student lending library shelved and ready for selection. She only hoped her new charges, arriving in the fall, would find the stories as meaningful and mesmerizing as she had.

"Oh, Keith!" Abbie exclaimed as she clapped her hands. "Thank you so much!"

Keith bent slightly at the waist and swept his arm across his chest. "I am your most humble servant, ma'am." As he stood, his gaze held hers for a long moment.

Once again, as she had earlier that day at lunch, Abbie felt there was more going on here than just his trying to be helpful.

Looking down at her watch, Abbie said, "Keith, it's almost five o'clock. I didn't mean to keep you so long. You'll be late for your appointment."

"You haven't kept me, Abbie," Keith said, with a smile playing across his face. "Remember, I offered to come help you. Thanks for letting me do so."

"You're right," Abbie replied as she turned to lead him toward the front door. "You have been most welcoming, especially on my first day at Timothy House."

Once out on the broad porch of the cottage, the pair said their good-byes. Afterward, Keith bounded down the steps and onto the graveled driveway. He stopped and turned back toward Abbie. After a few seconds, he spoke. "Abbie, I know today's been an extremely full day with a lot to process. I've missed you, and I want you to know that."

Abbie could feel a blush rise on her cheeks, just as she had experienced at lunch earlier in the day. She stood on the porch, too overcome with emotion to speak.

Keith continued, "Could we plan an evening together soon? There's much we need to talk about." His dark, indigo eyes held hers like a magnet.

She nodded.

"How about dinner on Friday night? There's a special place in Kingsport I'd like to take you to. We need a quiet place to talk, one that's away from school."

Suddenly finding her voice, Abbie said quietly, "Friday evening sounds perfect." Her radiant smile spoke volumes. "What time should I be ready?"

Keith seemed delighted with her answer. "Let's say five o'clock." He hesitated and then asked, "You do like Italian, right?"

"Love it," Abbie said.

Keith looked greatly relieved. "Although I hope I do, I may not see you again until Friday. This is a really busy week for me, as this meeting I'm headed to is the first of four."

"I'll be praying for all on your plate," Abbie stated.

"Thanks. I need all the prayers I can get," Keith said, his expression a bit worrisome. "I'll explain everything to you on Friday night."

"Sounds like a plan. Thank you again so much for all your help this afternoon." Abbie stood a little straighter and gave Keith a luminescent smile.

He beamed. "You're very welcome. Get some rest." He turned and headed down the drive.

"Goodnight, Keith," Abbie called out softly.

The wave of his hand told her he had heard her farewell. The knowledge that he had done so thrilled her heart.

CHAPTER
6

Abbie turned out the lights at ten o'clock and crawled under the covers, but sleep would not come. By eleven, she was still wide awake, her heart full of anticipation of what may lay ahead in a relationship with Keith. The airflow created by the whirring ceiling fan only tossed her thoughts around even more. One minute her emotions were soaring, thinking about how special he made her feel; the next, she felt paralyzed by fear at the thought of "What if?"

What if Keith turns out to be like Joe?

What if I'm so damaged by Joe's betrayal that I can't love and trust anyone again?

What if I hurt Keith's heart?

What if he breaks mine?

"What if?" wasn't the only question Abbie was trying to answer. Another dilemma—"How's this going to work?"—had to do with her new position at Timothy House and how she and Keith might proceed in their new relationship. She was about to be the house mother to six seventh-grade girls. Keith was second-in-command at this prestigious school.

As committed Christians, they had each made personal decisions to maintain strong boundaries regarding the physical aspects of attraction to one another. Although their conversations had never migrated to this topic, Abbie knew Keith and her heart well enough to know that marriage would be the only setting in which they would consummate their relationship. However, holding each other's hand, putting an arm around the other's shoulder, hugging, or kissing good night were another matter altogether.

As Abbie thought back over her arrival at Timothy House, she was amazed at the convincing signals Keith had already telegraphed in their brief encounters at lunch and when he came back this afternoon to help her unpack. Long gazes at the lunch table. Awkward pauses in conversation. Watching her intently from across a room. Standing close to her.

Joe had now been dead for five years. Sometime long before his death, a fracture had occurred in the Richardsons' marriage. A rift as deep as the Grand Canyon. Emotions as cold as a deep freeze. Abbie knew she was dreadfully out of practice regarding relationships with men. However, as a teacher and as an adult in a position of trust, she knew little eyes would be watching her and Keith. Abbie wanted to make sure they set a godly example. She knew in her heart that Keith did, too. It didn't matter to her what the world's standards seemed to be about the casual nature of physical relationships. As a Christian, her allegiance was to God. She hoped she would let neither Him nor Keith down.

Finally unwilling to lay awake in the dark any longer, Abbie got up and put on her robe. Wandering out to the great room, she peered out the cottage's front window. Moonlight cast a soft, white gleam over the lawn. She reached for the blanket from its place on the sofa as she crossed the room. Unlocking the front door, Abbie slipped outside. The night air was cool, the woods nearby silent and still.

Abbie sat on the top step of the stone porch and wrapped the blanket around her, tucking it carefully around her legs. She looked up at the large, white moon. For the longest time, words from Psalm 8, penned millennia ago by David, repeated themselves in Abbie's mind. "When I look at the night sky and see the work of your fingers—the moon and the stars you set in place—what are mere mortals that you should think about them, human beings that you should care for them? Yet you made them only a little lower than God and crowned them with glory and honor."

For minutes more, Abbie sat, quietly soaking in the hushed, tranquil night.

Finally, she whispered, "Dear Lord, I am fully aware that, for some unknown reason, You have crowned my life with honor, especially by giving me the gift of this new job. Thank You so much for this new season in my life and for this wonderful school at which to teach. I *do* know that my being here at Timothy House is part of Your plan for me. Thank you for the peace in my heart about this new position.

"Trying to figure out where this relationship with Keith will go, however, is another matter. I need Your direction. Keith is such a good and honorable man. His heart is so pure, and He loves You so much.

"You know how cold and hard my heart has been for so long." A silent tear trickled down Abbie's cheek, and she brushed it away.

"I desperately want to be free of the lack of trust that remains entwined around my heart. Like the roots of some unwanted weed, distrust bears its fruit in my life. Even if Keith never senses it, I know it's there, lurking deep within. If this relationship is going to succeed, I've got to be able to trust him wholeheartedly, with no holds barred."

Abbie bowed her head and wrapped her arms around her waist.

"Please melt these iron bars of suspicion and doubt that hold me prisoner. Give me fresh eyes through which to see Keith, solely as he is and with no comparison to Joe. Give me listening ears through which to hear not only Your direction and guidance, but also the sincerity and honesty of Keith's words. Blot out from my memory any of Joe's hurtful comments that still bind me. Give me Your heart to understand that love—*real* love—can be a reality in this world and is one of the best gifts You give."

Fresh tears, now flowing freely, streamed down her cheeks. Gentle sobs racked her body for a long while as Abbie allowed the river to run its course. Only the hardwoods and the gleaming moon were witnesses to her anguish. Finally, reaching for the hem of her robe, she wiped her face dry, then bowed her head again to finish her prayer.

"I am opening my heart and my life to You, Jesus. Guide me in this new season. I'm not sure, but I think I may be falling in love with Keith, and that terrifies me. Hold my hand, Lord, and walk with me. Protect and shepherd us both as we walk this new road together. Amen."

Long after her prayer had been lifted, Abbie continued to sit on the stone steps of Mistletoe Cottage, the moon protectively watching over her like a silent, vigilant defender.

CHAPTER
7

Abbie woke to find sunlight filtering through the blinds on the bedroom windows. Sheer, white curtains danced slightly in the breeze of the ceiling fan. For a few seconds, she found herself a bit disoriented. Raising her head off the pillow, she looked around the room. The wooden trim around the windows and doors was stained a rich amber color; the walls were freshly painted a soft white. The smile on her face dawned as brightly as had the morning sun. Placing her head back on her pillow, she remembered, *I'm at Timothy House!*

She continued to lie warm and still under the coverlet as she thought back over the events of the past day. The drive from McHenry to Robbinsonville. The unexpected help from Don, Keith, and Josh to unpack her car. The delicious luncheon prepared by Charmaine in the dining hall. The warm welcome from Don and Doris. The gracious dinner invitation from Evelyn Benson. The special offer from Keith to help her with unpacking.

Though she had enjoyed his visit, it had cost her almost all the emotional capital she had to spend for one day. She only had enough energy to make a sandwich from some of the groceries she had brought with her and unpack two more boxes. Too tired to move another muscle, Abbie had washed her face and fallen into the bed.

Today was the second day of this new season in her life. *What are you up to, Lord?* she thought as she got up, made the bed, and pulled on some clothes. Wandering into the kitchen, she loaded the basket of the coffee maker with her favorite hazelnut-flavored grounds and poured water into the tank. Turning on the machine, she returned to the bedroom to retrieve her Bible and her blessings book. It had been a long time—too long—since she'd written down the things for which she was thankful.

Once she had filled a cup with the fragrant coffee and added creamer and sweetener, she made her way to the comfortable sofa in the great room. Settling into its soft cushions, she pulled the crocheted blanket from the back of the couch and covered her legs with it. Even though it was summer, the mountain air could be quite cool until the sun stood high overhead. Taking a sip of the hot coffee warmed her.

Abbie opened the book of remembrance that her late friend, Audry MacDonald, had encouraged her to write in frequently as a spiritual sacrifice of praise. The concept was quite simple. Each day, Abbie wrote down five things for which she was thankful. Sometimes, it might be a significant achievement, like this new job at Timothy House. Other times, it might be something simple like thanking the Lord for food in her refrigerator and the means to buy it.

Audry's words echoed in Abbie's heart: "Gratefulness is a choice of the heart and will always draw you closer to God."

That's where I want to stay, Lord, thought Abbie. *Close to You.*

Abbie took another sip of coffee. A glance out the window told her this would be another beautiful day. Turning to a fresh page, Abbie chewed thoughtfully on the end of a black ballpoint pen before beginning to write:

Wednesday
1. *This new job at Timothy House*
2. *A chance to see Drew more often because of his new jobs at Timothy House and Wright's Creek Church*
3. *The kindness of my new department chair, Evelyn*
4. *The thaw that I'm beginning to feel in my heart*
5. *Keith's love and friendship*

Abbie stared at the word *love*. Although the prospect of this man caring for her was exciting, the thought of navigating the landmines buried covertly within her heart and soul scared her to death. How desperately she wanted to be free of all the hurt and pain Joe had caused.

Looking back at the list she'd just made, item four caught her eye. *The thaw . . . in my heart. You're the only one, Lord, who can melt the glacial wall that's held me captive these five years,* Abbie thought. *Although I don't know how it will happen, I'm choosing today to believe You will. To put feet to my faith and to leave the results up to You.*

For the next hour, after pouring herself another cup of coffee, Abbie read through various chapters in Psalms, one of her favorite portions of scripture. The delicate edges of the pages in this part of her Bible were worn from frequent use. How many times had she found solace and comfort for her troubled heart in the pages of this treasured book of wisdom? Too many to count.

Psalm 27:13 caught her eye, "*I would have despaired* unless I had believed that I would see the goodness of the LORD in the land of the living" (NASB 1995). For a long while, she remembered how close to the brink of losing her sanity she had come. Looking around the great room of this almost one-hundred-year-old cottage, she knew she was in the "land of the living." A fresh start in this new season of her life was another provision of "the goodness of the LORD."

Abbie laid her Bible aside, then went to her bedroom, where several boxes waited to be unpacked. Against one wall stood a small wooden bookshelf Abbie had brought from home. Josh had carried it in for her yesterday after she arrived. She'd found it years ago at a second-hand store, and a thorough cleaning with liquid wood cleaner and a rubdown with furniture restoration polish brought the old piece back to life. Abbie had brought it along to hold her personal collection of books and a few family photographs.

After searching through the stack of boxes Keith had moved to this room yesterday afternoon, she located the two boxes she wanted. The first box contained various photographs she had carefully wrapped before moving from her house on Flaherty Road in McHenry. As she removed each one, releasing it from its paper shroud, she smiled, thanking God for all the love and laughter He had brought into her life despite difficult circumstances and relationships.

One of the first framed photographs she unwrapped was her favorite picture of Drew on his first birthday, the little boy's impish grin surrounded by chocolate cake icing smeared all over the lower portion of his face. Abbie laughed aloud softly, lovingly running her finger across her son's little face. *Oh, Drewby*, she thought. *How much I love you!*

Another photograph was of Abbie, Lane, and Eric, one taken many years ago at a church gathering. *Another reason to thank You, Lord*, Abbie said in her heart, as she looked at the beloved faces of these dear friends. Lane and Eric had been instrumental in introducing Abbie to Timothy House and its directors, Don and Doris Fielding.

One of the last pictures Abbie unwrapped was a family photo of her Aunt Caty and Uncle Scott and their two daughters Lexie and Jan. Perhaps taken for a church directory when Abbie's cousins were still in college, it was one of her favorites. *Thank You, Lord, for the love and support of this dear family. How different my life would have been without their influence.* Abbie's father, Franklin "Lin" Ellis, had died when she was only ten years old. Once her protector was gone, Abbie had been forced to fend for herself, as her mother, Tina, was a woman more interested in consuming her next drink rather than ensuring the welfare of her only child. Aunt Caty, Tina's older sister, was all too aware of the dysfunction in the family.

In the years since Lin's death, Caty and Scott begged Tina to allow Abbie to live with them. The mother adamantly refused each time, accusing them of trying to drive a wedge between her daughter and herself. Tina Ellis could never quite wrap her mind around the fact that *she* was responsible for the ever-widening chasm in her relationship with Abbie. Over the years, Caty and Scott "rescued" Abbie in seasons when Tina's drinking spun out of control.

Throughout her tenuous marriage to Lin Ellis, Tina also tried to snuff out any hint of a relationship between herself and her mother-in-law, Ella. Tina built a wall around her life and around Abbie's, designed to keep Ella Ellis on the other side. The bond, however, between Ella and Abbie—established early on—was unbreakable. Abbie, like her father, was an only child. This fact endeared her even more to her grandmother.

Caty and Scott provided many opportunities throughout Abbie's childhood for Abbie and Ella to spend time together. Once, when she was seven and again when she was nine, Caty convinced Tina to allow Abbie to accompany their family on a vacation. Tina never knew that

Ella was also coming along. Furthermore, Caty served as postmistress for all written correspondence between Abbie and Ella.

Lin Ellis instilled within Abbie the drive to always give her best. Despite his valiant efforts, Abbie's tender spirit was wounded early on by the anger and venom spewed forth by Tina, especially when under the influence of alcohol. *You'll never amount to anything.* If Abbie heard this comment once from her mother, she heard it a thousand times. As a result of such damaging remarks and the lack of maternal warmth, Abbie retreated further and further within herself. It wasn't until graduate school that Abbie began to find the self-confidence her mother had all but snuffed out years before.

Soon after Tina's death, Caty and her family moved from Memphis to Portland, Oregon. A large company headquartered on the West Coast sought Scott's expertise as a chemical engineer. With the help of airlines, phone companies, the internet, and the U.S. Postal Service, Abbie managed to stay well connected with her Aunt Caty. Lexie and Jan had long been married and had families of their own. Emails and occasional phone calls kept the cousins connected.

Throughout the past few years, Abbie had revealed to Caty her unrest and dissolution with life, especially with her job at Kent Academy. With every call, her aunt could tell it was becoming increasingly obvious that Abbie no longer had the enthusiasm and drive to stay in that position. Less than two months ago, Abbie called Caty for advice regarding the Timothy House job offer. During the call, Abbie shared the details of what a move to Robbinsonville and the new teaching position would involve.

"What have you got to lose?" Caty had said. "Sounds to me that God has provided the escape."

Abbie remembered that Caty had chuckled at the word *escape*.

"You've lived in the shadow of Joe's misdeeds long enough. It's time you break up the concrete that's kept you cemented in the past. Get back to the business of living, Abbie. The rest of your life is ahead of you. Go and find it."

The verbal push was exactly what Abbie needed to hear. She dialed Don Fielding's number soon after ending her call with Aunt Caty.

Abbie readjusted the photo of Caty and her family, turning her attention instead to the second, much larger box she needed to unpack. This one contained the books that had been guiding lights for her: some old, others new, but all cherished. She filled two of the case's three shelves, moving many of the books around until their arrangement suited her.

While working to put the bookshelf in order, Abbie thought again of her childhood and all she had suffered at the hands of an alcoholic mother. Besides being neglected and having her self-confidence all but snuffed out, Abbie's spiritual development especially suffered, another casualty of alcoholism. Abbie had claimed the Lord as her personal Savior while a child, having been led to do so by the godly example of her father. Once he died, however, and especially during her teen years, Abbie lost her spiritual footing, convincing herself that God had forgotten her.

Enter Frances Thompson, Abbie's eleventh-grade English teacher. Miss Thompson became a lifeline for Abbie. A committed Christian, this gentile lady possessed a passion for the beauty of the English language and the study of it, fostering within Abbie an insatiable appetite for learning and literature. The teacher quickly recognized her student's bright mind and sharp academic skills and set about to nurture them in every way possible. Miss Thompson introduced Abbie to Jane Austen, Charles Dickens, John Steinbeck, and L.M. Montgomery. She also shared with Abbie her appreciation of outstanding Christian writers Amy Carmichael, Andrew Murray, C.S. Lewis, Elisabeth Eliot, and Oswald Chambers.

Abbie's beloved teacher had also introduced Abbie to classics of children's literature—marvelous stories like *The Secret Garden, Charlotte's Web*, and *The Velveteen Rabbit*. Abbie would need to prepare a proposed reading list for her girls—so many wonderful books to feed one's heart and mind. As she lovingly placed her copy of Lewis's *The Lion, the Witch, and the Wardrobe* on the shelf, Abbie made a mental note to include it in the books she planned to read each night to her girls.

Frances Thompson quickly became a mentor and role model in Abbie's life, serving as the inspiration for Abbie's decision to become a teacher. She had also taught Abbie how positive words, especially God's words, had the power to shape thoughts and change lives. Miss

Thompson and Aunt Caty were instrumental in getting Abbie back on track and renewing her faith in herself and in God.

Once order had been restored to her bedroom, Abbie went back to the great room and reopened her blessings book. She found the black pen and added a sixth and seventh item to the list she had written only a little earlier:

6. *The love and influence of Aunt Caty and her family*
7. *Miss Thompson's legacy that has shaped my life*

Choosing gratefulness does indeed make a difference, Abbie thought as she closed the book. She silently prayed that in the days to come God would honor her decision to thank Him for all in her life.

CHAPTER
8

Keith hung up the phone and grinned. Don had called to say he'd canceled the meeting they had scheduled on this Tuesday morning. Although Keith had been looking forward to the appointment with Bill Howard, the owner of a local automotive repair and supply store, Keith was grateful for this opening in his already hectic schedule. Breakfast at Gravlee's Diner would have to wait until next Tuesday, when the three men would gather.

This unexpected gift of time would be helpful as Keith continued shoring up the proposal for the Tentmaker's Project, a business mentoring program he and Don hoped to integrate at Timothy House. Thursday's board meeting was only two days away and the plans needed more tweaking. Chuck Hawthorne, a Timothy House board member from McHenry, had introduced the idea to Keith and Don. Both men immediately liked it. This week's meeting would introduce the program to the rest of the Timothy House Board of Trustees.

Odd, Keith thought as he reached for the file folder marked "Tentmaker's," *that both Abbie and Chuck are from McHenry. The town's turned out to be a pretty special place.*

For the next two hours, Keith worked out different scenarios for partnering business professionals in this corner of the state with interested Timothy House seniors. He filled copious sheets of yellow paper, scribbling numerous ideas for the program in black ink. If this program worked, as he and Chuck hoped it would, the students would not only build valuable relationships with their business mentors, but would also sharpen their entrepreneurial skills. The possibility that these same business mentors might serve as references for these young people was particularly appealing.

At last, Keith gathered the assortment of paperwork he'd produced. After shuffling the various sheets into an orderly pile, he placed the stack inside the file folder, closing the cover as he did so. He sat back for a moment and noticed the date on his desk calendar. June fifth. How was it even possible he had now been at Timothy House for almost eighteen months? Memories rushed in, taking Keith on a journey to remember the events that had brought him to this place.

———

After a series of more calls and several faxes, Keith found himself employed once again in pharmaceutical sales. The first few years following the deaths of his wife and children were marked with a dull routine from which Keith refused to stray. Buechner Pharmaceuticals was glad to have Keith back with them. He had been a rising star in their organization all those years ago when he had left the first time, and they wanted to do everything possible to keep him from leaving again.

One friend who kept close tabs on Keith, especially after the wreck, was Dan Levinson. Dan and his family lived in Chattanooga. A committed Christian and an old friend since their college days, Dan was the shoulder Keith cried on when he allowed himself such a luxury. Mainly Keith had bottled up all his hurt and anger and bewilderment following the loss of his family and crammed it deep inside where no one could reach it, especially God. He used the perks and the salary from his job like a drug to dull the pain he refused to deal with.

God had been a part of the perfect picture for Keith and Genny, but only in a superficial way. The Haliday family plugged right into the church scene as members of the Second Street Church in Chancellors. They went to Sunday School and church on Sunday mornings. Wednesday nights were reserved for children's activities and prayer meetings. Genny's faith was more anchored and secure than Keith's, but that never bothered him. Life was good, and to him, that equaled God's blessing.

Keith somehow managed to keep God at arm's length. His parents were good, honest, God-fearing people who tried hard to give Keith all he needed while growing up. Their greatest gift to their only son was a self-confidence they somehow passed on, a comfort with and a genuine like of himself. He was now an only child, having lost a younger sister, Ellen, to leukemia when she was only three years old. She was eight years younger than Keith, although his memories of her never dimmed throughout the years.

Dan patiently waited for Keith—waited for an opportunity to share God's love, waited until Keith reached a point in his life where he was open to receiving it. About two years into his sales job, Dan convinced Keith to accompany him for a weekend men's retreat. There, at age forty-eight, Keith came face to face with the risen, living Savior. On a remote mountaintop, Keith surrendered his life to the lordship of Jesus Christ, finally understanding what "casting all your cares upon Him" really meant. When he rose from his knees that spring afternoon, he had no more tears to cry. Surprisingly, he felt renewed and filled rather than depleted and washed out.

The pain from his great loss was still there, but where before it was like a wound left to fester, the heartache had now been cleansed and could heal properly. God was using the purifying pain of suffering to carve out and fashion a new heart within Keith Haliday. Where he was once lukewarm and merely acknowledged God, he now knew beyond a shadow of a doubt that Christ was real and that He wanted to do some exciting, serious work in Keith's life. He also knew that somehow God wanted to use him to reach others in His name.

Keith and Dan had several lengthy, long-distance conversations about the matter. On a few calls, Betse, Dan's wife, joined to provide a woman's perspective. After prayer and several extended talks with his administrators at Buechner, Keith decided to move to Chattanooga and affiliate with the company's office there. Dan and Betse even had an extra bedroom for Keith to stay in until he could find his own place. Their church, Wildwood, was a warm, inviting congregation, making Keith feel at home. He and Dan met weekly on Thursday mornings at six-thirty for Bible study and prayer.

After Keith's life got back on track spiritually, the direction of his work changed drastically. By nature, Keith was not an extravagant spender, but neither was he thrifty. He started searching the Word for verses concerning money and stewardship of material possessions. Over three months, he took inventory of his spending habits, poring over his bank statements and tax returns from the last few years. Keith felt led to cut down on his expenses and find an income figure below his salary level on which he could comfortably live. He also began tithing.

Earlier in his life, when Genny was alive, he always gave money to the church, but it was on Keith's terms. Now, though not technically required in the New Testament, Keith felt a monetary goal of at least ten percent was what he would give. The extra money in his income beyond his "budgeted" amount, tithe, and what he actually made was put into a savings account. Keith wasn't sure what God wanted him to do with the money, but he believed this was what God wanted done for the time being.

Another change in Keith's life was that he began to spend vast amounts of time with God each day—reading his Bible and earnestly praying before the Father. Some days Keith found himself begrudging work because it cut into his daily quiet time. God was also cultivating within Keith's heart an awareness of and concern for people in unfortunate circumstances, particularly children. Many of his doctor clients recounted stories of needy children and how the medicines that Buechner Pharmaceuticals provided positively impacted their lives.

One evening Dan asked Keith to join him at a men's dinner. Don Fielding was the guest speaker. Don talked to the men about Timothy House and the needs of the children there. He also spoke to them about considering serving as volunteers with the Camp 4Ever program and supporting Timothy House financially. He explained that the school's operating expenses came from the proceeds of a trust fund started by the school's founders, but that programming beyond the eight-to-five operations always needed more support.

After dinner, Dan invited Don and Keith back to his home for coffee and a slice of hot apple pie. Betse had everything ready and waiting when the men arrived. Even though it was a weeknight, the three men visited well past midnight. Keith felt moved that night to become involved with the ministry of Timothy House. He asked Don many questions and left Dan's home with much he needed to think and pray about.

Over the next two years, a fast friendship developed between Don Fielding and Keith Haliday. Keith revealed to Don, bit by bit, over the course of many more lunches and dinners, long walks, and cups of coffee shared in Don's office, the story of the terrible wreck, the devastating loss of his family, and the way God had reclaimed his life out of a dark abyss.

Keith also shared with Don the guilt he still carried, that he had never been the spiritual leader he should have been for his family, and how he was trying to do a better job walking as a man of God. Keith believed his main task now was to be obedient to God, no matter the cost. He also told Don that he knew the job with Buechner was not a forever thing, merely a holding station until God showed him the next step. That was the news Don had been waiting to hear. Four months later, Keith joined the administration of Timothy House.

————

Movement outside Keith's office window caught his attention, pulling him back from the past to this present moment. Don Fielding was headed away from Sanctuary Hall and toward the back of campus in the direction of Serenity Cove, the lakefront portion of the campus. A twenty-two-acre lake, christened Shelter Lake by the school's founders in the late 1930s, served as the centerpiece of this area. Sand had been brought in many years ago to form a beachfront. A boathouse and dock area on the lake's left shore housed canoes and small watercraft. Consecration Point, a long, slender bit of land jutting out into Shelter Lake, was where special outdoor services at Timothy House were held. A tall, wooden cross stood at the end of the point closest to the lake, forming the backdrop for morning devotionals and nighttime ceremonies.

Don must be going to check on the work crew, Keith thought. A group of workers had arrived three days ago to place new flat rocks in the outdoor amphitheater seating area at Consecration Point.

Don was a treasured friend. Keith smiled as he watched the figure of his boss disappear in the curve of the pathway, and he silently thanked the Lord for this godly man who had helped Keith grow so much in his walk with Jesus Christ. Keith only hoped he could be used in the same way in the lives of the students at Timothy House.

CHAPTER
9

Keith walked across the Timothy House campus toward Sanctuary Hall. He had been looking forward all week to this Thursday meeting. He was especially eager to greet his new friend, Portia Dockery. A legend in Robbinsonville, she had been one of the first trustees of the school to pay him a welcome visit when he joined the Timothy House staff. As he bounded up the steps of the administration building, his mind wandered back to a comment Don made about Portia: "She has the heart of a lion." Keith knew right then and there that Portia Dockery was a woman he would like.

Sounds of friendly, enthusiastic banter greeted him as he approached the doorway of the conference room. Keith slipped into an empty chair between Chuck Hawthorne and Eric Wyatt, both from McHenry. The three men exchanged handshakes and hellos. Don and Doris Fielding, Elton and Summer Tidwell, and Portia shared their how-are-you's and good-to-see-you's.

Portia beamed at Keith from across the table, giving him a conspiratorial wink. Despite her age, she still cut an imposing figure. Clothed in a conservative business suit draped elegantly over her ample five-foot-eight-inch frame, she stood out in the room. A head full of wiry, wavy hair that had years ago surrendered to the inevitable was now the color of burnished silver. Constrained somewhat in a bun at the nape of her neck, the sterling strands formed a regal crown, the perfect complement to her azure-blue eyes. Rosy pink cheeks rarely needed cosmetic embellishment, hinting at Portia's Danish heritage.

"Sorry I'm late," said Keith, looking around the room to greet the committee members. "Several of my eighth graders had some questions after class. Just took longer than I planned."

"No problem, Keith. Glad you could make it," said Don, rising to stand at his place. He nodded toward Keith as he spoke. "I want to thank all of you for agreeing to serve on this committee. From its inception, Timothy House has been committed to enriching the lives of its students far beyond the bounds of the classroom. The Tentmaker's Project will be a way for us to further that pledge. For some time now, Doris and I have wanted to address the ever-changing needs of our eldest students here at the school. Although most of our seniors continue on to junior college or a four-year program, they could use a helping hand when it comes to deciding upon their life's work."

Looking over at Chuck, Don continued. "Chuck approached us last fall about the Tentmaker's Project. He's been involved with a similar program at another school. I'm going to turn the meeting over to him and let him tell you more about this exciting opportunity."

Chuck radiated a quiet confidence. "I'm excited to share this concept with each of you. Keith and I had the opportunity to talk about it several times throughout the past nine months. As Don mentioned, I've been involved with a similar project at Hickory Ridge School in Lexington, Virginia. I've seen God do amazing things in the lives of both the students and adults involved."

Chuck picked up some brochures from the conference table, handed them to Eric, then waited a few minutes as the stack made its way to each member seated around the conference table. "As you will see, Hickory Ridge has been involved with the Tentmaker's Project since 1991. I don't know if many of you are familiar with their program, but they're a school built on a similar model as ours."

Several heads nodded.

"For those of you who might not be familiar with the Tentmaker's concept, it's a mentoring program that pairs high school seniors with a sponsor in the business community. As you have probably surmised, it's based on the New Testament patterns set down by Paul and his friends Priscilla and Aquila. As tentmakers, they shared the Gospel primarily through sharing their business skills. The purpose of the Tentmaker's Project is to not only pass on to the next generation the values and skills necessary to be effective business leaders, but also to equip them with foundational principles for godly living. Don is going to help me with a PowerPoint presentation that will give you some more insight into the project."

As Chuck sat down, Don moved to the end of the table and to the laptop located there. Keith stood and flipped the room's light switch. Soft light filtered through the wooden blinds of two windows on the wall behind the table. A soft whirring noise filled the room as the computer sprang to life. After a few clicks of the mouse, the program started. Don sat down and watched with the others.

Ten minutes later, Keith rose again and turned on the lights. No one said a word. It seemed to Keith that the silence was the result of how moved the group had been by what they had just seen. Candid photographs, soul-stirring music, and heartfelt testimonies made for a poignant account of young people whose lives had been changed by the Tentmaker's Project. If the tears glistening in the eyes of several board members around the table were any indication, Keith knew the program had also touched them.

Chuck said softly from his seat, "I think you can understand why this program could have a tremendous impact on our students. Does anyone have any questions or comments?"

An hour and many good questions and comments later, the program was approved. Everyone in attendance had given their hearty agreement to lay the groundwork for the project. To no one's surprise, Chuck was chosen as chairman of the committee. The Tidwells and Eric had agreed to work with Chuck to secure the names of individuals from the business community in the Robbinsonville area who would serve as sponsors for the program's inaugural launch.

"Before we end," Keith said as all heads around the table turned to him, "I wanted to let you know that we'll be adding a new board member in August. Lance Tate, a retired two-star general and former high school classmate of mine, will be joining us. He and his wife, Claire, recently moved to the Knoxville area. Although career-Army, Lance and his family have been working with youth programs throughout their marriage, and various deployments throughout his career have brought him face-to-face with children in impossible situations. As a woodworker, a hobby he's honed and developed into a booming side business, he is excited about the entrepreneurial opportunities our students will have through the Tentmaker's Project."

After Keith's brief announcement, board members stood from various positions around the room. As the group broke up, he went over to Portia's side of the table. She rose from her chair and reached out to hug him.

"Mama Dee," Keith said with great affection, "how wonderful to see you." He bent down and kissed her cheek.

"My dear Keith," said the matriarch. The warmth in her voice was obvious as well. It was evident she held Keith in the highest esteem. "How have you been?" She pulled back to look up into his face.

"I've been great." Keith helped Mama Dee gather her notebook and purse. "How about taking a walk with me across campus? Do you have time?"

Mama Dee beamed at the attention. "Why, son, I always have time for you." Well into her seventies, Mama Dee, as she was affectionately called, had seen enough suffering to last a body a lifetime. Her daughter and only child had taken her life in her late teens. Mama Dee's husband, finding the emotional toll too heavy to bear, lost his mind, spending the remainder of his life at a residential mental health facility. Mama Dee visited him faithfully twice a week until his death twelve years later. Despite all her many trials, she hadn't lost her hilarious good nature and unswerving love for the Lord. Perhaps it was this bond of affliction that had instantly drawn Keith and Mama Dee together. She had become a safe harbor and an instant friend.

The temperature was amazingly cool for this Thursday afternoon in June. Bright green leaves fluttered on the hardwood trees as if they reveled in the crisp mountain air. The pair walked arm in arm across the immense courtyard that linked the four main buildings of the Timothy House campus—Sanctuary Hall, Peter's Chapel, Covenant Kitchen, and Timothy Hall, where the classrooms were located.

"Tell me, Keith, how's life been treating you?" Mama Dee looked at the younger man. "I haven't seen you in a while."

"I know, Mama Dee. It's been too long." Keith patted her arm gently as they walked across the stone walkway. "I'm still trying to get my bearings around here. It's just taking more of my time than I realized."

"Well, young man, you'd better hurry over to my house for a home-cooked meal soon. I've missed our talks. Otherwise, I'll think you don't love me anymore." She winked at him, grinning like a Cheshire cat.

"I do have a prayer request," said Keith. By now, they had reached the spot where Mama Dee's tawny brown Buick LeSabre was parked. The pair stopped as the older woman reached inside her purse to find her keys.

"Is it about a woman?"

Bewildered, Keith's mouth gaped open. "Why? How did you know?"

"Let's just say, son, I've been around the block a time or two. There's just something different about you, a difference only a female can make." Mama Dee looked certain of her pronouncement. "I noticed immediately when you came into the conference room today. What's her name?"

Keith stepped back and scratched his head, amazed by Mama Dee's astute observations. "Her name is Abbie Richardson, and she's quite a lady. I hope you can meet her soon."

"Well, I would love to. All I've got to say is she better not break your heart. She'll be answering to me if she does." Mama Dee let out a low, soft chuckle. "It's time for this old woman to get on the road."

Keith opened the car door and kissed Mama Dee once more on the cheek before helping her into her seat. "Just pray that I don't scare her away. She's been through a great trial herself, and she's hesitant to trust. I'm trying not to think too far into the future—just taking this a step at a time. I covet your prayers." Keith leaned over the top of the open door as Mama Dee cranked the ignition.

"I'll talk to the Lord. He'll know just what to do." Mama Dee buckled the seat belt across her stout frame and blew a kiss to Keith. "Come see me soon."

As Keith watched the older model car drive out the driveway, he couldn't help but smile, chuckling to himself about the wonderful provision of Mama Dee's friendship.

CHAPTER
10

Drew Richardson had waited a lifetime for this day. His graduation only three weeks earlier seemed light years ago. Finally, he had completed college and was entering the wide world on his own. He smiled as he fondly remembered the happy memories made with his mother, Abbie, in his last days as a college student. His great-aunt, Caty, and her husband, Scott, had surprised them, flying in unexpectedly from the West Coast to attend the graduation weekend festivities.

As he made the three-hour drive from McHenry to Robbinsonville, he looked forward to his first adult job. *Two of them,* he thought.

Rod Eichman, the senior pastor of Wright's Creek Community Church, had hired Drew on a part-time basis to help Josh Hastings coordinate a youth mentoring program. Don Fielding had also hired Drew, again on a part-time basis, to serve as a coach and coordinator for special sports camps offered by Timothy House several times throughout the upcoming year.

A quick glance in the rearview mirror confirmed that Drew had indeed crammed "everything but the kitchen sink" into the back of his GMC Jimmy. He checked both side mirrors, as boxes prevented him from seeing anything out the vehicle's back window. A green highway sign near the shoulder of the road caught Drew's attention. Its printed white lettering announced that Robbinsonville lay eleven miles ahead.

The young man reached down to retrieve the piece of paper from the seat beside him on which he'd written down Barb Turner's address. Pastor Eichman had connected Drew with this member of his church who owned the garage rental. She had sounded nice when Drew called her to work out the details of the lease. He would find out soon enough when he arrived at her home.

The road wound upward, and as Drew crested the top of this stretch of road, he could see the city of Robbinsonville spread out below. Gentle, rolling hills surrounded the area like strong shoulders to protect it from harm. As he passed the sign marking the city limits, a wave of excitement and promise washed over him, one he had seldom experienced. *Lord,* he thought, *I'm ready to see Your goodness in the land of the living. Thank You for this new chapter in my life.*

Ten minutes later, Drew was turning into Mrs. Turner's driveway. The lane wrapped around a well-manicured lawn shaded by several maple trees and then wound around to the rear of the ranch-style brick home to the detached garage behind. As soon as Drew's Jimmy cleared the corner of the house, he saw his mother's SUV parked in the driveway and Abbie standing beside it.

Abbie squealed with delight as her son opened the door of his car. "Drew," she exclaimed as she wrapped him in a bear hug.

"Hey, Mom," said Drew, returning the embrace. Despite the fact that he was twenty-three, he never wanted to grow too old to stop receiving hugs and kisses from his mother.

"So glad you made it here safely." Abbie stepped back to look at Drew and peer into the back of his car. "What do you have back there?" she asked, a broad grin spreading across her face.

"Oh, Mom, you know how you've always taught me to be prepared? Well, I finally listened."

Both laughed. The sound of a screen door slamming from somewhere across the driveway caught their attention, and they turned in the direction of the noise.

Barb Turner, the homeowner and Drew's new landlady, walked across the gravel driveway.

Drew immediately stepped forward to introduce himself. "Mrs. Turner," he began, offering his hand in greeting, "I'm Drew Richardson, and this is my mother, Abbie."

Pride washed over Abbie as she watched her grown son.

"Hello, Drew," said Barb, shaking his hand. "And hello, Abbie." Barb took Abbie's hand. "I'm delighted you're both here." Shielding her eyes from the sun, Barb looked up at Drew. "I've heard many nice things about you, and I'm glad you'll be living in the apartment. I always feel safer when there's a man around."

Grinning, the older woman looked at Abbie conspiratorially and winked.

In this first conversation, Abbie determined Barb was someone with whom one felt instantly at ease. Her short, naturally curly hair was dyed a light shade of blond. Tailored clothing softened the angular features of her chunky body shape. Rosy cheeks and the constant twinkle in her soft brown eyes made anyone in her presence feel as if they were talking to Mrs. Claus.

Through mist-filled eyes, Barb revealed that her husband, Larry, had died several years ago in an accident at the manufacturing plant where he worked. Wiping away a stray tear, the lady turned the conversation to a brighter subject, sharing with Abbie and Drew about her three children and seven grandchildren. They were obviously her pride and joy. Abbie already had a soft spot in her heart for this older woman who generously shared with others what God had given her. How well Abbie knew that the best love was often that lavished by others on one's own children.

Motioning for them to follow, Barb called out over her shoulder as the trio walked across the driveway to the stairway on the side wall of the three-car garage. "Drew," she said, sounding a bit winded, "please call me Miss Barb. Mrs. Turner's way too formal for me."

"Yes, ma'am," said Drew, following close behind.

Barb Turner's footfalls on the stairwell treads were rhythmic and sounded like those of soldiers marching in line. The waves in her permed hair moved up and down with each step. By the time they reached the landing above, Barb was panting heavily and seemed to need a few minutes before speaking.

Abbie and Drew waited while the older lady caught her breath.

"The apartment's been thoroughly cleaned," said Barb as she placed the key in the knob. Opening the door, she turned back to them and continued, "I hope you'll find the place to your liking." She flipped on the light switch and stepped back, allowing mother and son to enter the apartment first.

Abbie waited until Drew entered. *This is his big day*, she thought, *and he'll have to decide if this is what he needs. I'm just happy to be here with him.*

Drew was pleasantly surprised with the room before him.

No more than nine hundred square feet, the space was small but clean. The rectangular room held everything he would need in his first venture into the wider world. A tidy kitchenette was located in the far-right corner. A single oven with a gas cooktop sat beside a refrigerator. A small counter separated the stove from the sink. Another counter on the far side of the sink connected to a floor-to-ceiling pantry. The dishwasher was under the counter to the right of the sink.

A small dinette table and four chairs filled the main space of the kitchenette. A comfortable set of den furniture was arranged to the right. Two small leather sofas, a recliner, and a footstool were positioned to focus on the large-screen TV placed on a table in the corner. Several small wooden end tables were scattered throughout the living area as well. Two wrought-iron floor lamps offered lighting for this part of the small apartment. Light from recessed canned fixtures provided a gentle glow to the rest of the room.

A queen-size bed stood in the far-left corner. A small chest was beside the bed and upon it was a brass lamp. Next to the chest was a three-shelf bookcase. The quilt spread over the top of the bed reminded Drew of many his mother had made for him over the years.

The front right corner of the efficiency apartment was where the closet and a small bathroom were located.

After completing the 360-degree tour of his new living quarters, Drew turned to Barb Turner and gave her a thumbs-up. "It's perfect," he exclaimed.

From the smile on her son's face, Abbie knew the compliment was sincere.

Before leaving her new tenant to move in, Barb gave Drew and Abbie each a small piece of paper on which she had written her name, address, telephone numbers—home and cell—and email address. "If either of you need anything, please let me know. It's been a while since I've had a boarder, and I've missed the company."

Once mother and son took the neatly written notes from Barb, Drew stepped forward and put his arm around the older woman's shoulder. He gave her a gentle hug and said, "Thanks so much, Miss Barb. I'll take good care of this place." His enthusiasm was palpable.

Barb reached up to pat his hand. "I know you will."

Drew, suddenly aware he was still hugging his new landlady, moved his arm as inconspicuously as possible from Miss Barb's shoulder and stepped back.

Abbie reached for Barb's right hand and took it in both of her own. "Thank you, Barb, for your kindness to Drew and your hospitality." Holding up the sheet Barb had given her, Abbie continued, "I especially appreciate getting this. Drew has my cell number if you ever need to reach me. I moved to Robbinsonville earlier this week and will be teaching at Timothy House in the fall. I'm not far."

"That's what I heard," said Barb, looking admiringly from Drew to Abbie and then back to the son again. "This will be a special year as you'll both be working together. Know I'll take good care of your boy."

"That means a great deal, Barb," Abbie said as tears glistened. "Thank you."

Once out the door, Abbie followed Drew and Barb down the stairs. Abbie's heart was full as she silently thanked the Lord for this kind woman's generosity, now allowing Drew to establish his first adult living space.

By the time they reached the driveway, all Abbie could do was raise a hand in farewell. Mother and son watched Barb head back across the driveway to her home.

———

Three hours later, Drew and Abbie had unpacked most of the boxes crammed in the back of his Jimmy. Clothes now hung in the closet. Canned goods, snacks, and cereal stocked the pantry. The kitchen table was moved closer to the wall and the electrical outlet as it would double as Drew's desk. Two rows of books lined the shelf near the bed.

Abbie watched as Drew inspected the room, making small adjustments to the items already in place. *Another sign he's putting on his man clothes,* she thought, as she smiled. Looking around the cozy room, she silently thanked the Lord for yet another provision in Drew's life.

Suddenly, he exclaimed, "Gee, I'm going to be late."

"Late to what?" Abbie asked. "You just got here."

"I forgot to tell you, but Josh and Pastor Eichman are taking me to dinner tonight. We're supposed to meet at Gravlee's in ten minutes."

"Well, then. You better get going." Abbie walked over to pick up her purse from the kitchen table.

As Abbie exited the apartment, Drew made sure the door closed tightly behind them and then locked it.

On her way down the stairs, Abbie called out, "The restaurant's not far. You'll make it on time."

"Thanks again, Mom, for helping me move in," said Drew, placing a hasty kiss on Abbie's cheek. "Sorry, I've got to run." He climbed into his SUV and turned the key in the ignition.

"Have fun," replied Abbie as she stood in the driveway watching him.

Drew placed the car in reverse.

Suddenly remembering something, Abbie ran over and knocked on the driver's side window. Drew rolled it down halfway.

"Pencil me in for dinner on Saturday night," his mother said brightly. "We have a date!"

"Will do," said Drew. "Bye, Mom." He rolled the window up and headed out of Barb Turner's drive.

As she watched her son's car disappear down the tree-lined path, Abbie hoped the kitchen at Gravlee's was well stocked. A mighty hungry customer was soon to arrive.

CHAPTER
11

This morning was off to a busier clip than Keith had planned. He left Sanctuary Hall and hurried to the parking lot. Opening the door of his Explorer, he slid into the seat and glanced at the clock on his dashboard. Eight thirty-two. He was late for his breakfast meeting with Trent Lockhart, Robbinsonville's chief of police. Keith grinned, knowing Trent would understand. Soon, Keith was parking his Explorer on the street that ran alongside Gravlee's.

After pulling open the front door to the diner, Keith stepped inside. Delicious smells of bacon sizzling on the grill and pancakes cooking welcomed him. He could see Trent Lockhart's large frame already seated in the booth where they usually met. Light brown hair, closely cropped in an almost military style, framed Trent's chiseled features. The skin of both his face and his arms was well tanned, giving evidence to the fact that he spent a great deal of time outdoors. From the bulges in his uniform sleeves, there was no doubt the man spent a substantial portion of every day lifting weights. His boots, surely larger than a size thirteen, looked more like those of a cowboy than an urban law enforcement official.

The man was absorbed in the menu as Keith approached. However, Keith's shadow quickly caught Trent's attention.

"Hey, man," Keith said as he slid into the booth. "Sorry to be late." He extended a hand across the table.

"Not a problem," said Trent, clasping Keith's hand in a firm handshake. "Glad you could make it. It's been a while since I've seen you. Wanted to see how things are going in your world." He flashed a broad grin Keith's way.

"Life is good," Keith replied as he picked up the menu before him. "It's hard to believe, though, that June is almost over. This summer's been hectic."

As the two men caught up with each other in broad generalities, their conversation was soon interrupted by the waitress.

"Teencie," both men said almost in unison, giving her their full attention.

"Good morning, gentlemen," said Teencie Curtis, their favorite waitress. "Haven't seen either of you in quite some time."

"It's been a while," said Keith, offering a smile. "We've been really busy at Timothy House."

"I know, I know," said Teencie. Nodding toward Keith, she continued, "One of you's trying to help kids stay out of trouble." She turned to look straight at Trent. "The other one's dealing with those who get in it." She reached up and pulled down a pencil that had been tucked over her right ear amid the soft red curls that covered her head. "What can I get for you?"

Keith pointed to Trent and said deferentially, "Chief."

Trent ordered the breakfast special for this Monday morning—two eggs over easy, grits, hashbrowns, two slices of turkey sausage, wheat toast, and a cup of coffee.

"I'm going to second that order, Teencie," said Keith.

"I'll bring your coffee and put in your order." Teencie tucked the pencil back over her ear and turned toward the kitchen, her curls bobbing gently with every step.

"She's quite an amazing lady," Keith admired as he nodded his head in the direction Teencie had taken. Keith well remembered how kind Teencie had been to him and Abbie when he had brought her to Gravlee's for hot chocolate on an impromptu late-night date last December. Teencie seemed to have an internal radar, an awareness of suffering and pain that lay hidden under the surface in other people's lives.

"That she is," Trent agreed. He, too, knew of her kind heart.

Fortunately, Teencie's return to the table occurred right after the two men had shifted the subject of their conversation to the latest rankings in the college baseball playoffs. The friendly waitress set two steaming mugs of coffee on the table. The expert server that she was, she'd memorized many of her best customers' preferences. These two men both liked their coffee hot and black.

Shortly after, she returned with their breakfasts. Keith and Trent said little as they began the task of consuming the heaping plates of food. Occasionally, Teencie returned to the table or made several trips back and forth from Gravlee's kitchen—once to retrieve more butter, a second time to deliver another order of wheat toast for Trent, and a third time to refill their coffee cups. Otherwise, she gave the men at table twelve a wide berth and privacy to enjoy their meal in peace.

Trent opened the conversation. "So, my friend, now that you've completed your first full year at Timothy House, what do you think? Still glad you decided to move here?" The chief sprinkled salt and pepper over his eggs and diced them neatly with his fork.

"This year, although different," Keith began, "has been one of the best I've had. It's been a long time since I've been able to say a year has been a good one."

Trent nodded silently, knowing the pain and suffering Keith had endured following the loss of his wife and two teenage children killed by a drunk driver.

Keith had met Trent after joining the administration of Timothy House. Don and Doris Fielding hosted a get-together in their home, The Manse, and invited their friends in town to come for light refreshments and a chance to meet Keith. The police chief and Keith hit it off immediately. Both were about the same age and resembled each other. Each man was well over six feet tall and in good physical shape. Each was a sports fanatic and enjoyed the out-of-doors. The two quickly discovered, however, that the common thread that bound them together was their shared faith in the Lord and a no-nonsense approach to life.

Since that initial introduction, Keith and Robbinsonville's police chief met almost every month for breakfast at Gravlee's. Over these early-morning meals, the two men got to know one another. Every other month, Trent and his wife, Kelly, invited Keith to their home for dinner. The three would enjoy rousing conversation, always laced with plenty of laughter, as they savored a delicious home-cooked meal.

After one of the first of those dinners had ended and the men finished helping Kelly stack the dishwasher and tidy the kitchen, Trent and Keith went back to the den after Kelly said good night. Both the Lockharts and Keith attended Wright's Creek Church and had been challenged and encouraged by the preaching of Rod Eichman. Following up on recent comments the pastor had made to the church's deacon body concerning the importance of prayer and the vital role men were called to play in their families, Trent asked Keith if he would consider being an account-ability prayer partner with him. Keith instantly agreed.

Keith, too, was in a place in his Christian walk where he needed the type of iron sharpening that a solid brother in the Lord would provide. Don Fielding was certainly one of those blade grinders in Keith's life, but Trent and Keith were practically the same age. The fact that Keith didn't see Trent every day nor work with him offered a different perspective than the one Keith and Don shared. Leaving the Lockharts' home that evening, Keith had thanked the Lord for this new friend.

After each subsequent monthly dinner Keith enjoyed with Trent and Kelly, he and Trent would follow the same routine. Once the kitchen had been cleaned and Kelly headed upstairs to bed, the two men would retire to Trent's study, a small office off the family den. There the two would share more serious matters and open their hearts to the Lord as they prayed together. Keith always left those evenings invigorated and full of hope.

Keith continued, "I'm enjoying the work at Timothy House immensely. My work with Don has involved a steep learning curve, but he's been a patient teacher. I know I don't have to tell you what a wonder-ful person he is and how fortunate the school is to have him at the helm."

"So glad to hear the job's one you enjoy," Trent said. "You're certainly right about Don." As both Trent and Don had grown up in Robbinson-ville, they had known each other's families. Experience and friendship had taught him there weren't many men as fine as Don Fielding. "How's Abbie?"

Trent's question caught Keith off guard. Abbie had only been in Rob-binsonville for three weeks, and because the monthly prayer time he and Trent shared was coming up later this week, Keith had not filled in his friend on how the relationship with Abbie was progressing. The rush of color on Keith's cheeks told Trent all he needed to know.

Trent let out a low whistle. "Man," he said, trying hard not to laugh, "you are smitten." He grinned like a Cheshire cat as he watched Keith's attempt to downplay the blush.

"We're still trying to figure this thing out between us," Keith said tentatively.

"If the look on your face is any indication," Trent replied, "you've already got this relationship figured out. Has Abbie?"

Keith dropped his gaze from Trent and shook his head slightly. "She hasn't." His tone turned more serious. "I'll fill you in on Thursday night after dinner, but she's still really cautious. We're also trying to figure out the dance steps to this faculty-administration dating relationship. Don, of course, knows how I feel about Abbie, but this is uncharted territory. I'd be grateful for your prayers." Keith took a sip of his coffee, which by now had grown tepid.

"You've got them," Trent said quietly. *This new lady in Keith's life must be someone special*, he thought.

Catching Teencie's eye and raising his cup slightly, Keith made small talk until she returned to their booth, a carafe of steaming coffee in her hand.

"Gentlemen," she said, looking at both of them. "A cup for each of you?"

Their heads nodded their consent.

Once the curly-haired waitress left their table, the men concentrated on finishing their breakfasts.

"Tell me, Trent," said Keith as he wiped away evidence of the last bite of grits from his mouth. "How are things going at the police department?"

"Pretty good," the chief replied. He took another sip of coffee and then loaded his knife in preparation to butter the hot, toasted wheat bread Teencie had delivered only minutes before. "The beginning of this summer's been pretty quiet. To tell you the truth," the police chief said in a tone that implied concern, "it's been too quiet. Makes me wonder if this lull we're experiencing is the calm before the storm."

Trent spread strawberry jelly onto a new slice of toast and took a bite.

Keith took another sip of his coffee and waited for his friend to continue.

"One of the main problems we've had throughout the years in this part of the state is drug running. Most of it's been small stuff—a couple of ounces of weed, a few stolen Adderall pills, kids selling some of their mommas' sleeping pills . . ." The chief took another bite of toast.

"Are the pushers local?" Keith asked.

"No, not really, although there are a few knuckleheads we keep our eyes on." Trent wiped his mouth with his napkin and took another long sip of coffee. "There have been rumors, however," he continued, a worried expression filling his eyes, "that some unsavory types are making plans to move into the Robbinsonville area because of the location in the far corner of the state."

"Where do you think trouble may be coming from?" Keith asked as he speared the last piece of sausage with his fork.

"Possibly Jonesborough or even Oak Grove. Kingsport, near the Kentucky line, is always a good possibility. Do me a favor," Trent said as he laid his knife across the back of his plate. "Keep your eyes open and your ears to the ground. If you hear any buzz from any of the kids on campus, be sure to let me know."

Keith looked across the table at his friend as Trent's voice had taken on a grave tone. "I will. I definitely will."

Teencie brought their bills to them and waited for the men to open their wallets.

"Gentlemen," she said, smiling brightly at two of her favorite customers as she took their payment, "it's been a pleasure. Hope you have a wonderful day!"

"You, too," said Trent.

"Thanks so much, Teencie," replied Keith.

Once Keith and Trent said their goodbyes, each left the diner, fortified by good food and invigorating fellowship, to meet the day before them.

CHAPTER
12

Keith spent most of Friday afternoon preparing for his special date with Abbie. Though he'd only asked her out four days ago, his imagination had been busily planning every detail in panoramic color. Throughout the past several months, Keith spent countless hours talking to the Lord about Abbie, his love for her, and the direction he hoped their relationship was headed. This was a journey for which he had no map, only the compass provided by the Lord's guidance. Strangely, though, he felt like he was headed into friendly territory.

He took his car through the local car wash and detailed it from top to bottom. On the way back to campus, he stopped by a specialty bakery in town and selected two pieces of tiramisu. The chef packed it in plastic boxes and included small containers of extra chocolate sauce and heavy cream. Keith tucked these treats in a small ice chest, placing it on the floorboard of his back seat. Two bottled waters were also in the cooler. A plastic grocery bag containing paper plates, forks, and napkins sat nearby.

As Keith drove through the gates of Timothy House, he glanced at the digital clock on his dashboard—four forty. By the time he reached Stone's Throw, it was four forty-four. He bounded into the house and headed for the bedroom. He pulled off his shirt and tossed it onto a side chair. Picking up the pressed button-down plaid shirt from the bed, he pulled it on, fastening the buttons as quickly as he could. It was now four fifty-two, and he didn't have time to unbuckle his belt to tuck the shirt in properly. He crammed the shirt inside the top of his pants. A quick glance in the mirror showed which strands of dark hair needed smoothing, having been disturbed by the change of shirts. He did so with his hands, and then headed back to his SUV.

"Dear Lord," he whispered as he turned the vehicle around and drove toward the other end of campus, "please bless this night. I love this girl so much, and I'm so ready to find out exactly how she feels about me. As this is a path neither of us has been on before, we need You to be our Guide and Shepherd."

As he jammed the gear shift into park, he uttered, "Amen."

No sooner had he stepped onto the porch of Mistletoe Cottage than the front door opened. Abbie stood before him. Keith was speechless for a few seconds as he took in the light coral linen sundress that made her toffee-colored hair look even darker. The wheat-colored, open-weave sweater thrown over her shoulders brought out the highlights in her soft green eyes. Strappy summer sandals and a small leather purse completed the outfit. Abbie looked like a model in a ladies' summer clothing catalog.

Realizing he still had not uttered a word, Keith tried to appear nonchalant. "Good evening," he said, his eyes alight with hope for this special evening.

"Good evening, yourself," said Abbie, closing the heavy door behind her. "How are you?"

"Tired, but good." He extended his elbow for Abbie as they descended the front steps of the cottage.

Once they were both in the car, Keith cranked the ignition.

"Sounds like you've had a busy day," Abbie said, looking over at him. "I'm a little tired myself. I've been at Drew's most of the day helping him unpack."

"Oh, that's right," he said. "Didn't he move yesterday afternoon?"

As he guided the SUV down the drive of campus and headed out onto the main road, Keith listened as Abbie talked excitedly about the arrival of her son in Robbinsonville.

"Barb Turner's place is perfect for Drew," Abbie said, excitement evident in her voice. "I was amazed at how spacious the one-room apartment has turned out to be."

"Did Drew bring much with him?" Keith inquired.

"Practically everything he owns. We did our best at least to get things in their general area of the apartment. I'm taking him to dinner tomorrow night. It'll be interesting to see how he's settled in. This is his first real home away from home, and I can tell he's pumped about it."

Keith smiled to himself as he drove, hearing the passion and pride in her voice for this son who would now be working at Timothy House with her.

As they headed out of town and reached the main highway, Abbie inquired, "Where are we going tonight?" Her voice was soft and lilting, like she knew he had planned something exciting for this evening but did not want to spoil the surprise.

"We, dear lady, are going to Kingsport," said Keith. "I'm taking you to Giuseppe's, a family-owned Italian restaurant that's a favorite. Don and I ate lunch there early this spring during a meeting with several board members. This will be my first time trying the dinner menu, but if that selection is as good as our lunch was, we're in for a treat."

Abbie's eyes glistened with excitement. Touching his arm, she said, "Tell me about your week. I know you said it would be a long one."

As they drove through the summer evening, Keith shared the details of his many meetings. While sharing bits and pieces of the seemingly inconsequential yet monumental aspects of his work, he relished describing the details to someone he cared deeply about. That was one of the things he had missed the most since Genny's death eight years earlier. There was no one but the bare walls to share his thoughts with.

Her next question interrupted his thoughts. "How did the board meeting go yesterday?"

"It went really well," Keith said brightly. "In fact, Chuck Hawthorne and Eric Wyatt were here from McHenry."

"Yes, I know," replied Abbie. "They stopped by the cottage on their way out of campus. I met Chuck one other time, and it was good to get to see him again." Abbie's voice sounded a bit dejected. "Lane was supposed to come with Eric and spend the day with me while he was in the meeting, but her schedule fell apart, and she couldn't come. It was wonderful, however, to get to see him."

The tone in her voice brightened as she shared her last bit of news about the Wyatts. "They're both working again this summer at Camp

4Ever, and they're planning to come a few days early and stay with me before camp starts. We'll have a great time."

Keith glanced over briefly at Abbie as she rambled on about the plans she was making for the Wyatts' return visit in July. *Dear Lord,* he thought, as they drove on toward Kingsport, *I don't think I can live without this woman much longer. Oh, how I pray she feels the same.*

As they reached the city limits of Kingsport, Keith shared some of the city's history with Abbie. Founded during the Revolutionary War, the town had a past both rich and colorful. Long a leader in both industry and commerce, Kingsport was also part of a trio of cities in the northeastern corner of Tennessee, commonly referred to as the "Tri-Cities." Keith steered his way through the busy city streets, finally arriving at their dinner destination. Once parked, he helped Abbie out and they headed toward the door. He prayed silently that the requests he had made when making the reservation earlier in the week would be fulfilled.

Soon they were seated in a quiet booth at the back of the restaurant. Small votives with glass shades twinkled on each table. The dark green tufted upholstery offered guests a comfortable spot to enjoy their meal. Starched white tablecloths and crimson napkins complimented the green velvet, bringing to mind the colors of Italy's flag. Small pedestal sconces adorned the restaurant's whitewashed walls. Upon them sat handmade pottery from the artisans of Italy's Amalfi Coast. Guests would be hardpressed to find a more authentic dining experience in Italy itself.

The waiter was courteous and attentive but not obsessive. Keith ordered an appetizer for them to share. Bruschetta Al Pomodoro, a house specialty, was a generous portion of homemade Italian bread toasted and topped with garlic, olive oil, onion, and minced tomatoes. At the same time, he and Abbie placed their entrée orders. He selected the Seafood Linguine; Abbie chose the Chicken Piccata with Penne. Two tall glasses of unsweetened tea, along with ice water, were served to each.

The pair talked about everything and nothing as they made quick work of the first course. The sauce on the bread was not one they wanted to waste, and they used spoons to savor the last morsels of the appetizer's topping. Before Keith and Abbie knew it, their waiter arrived at the table, juggling hot ceramic plates loaded with food.

Once the entrées had been served, Keith reached his hand across the table. "Let me bless the food." Abbie placed her hand in his as they bowed their heads.

"Dear Father," he prayed quietly, "thank You for this evening and for this time to be with Abbie. Thank You for bringing her and Drew to Robbinsonville and Timothy House. You have brought us both safely through many dark valleys, and I pray You will continue to guide us in the days ahead. Thank You for this food. May it nourish us as we serve You. In Your Son's name I pray. Amen."

Keith gave Abbie's hand a gentle squeeze before releasing it. As he looked up from the prayer, he found that she was already gazing at him with eyes the color of summer ferns. He hoped his own eyes returned the deep emotion he saw in hers. Keith also trusted their conversation would lead them to a positive conclusion by this date's end.

"I'm sure you've missed your friends from McHenry," he began, taking a bite of his linguine.

"I have," she said, "but not as much as I thought I would. I don't mean I've forgotten about them, but this place—Robbinsonville, I mean—feels so like home. It's funny. I don't quite know how to explain it."

Keith smiled. "Sounds like you've done a pretty good job of doing so."

"Sure, I'll miss many aspects of living in McHenry, but the friends I have there are heart friends, the kind that will be my friends no matter where I am in this world. Those friendships are a great gift God has given to me."

Chalk one up for the home team, he thought.

Keith inquired again, "You've told me before about your friend Winnie's suggestion to use The Target Plan. Has that helped you?"

Abbie smiled and finished chewing a bite of her piccata. After wiping her mouth, she replied, "Winnie's wise advice has been like receiving a new set of glasses to view the world. In the past, I worked hard to overcome difficulties as they arose in my life. Guess I relied mainly on my own strength. The damage, however, that Joe's betrayal brought into my life was too much for me to handle. Not only did he cause pain and heartache in my life, but especially for Drew."

Keith quietly sat as he listened to Abbie. Her tone of voice in earlier conversations about Joe was brittle, her eyes cold and hard, as she described the man who had almost ruined her life. Tonight's description of her former husband, however, was somehow different. Abbie leaned toward Keith as she talked rather than away from him, her arms crossed as he'd often seen her do. Tonight, her eyes were warm and velvety, the glow of the flickering candles dancing within them with a newfound joy. Her eyes were the windows to her heart, where he could see that God had slowly moved away the stones of bitterness and unforgiveness. He could almost feel the softness and vulnerability of her heart.

"I'm so proud of my son," Abbie said softly. "He's become quite the grown-up. Helping him get settled has shown me how much healing has taken place in his mind and his heart. Rod Eichman, Josh Hastings, Don Fielding, and you will be wonderful role models for him to follow."

The fact that Keith's name was mentioned along with the others, whom he considered some of the godliest men he knew, thrilled him beyond measure. *Run #2 for the home team.*

Keith took a sip of his iced tea before venturing to ask his third question. *Lord,* he thought, as his throat went suddenly dry like cotton. *Please let Abbie say the words I long to hear.*

"When I came to Mistletoe on Monday afternoon," he began, "we talked briefly about our relationship. Where it's headed and how it might progress, as we both work at Timothy House." Keith felt like his chest was about to explode.

Abbie smiled, her eyes never leaving his. "I've thought a great deal about that this week."

"You and I have both been hurt before. Deeply wounded by people we loved and betrayed by life circumstances beyond our control. It would be easy to pull up the drawbridge of our hearts and never let another get close enough to hurt us."

Still silent, Abbie's gaze was unwavering, her eyes gentle as they gleamed in the candlelight.

"I love you, Abbie. Of that, I am certain, and that has not changed. If anything, that feeling has only grown stronger. If we were teenagers, with our whole lives before us, I could understand dating for a prolonged period, maybe even years, before deciding to marry. You and I, however, are not exactly spring chickens."

At this, Abbie smiled. *Like mother, like son,* Keith thought.

"I've never met anyone like you," Keith continued, "and I don't think I ever will. I want a chance to see where this relationship might lead. Would you give me that chance?"

Just at that moment, the waiter appeared. Both Abbie and Keith declined dessert. After glancing over the bill, Keith handed his credit card to the server, and the man disappeared to process the payment.

As soon as the waiter stepped away from the table, Abbie spoke up. "Keith, I've never met anyone like you either. And although I'm scared to death, I don't want to lose you." As before, her eyes never left his.

Keith wanted to shout. *Home run for the Haliday team!*

Their waiter, who seemed to have an uncanny sense of timing, returned to deliver the transacted bill. Keith signed the ticket and thanked the man for his attentive service. After he left the table, Keith and Abbie sat and stared at each other for the longest time, a silly grin on both their faces. He reached across the table for Abbie's hand and took it in his own. "If you don't mind, I have a surprise for you."

"Let's go," she said as she squeezed his hand.

CHAPTER
13

Was this a dream? Keith could hardly believe that Abbie had moved to Robbinsonville and, because of their work, they would see each other practically every day. He had dreamed for so long about growing closer to her, and now here she was. Neither said much as they drove west from Kingsport. Some twenty minutes later they reached Bays Mountain Park. As they passed through the main gate and headed down the lake road, Abbie turned and asked, "What is this place?"

Wonder was evident in Abbie's voice as the sunset unfolding over the lake came into view. The sky was a golden vault spread high above them. When they arrived at an area where several picnic tables sat near the water, Keith parked the Explorer.

"This is Bays Mountain Park, a newly discovered place I come often to clear my head." Keith got out of the car and headed around it to get Abbie.

Opening her door, he said, "Madame," and bowed slightly. Employing his best impersonation of a British butler, he said, "If you please, I will escort you to your table."

Abbie giggled but played along, allowing Keith to lead her to a nearby table. After seating her on the far side, looking out toward the lake, Keith continued his monologue. "Please enjoy the spectacular view here at Bays Mountain Lake. Although you may hear strange noises behind you, have faith that they are related to the delicious treat prepared especially for you. Turning around would spoil the surprise. Dessert will be served shortly."

Keith turned back toward the truck, glancing back every few seconds to check on Abbie. She would definitely earn the Good Sport Award tonight, as he could tell she was doing her best to play along. Thankfully, the weather was perfect, and the panorama of the setting sun over the lake was stunning. Reaching into the back seat, he grabbed the cooler, sack of utensils, and a red checkered tablecloth Doris had lent him.

He quietly approached the picnic table, but Abbie heard him. When she tried to turn around, Keith's butler affectation had her convulsing in laughter, but she nonetheless turned back, keeping her gaze toward the lake and away from him. Soon, he had two place settings side by side on the near side of the table. A generous portion of tiramisu, smothered in chocolate sauce and heavy cream, filled each plate. After placing bottled water at each of their places, he tucked the small cooler and grocery sack under the table and went around to stand in front of Abbie.

Again, he bowed and held out his hand to her. "Madame," he said as he helped her up and led her to her seat.

A small gasp escaped from Abbie as she saw the surprise he had specially prepared. "Oh, Keith," she said, turning to him. "Tiramisu is my favorite!"

Taking a seat next to her, he picked up his bottled water. Raising it in a mock toast, Keith said, "To us," and clinked his bottle against hers.

As they savored the treat, several geese flew by, honking as if to send a greeting to them. An owl hooted quietly somewhere in the woods nearby. It was as if Nature had conspired with Keith to create the most romantic evening possible.

Once they had finished, Keith swung one leg over the bench to face her, and she turned toward him. Gently, Keith took both her hands in his.

"Dear Abbie," he began, "I pray tonight will be the start of something new and wonderful."

She held his eyes with her own as she softly moved a thumb over Keith's knuckles. Breaking her gaze to look down at her small hands clasped in his strong ones, she knew she never wanted to let them go. She looked back up, and the emotion that had been building from deep within her spilled over in a tear that made its way down her face. Her lips began to quiver.

Alarmed, Keith tenderly wiped a tear away with his thumb and said softly, "What's wrong? Did I say something wrong?" Fear and apprehension filled his heart.

"No," sniffled Abbie. "It's that I'm afraid I'll say something wrong."

Laughing gently, Keith lifted her chin slightly. "What could you ever say wrong, my dear Abbie?"

"It's not what I might say, but rather what I'm unable to say, at least not tonight, that I'm afraid will make you want to walk away."

Keith sat for a few minutes, soaking in the true meaning of her words. "Oh," he said, a slight smile playing across his face, "you mean the 'L' word—the one I said to you in the chapel two months ago?"

Abbie nodded as more tears trickled down her cheeks.

"Abbie," Keith began, his words earnest and sincere, "listen to me." He squeezed her hands tightly. His dark blue eyes glistened with emotion he'd long tried to hide. "I love you, and nothing's going to change that. Not your fear of being hurt again. Not knowing what this relationship will look like going forward as we both work at Timothy House. Not the fact that we can't say with certainty that our story will end in a happily ever after. And certainly not because you can't yet articulate your feelings for me. I believe you love me, and I'm willing to wait for you until you are ready to believe that for yourself."

As the sun slipped lower in the summer sky, Keith gently let go of Abbie's hands. Never breaking his gaze, he gently took her face between his hands. Leaning close, he kissed her tenderly. As he pressed his lips against hers, he prayed she could feel and taste and see the depth of his feeling for her. All at once, he had his answer as she wrapped her arms around his neck and pulled him closer, her lips warm and sweet with her tears. When the kiss ended, Abbie laid her head on Keith's shoulder, and they held each other tightly until the sun had set.

Just as He had before, God once again assured them that this journey of discovery would be traveled one second, one minute, one day at a time, and He Himself would be their guide.

CHAPTER
14

Working under the hood of a car gave C.J. time to think. In fact, it was all he had been doing since his arrival in Robbinsonville last fall. He had used these many months to bide his time and build a cover of respectability for himself. Securing a job at Howard's Tire and Auto had been a stroke of genius. He grabbed a wrench from the tool chest with one hand, and used the other to wipe away a bead of sweat trickling down from beneath the red bandana tied around his forehead. *What a perfect place to hide in plain sight*, he thought as he reached back to tighten the housing on the oil filter.

This particular morning, he was working on a 1998 Chevy Suburban. The client needed an oil change and the filter replaced. The man had also asked C.J. to check the spark plugs.

As he worked, the mechanic made mental notes of the plans he hoped to execute soon. Part of the reason he had come here was because his contacts in Illinois had told him this section of eastern Tennessee might offer a new market for his side business. Pushing pills was C.J.'s preferred way of making a living, but one little problem—running afoul of the law—forced him to find a day job that appeared as respectable as possible.

C.J. liked to think of himself as a businessman in an elaborate supply chain that had proved lucrative once before. Unfortunately, much of the profit made from the last place he lived was gone—it had taken more than he thought it would to make this move. The sheriff of a certain Illinois county had come close to connecting C.J. with a drug ring in the southern part of the state. The man had arrested him twice on speeding charges but had never been able to pin any drug-related charges on the young man. More slippery than an eel, C.J. had managed to escape the lawman's dragnet.

Fortune has smiled on me, C.J. thought, as he checked the Suburban's spark plugs. The mechanic had done all he could to ingratiate himself to his boss, Bill Howard. The name the mechanic had supplied on his paperwork was Durrell Dykes. Bill's trusting nature, coupled with the fact that he rarely used more sophisticated means of verifying information, was the hole in the net through which C.J. had slipped into this new persona. If Mr. Howard had dug a little deeper, he might have discovered that the initials were actually the first two initials of C.J.'s real name—Cash Jones Durrell. One of the older guys in the Illinois drug ring had once told C.J. that telling enough of the truth was one way to make a lie believable. So far, Bill Howard had bought the young employee's story.

C.J.'s Illinois supplier had been pressuring him to find someone to help push product. This was the part of establishing a territory that was always the hardest and took the longest. Finding someone who was either too naive or too desperate to really think about what the actual consequences of getting caught by the law might mean. C.J. was hoping to find someone in the Robbinsonville area who was both.

Throughout the past month, C.J. had been working on a plan he thought might be perfect. Besides being a local car repair shop and auto parts store, Howard's Tire and Auto was also a wholesaler to other auto shops within a thirty-mile radius. Throughout the past ten days, C.J. had made several deliveries for Mr. Howard: one trip to Fall Branch and two to Jonesborough. While in these nearby towns, C.J. had carefully noted the names of the auto body shops and employees he met at each. Perhaps one of them might be interested in making some extra cash.

Reaching once again for a wrench, he congratulated himself on his plan. As he replaced the filter, he smiled. *Simple, but brilliant. We hide a small stash of pills inside a radiator hose, then bury that part within a larger box of similar hoses. The hose containing the product will be marked with a dark blue circular sticker, like those at the office supply store. Once the box is delivered to its next stop in the delivery chain, our man carefully opens the*

box, recovers the drugs from the marked hose, and then reseals the box and
places it on the shelf of the supply room of another auto parts store.

C.J. had been involved in a similar operation in Illinois. Each distribution ring member was supplied a pair of twelve-inch stainless-steel tweezers to extract the pills packaged within should they have shifted while being transported. *Ingenious*, he thought, as he wiped down the engine with a grease-stained rag and then slammed the Suburban's hood shut.

C.J. smiled to himself as he thought about his next move.

Now all he needed was a mule.

———

Two days after school ended, DeSean took Max's older model Honda sedan to Howard's Tire and Auto in Robbinsonville for a tire change and balance. The drive was short, only about twenty minutes. While waiting in the lobby for the repairs to be completed, one of the mechanics came through the room and spoke with DeSean. He said his name was C.J. By the time the two finished talking, DeSean felt he'd found a new friend.

A few weeks later, DeSean had been out running errands in town for Max and Edna. While walking back to his car on the main street downtown, he heard someone call his name through the window of a vehicle driving slowly past him. He looked up to see C.J., the mechanic he'd met at the tire shop. Two other guys were in the car. Not anyone DeSean knew.

"Hey, man," C.J. called out.

"Hey, C.J.," DeSean said, raising his hand in a wave. "What are you doing here?"

C.J. motioned for DeSean to come over as he pulled the car into an empty parking space ahead. By the time DeSean reached the spot, cigarette smoke curled from the open right rear passenger window.

DeSean leaned down and looked into the car. "How are you?" he asked, looking into C.J.'s brown eyes and then glancing past to the faces of the other two guys.

The one in the front seat had a greasy, dark brown ponytail. The fellow in the back, dragging hard on the cigarette, had a pale, pimply complexion and stringy strawberry-blond hair. They didn't look much older than he was. DeSean could feel them sizing him up.

"I'm good," C.J. said. Nodding toward the other guys in the car, he continued, "We're making a delivery for Mr. Howard. How's your summer? Been practicing basketball lately?"

"Sure have. Practice won't officially start until September. We're hoping to make it to the playoffs. We came close last year."

The two guys in the car with C.J. still hadn't said a word, only stared coldly at DeSean as if trying to make him feel small and insignificant.

"Where are my manners, DeSean?" said C.J., looking remorseful. Nodding to his right, he continued, "This is Ted, and this"—jerking a thumb over his shoulder toward the back seat—"is Nico."

More smoke wafted up from inside the car.

"Look," C.J. continued, "I'll be in Jonesborough this weekend to see some friends. Why don't you come hang out with us? We'll grab a bite at a diner on Second Street on Friday night." He handed DeSean a grease-smudged business card through the car's open window. "Call me. We'll save you a place at the table."

"I'll see," DeSean replied. "We may have a late practice. Let me check and I'll let you know."

C.J. extended a closed fist out of the open window and bumped DeSean's. "Later," C.J. said, tipping his chin up slightly and putting the car in reverse.

DeSean couldn't be sure if the other two guys nodded to him or not. At least he thought they did.

As DeSean watched the car move slowly out of sight, a warm feeling rose within him, one he hadn't felt in a while. From the depths of his mind, a vague memory arose. Something about a child in the trailer next to his inviting him to come over to play. The little boys had played with toy trucks and cars, and the boy's mother had fixed cookies and hot chocolate for them. The afternoon had been one of the happiest DeSean had spent in his four-year-old life. Just as the neighbor's boy had done all those years ago, someone had thought to include him in their plans. He smiled to himself as he headed back down the sidewalk to Max Smith's car.

What DeSean forgot to remember is that emotions can be deceiving.

CHAPTER
15

Abbie drove up the long, shady drive of Drew's new residence and parked beside his SUV.

As she put her car into park, the movement of a curtain in the upstairs apartment caught her eye. She watched her son's handsome face come into view as he waved to her. As Abbie opened the door and stepped out onto the crushed pebble drive, she heard the apartment door open.

"Hey, Mom," Drew called from the top of the stairs.

"Hello, yourself!" Abbie made her way up the wooden stairway.

Drew met her halfway and wrapped her in a tight hug. "You won't believe the progress I've made since you were here on Saturday."

Abbie followed her son into the apartment. Though Drew had lived in rental housing before, this was his first foray into paying his own way as a grown-up. Her heart swelled with pride as she listened attentively as Drew led her around the small apartment, drawing her attention to his many improvements. The chairs and sofa in the living area had been rearranged. The tops of the kitchen counters were clean and neat. Drew's bed looked like one in a nice hotel, the covers pulled up tightly without a wrinkle in sight.

After the tour, mother and son piled back into her vehicle. Abbie backed away from the garage and headed down Barbara's tree-lined drive.

"Where are we going, Mom?" Drew asked. "I'm starving."

"Thought we'd try Mexican cuisine tonight," his mother replied. "We're headed to the Lime Tortilla, a relatively new place that Don and Doris recommended. Don told me their enchiladas were especially good." Abbie knew this selection was one of her son's favorites.

The pair chatted noisily for a few minutes more until they reached their destination. An almost full parking lot bolstered the Fieldings' recommendation.

Abbie and Drew didn't have to wait long to be seated and were pleased to learn that a table was open on the restaurant's back terrace. Beyond the seating area, a broad lawn stretched out a few yards or so to meet a mountain stream that gurgled cheerily as it wound its way toward lower ground.

Once the waiter brought dinner to them, the man left Abbie and Drew alone to enjoy their dinner, only reappearing occasionally to refill their glasses.

"How's your enchilada?" Abbie asked as she dipped a tortilla chip in the queso.

"This is fine, Mom," Drew said, barely reaching up in time with his napkin to wipe away a glob of sour cream that escaped from his fork. "How's your taco salad?"

"It's really good."

Abbie let Drew direct the conversation. As she listened to her now-grown son, she was amazed at how far he'd come over the past five years since Joe's death. The young man's father had been verbally abusive at best and emotionally abusive at worst. Abbie uttered a silent prayer, thanking God that Drew seemed to have found solid ground in his recovery from such an emotionally detached father.

Drew sounded excited about his new jobs and chatted away about how he looked forward to getting to know the men he would work with—Rod Eichman, Josh Hastings, and Don Fielding. An added bonus was that Jason Wyatt, Lane and Eric's oldest son and Drew's best friend, would also be working at Wright's Creek Church. Abbie smiled to herself as she listened to the positive, hope-filled tone in Drew's voice. God was definitely at work in her son's life.

The waiter appeared at the table with a dessert menu. After looking it over, the mother and son ordered a sopapilla, and the waiter left to place the order. Surprisingly, the man reappeared as quickly as he had left, setting down a warm fried Mexican pastry with a coating of powdered sugar. The server placed two small plates and a container of honey on the table, as well as a cup of hot coffee and a pitcher of creamer.

"Enjoy," the waiter said politely before turning his attention to other tables.

Abbie used her fork to break off a portion of the pastry and moved it to her plate. Drew did the same. Both drizzled amber-colored honey generously over their dessert. For a few minutes, neither spoke as they savored the delicious treat.

After taking a sip of her coffee, Abbie dabbed at her mouth with her napkin and looked over at Drew. "Son, I wanted to ask you something."

Drew looked up, his eyes full of questions.

"It will be so wonderful living in the same town together, as we've been apart during your time away at college."

"I am definitely excited about that," Drew replied.

"Me, too, but . . ." Abbie paused, not quite sure how to put into words what she had in her heart. "I hope you'll take this the right way."

The expression on Drew's face let her know he wasn't quite sure what she was about to say.

"I want to make sure you have your own space," Abbie continued. "You're a grown man embarking on your first real work in the world. You don't need your mother hovering over you like a helicopter."

Drew laughed aloud, relief evident on his face. "Mom," he said, "are you kidding me? The fact that you also live in Robbinsonville is one of the main reasons I took these jobs."

Abbie's heart swelled at these tender words from her son. "That's sweet, Drew."

"It's not sweet," he continued, "it's the truth. I love you with all my heart and am incredibly proud to be your son. I love the fact that you and I are close. So many of the people I met in college came from homes where no one cared or where the problems were ugly and unimaginable."

"Drew," Abbie said softly, "our home life wasn't always the best." The coldness and isolation Abbie and Drew both suffered at Joe Richardson's hands had left permanent frostbite wounds on their hearts.

"I know," Drew said, looking somewhere past Abbie as they sat at the patio table. "Dad was the worst."

Abbie's heart sank. She'd always suspected this, but hearing her precious son say these words aloud made her want to put her head in her hands and weep. Through tear-filled eyes, she said, "Oh, Drew. I'm so sorry."

Drew reached out and took one of his mother's hands in his and squeezed it tightly. "I know you are."

Mother and son exchanged a long, knowing look. Releasing her hand, Drew sat back in this chair.

"One of the things God has taught me this past year is that although I don't always have a choice about the circumstances of my life, I *do* have a choice about my responses to those circumstances. Yes, Dad was not a good dad.

"But I can choose to be a victim the rest of my life and feel sorry for myself because of the way my dad treated me, or I can look to my Heavenly Father for help to forgive Dad, to learn new patterns of love and faith from Him, and make sure that when and if marriage and a family become a part of my own life, I do all in my power to be the best husband and dad I can be. With God's help is the only way all that will happen."

For a long while, Abbie sat silently as she looked at this new adult version of her once little boy. "Drew, you amaze me," she said softly.

"This isn't anything I've done. This is the Lord at work in my heart and mind. Although sometimes, when I look at other guys' fathers, like Mr. Eric, I'd be less than honest if I didn't tell you I've been a tad jealous of Jason and Jonathan at times. What a great dad they have.

"*However*, what I've decided to do is give thanks and focus on what I *did* get in my family, and that is that God gave me the best mom in the world. Without your constant love and support, I don't even want to think about where I'd be." He reached over and grasped Abbie's hand again.

Tears trailed quietly down Abbie's cheeks as she gripped her son's hand with a ferocity of love that surprised even her. Mother and son sat looking at each other for long seconds, still so much yet unsaid between them. Finally, after wiping the tears away, she said, "I don't know what to say. The mom you describe is not the one I remember being, but I'm thankful it was the one you needed and found in me."

As if at the precise moment, the waiter appeared with the check. Abbie gave him her best smile as she reached into her wallet for her credit card. She hoped it wasn't too evident that she had been crying. The man took the ticket and her payment and headed back into the restaurant.

"You just promise me," Abbie said, wanting to finish what she had started to say to Drew earlier, "that if I get too pushy or call you or come over too often, you'll let me know. I want to be mindful of your life, especially this season of it, and allow you the freedom and space to live it."

"That's a deal, Mom," Drew said, reaching over and kissing her tenderly on the cheek.

The waiter returned with the receipt and thanked Abbie and Drew for their business. "Adios," he called out as he left the table. "Come back to see us!"

"Gracias," said Abbie and Drew, practically in unison. "We definitely will."

Before she left the table, Abbie tucked the receipt from the Lime Tortilla in her wallet. As she did, she silently thanked the Lord for what He delivered tonight to their table on the patio: manna from Heaven to feed their stomachs, and words of encouragement to sustain their hearts.

God was indeed up to something good.

CHAPTER
16

Coming to this basketball clinic today had been Coach Denning's idea. The gym at the Jonesborough Community Center was the last place DeSean wanted to be on this Saturday morning. Now that summer had arrived, he had hoped to spend much of the first full day of each weekend sleeping as late as possible. The day-long skills builder workshop was sponsored by Timothy House, some school DeSean had never heard of. *Man,* he thought, *the school isn't even here in town.* DeSean couldn't figure out why Coach was so jazzed up about his being there. A few other guys from the team would be here, too, but not anyone DeSean was close to.

Edna Smith had been nice to get up early and prepare a hearty breakfast before sending him on his way. Scrambled eggs, toast, jam, and butter were already on the table. A tall glass of water and a shorter one filled with orange juice sat beside his plate. Bacon, however, was taking its own sweet time, according to the cook.

Slouching in his seat at the table, DeSean muttered under his breath, "Basketball practice doesn't even start for another three months."

Mrs. Smith glanced up from the stove and looked back at DeSean. "What did you say, honey?"

"Oh, only that we're getting an early start to the basketball season," said the teen with a smile as plastic as a child's toy. He stabbed a mound of scrambled eggs with his fork and stuffed them in his mouth. As much as DeSean hated to admit it, Mrs. Smith was an excellent cook. *These eggs taste great,* he thought. However, he stingily held on to the compliment, swallowing it instead as he inhaled a piece of buttered toast slathered in strawberry jam.

A few minutes later, Edna added a plate laden with four hot slices of bacon. By the time she had turned away from the table, DeSean had wolfed down two of them. By the time she reached the sink halfway across the room, the other two slices had disappeared. The ravenous teen washed down the home-cooked breakfast with the last of his orange juice.

"Thanks, Mrs. Smith," said DeSean, wiping his mouth with the back of his hand. Noticing the stricken look on Edna's face, he reached for the paper napkin on the table and wiped his mouth again. The pained expression on her face lessoned and looked more like a slight smile.

"What time is the clinic over this afternoon?" inquired Edna as she began collecting the various dishes scattered across the rectangular wooden table.

"I think around four, but I'm not sure," DeSean said politely. "Coach Denning will be there, or at least he said he would be." Seeming to talk more to himself than to his foster mother, DeSean continued, "I'm still not really sure why he wants me at this clinic."

"It's because Coach cares," said Edna, looking straight into DeSean's ice-blue eyes. "He sees something in you that has great promise, and he wants to develop that something in you."

DeSean blinked quickly to stem the angry tears that had sprung up unexpectedly. *No one* cared for him; of that he was sure.

But, oh, how he wished someone would.

———

When Keith pulled into the community center parking lot, a few teenage boys were sitting along the front sidewalk as if waiting for him. Once he parked and stepped out of his car, several stood, waved, and disappeared into the gym through a door behind them. *Hope that's not the welcoming committee,* Keith thought wryly. No sooner had that thought run through his mind than Coach Jackson Denning stepped into the morning sunlight through the door the boys had just entered.

Crockett High School's coach raised a hand in greeting as he headed toward Keith and his passengers.

"Welcome, Keith," said Jackson. The man was one of the most storied coaches in this part of Tennessee.

"Glad to be here," replied Keith as he shook Jackson's hand. It was like a small ham and hid the strength that lay within the man.

Josh had come around the front of the Explorer. "Coach," he said, not waiting for an introduction. "I'm Josh Hastings. Great to meet you." As Keith had already done, Josh likewise shook Jackson's hand.

"Do you guys need any help?" Jackson asked, turning his attention to Andy and Davis, who had piled out of the back seat and were now raising the Explorer's rear door.

"No, sir," they practically answered in unison. "We've got it."

Keith turned and rescued the young men. "Coach, where are my manners?" he said, extending a hand toward the young men working to remove several ball bags, two clipboards, and a stack of orange plastic cones. "This is Andy Beason and Davis Landrum. Gentlemen, this is Coach Jackson Denning." Keith was proud to see each young man step forward, look the older coach square in the eye, and shake his hand firmly.

"My pleasure, guys," replied Jackson. "Welcome to Jonesborough." Turning back to Keith and Josh, Jackson continued, "Come on in, and we'll help you get set up. It's time to get this show on the road." He grinned broadly and turned to lead them into the building.

The Jonesborough Community Center was one of the hubs of this town. It boasted an indoor swimming pool, two racquetball courts, a small exercise room, and a basketball court large enough to accommodate spectator stands on either side. Visitors entered through a lobby, off of which the business office was located. The center also had a kitchen and a large dining room. These two rooms, along with a series of meeting rooms on the second level of the center, were often used by organizations in the Jonesborough area.

Once in the gym, Keith saw a sizable group of teenage guys sitting in the stands on the far side of the court. Several grown men stood nearby talking. Nodding to Jackson, Keith said, "Are those yours?"

Jackson replied, "Eleven of them are. The others are from various schools in this area. I'll introduce you in a minute to the coaches that are with them. One is my assistant—the two other assistants are from Fall Branch."

"Looks like a good group to me," said Keith. "Give me and my guys about ten minutes to get our gear in order, and then we'll start. I want to make sure we begin and end on time today."

Jackson's only reply was a nod as he walked across the court to visit with the high schoolers and coaches.

Keith, Josh, Andy, and Davis used the next few minutes to take balls out of bags, set up cones for drills, and lay out the clipboards Keith and Josh would use. Once all was in place, Keith walked out in front of the stands, and the other three attendees from Timothy House joined the crowd on the bleachers.

Jackson Denning joined Keith and reached for the whistle hanging from a lanyard around his neck. He gave two quick blasts on it, and all in the stands grew quiet. His stocky build and salt and pepper crew cut made him look more like a Marine drill sergeant than a coach.

"Gentlemen," he began, "welcome to the Summer Skills Clinic. It's our distinct pleasure to have Timothy House Crusaders basketball team players Andy Beason and Davis Landrum, Coach Keith Haliday, and Josh Hastings. Please give them a warm welcome."

The foursome from Timothy House waved as the small group applauded. Keith was drawn to a somber-faced, sandy-haired teen sitting by himself a few rows behind the others. *Wonder what his story is*, Keith thought as he panned the group of students.

Before turning over the reins of the clinic to Keith, Jackson introduced the three assistant coaches who were also joining the group. As before, polite clapping followed.

For the next few minutes, Keith gave a short introduction and brief overview of how the clinic would run. The morning drills would focus on strengthening offensive skills—dribbling, passing, shooting, and rebounding. The afternoon drills, he explained, would focus on enhancing defensive tactics—blocking and stealing the ball. The last hour of the clinic would include discussions on the art of the game itself—conditioning, foot placement, mental discipline, and sportsmanship. After he finished, Keith asked all the coaches and players to join him and the others from Timothy House on the court.

The morning activities ran smoothly. Keith was impressed not only with Josh and their two players but also with the three assistant coaches working with them. Jackson kept one eye on each skill station and lent a hand where needed. Several times throughout the morning, Keith's attention was again drawn to the teen he'd noticed earlier sitting alone in the bleachers. The kid was tall, about six feet by the looks of it, well proportioned, and had a wiry, muscular build.

While Coach Denning led the players through several drills, Keith watched DeSean run the paces. He was confident when holding a basketball and handled himself exceptionally well on the court. *This kid's got some moves*, thought Keith. Though the boy followed instructions well, he seemed awkward around the other players. DeSean's Crockett High teammates appeared to feel the discomfort as well. Keith noticed how they seldom passed the ball to DeSean or called out to him while running the drills. Keith made a mental note to ask Jackson about DeSean later.

By the time Jackson Denning blew the whistle for the lunch break, most of the teens were drenched in sweat and relieved to have a chance to sit down and relax. A local sandwich shop provided box lunches for the clinic, set up on a table along the far wall of the gym. A large cooler filled with ice and bottled water sat nearby. Several mothers of Crockett High players had arrived at the gym in the late morning, handed out the lunches, and served homemade chocolate chip cookies and brownies to the players and coaches.

The teens swarmed the food table. Keith noticed that his students, Andy and Davis, waited toward the end of the line while those from Crockett and the other area schools were served first. *Maybe some of our lessons on servant leadership are paying off*, he thought.

CHAPTER
17

Once Keith had picked up his lunch, grabbed water from the cooler, and nabbed a cookie, he glanced up in the stands to see the sandy-haired kid sitting all alone again. *That's where I'm headed*, he thought as he turned back to the bleachers, taking the steps two at a time.

"Mind if I sit down?" Keith asked. He noticed at once that DeSean seemed to tense up.

"Nope," the kid said. "I mean, no, sir," he quickly corrected himself.

"Thanks," Keith said. He sat a row below the kid, then set his box down on the metal platform and put his chilled water bottle on the step beside his feet. "My name's Keith. What's yours?"

The teen looked over at him with a look Keith couldn't quite discern. Apprehension perhaps? "My name's DeSean. DeSean Matthews."

"Well, nice to meet you, DeSean," Keith replied, trying to sound upbeat. *It's like this kid wishes he were anywhere but here at this clinic*, he thought as he opened his boxed lunch.

For the next few minutes, the two ate in silence. As time went by, and they ate more of the contents of their boxes, Keith made a few more attempts at conversation. All DeSean offered were vague, flippant answers. Usually, Keith found this type of behavior incredibly disrespectful and selfish in a teen, but as he took bites of his ham sandwich, Keith had a strong impression that this particular young man was working hard to protect himself. From what, Keith wasn't quite sure.

Trying a new approach, Keith said, "Son, you've got a real talent for the game. I was watching you this morning. You're a really good player."

He wasn't sure, but he thought the boy sat up a little straighter after this comment.

"Thank you," was the reply, but Keith noticed that DeSean said it without looking him in the eye. In fact, the teen had looked anywhere but at Keith for most of their short, awkward conversation.

The blast of a coach's whistle had everyone turning around to the source of the sound. Jackson Denning stood at mid-court, his hands behind his back. "Eat up, men," he said, a slight grin on his face, although his voice sounded like that of a drill sergeant. "The afternoon session begins in ten minutes."

DeSean seemed relieved that the lunch break was ending. Keith wadded up his sandwich wrapper, the chip bag, and his napkin and placed them inside the white cardboard container. After drinking the last of his water and capping the bottle, he stood.

"DeSean," Keith said, extending his hand toward the teen, "it was nice to meet you. Thanks for letting me eat with you." *Let's see how this goes*, Keith thought as he waited for the young man's response.

Surprisingly, DeSean grasped Keith's hand and returned the handshake. The teen, unlike a few minutes earlier, looked Keith square in the eye. *Those are sad and weary eyes for someone so young*, Keith noticed.

"Nice to meet you, too, Coach Keith."

For the second time in a brief period, Keith had a strong intuition that this young man had many great needs. What they were, however, he didn't know. Realizing the gentle nudge of the Holy Spirit that he had long ago learned to recognize, Keith reached into his shorts and pulled out his wallet. Flipping it open, he grabbed a business card and extended it toward the boy. "DeSean, here's my contact information. If you ever need anything, don't hesitate to contact me. I'll be glad to help."

DeSean again met Keith's gaze head-on. "Thank you, sir," he said quietly. Taking the card from Keith's extended hand, the teen looked at it carefully and then squirreled it away in a pocket.

As Keith headed down the steps of the bleachers, he thought, *Lord, what was that all about?* He hoped, in time, he'd get an answer.

The end of the clinic went well, and before they knew it, Keith, Josh, Andy, and Davis were once again loading equipment into the back of Keith's Explorer.

Jackson Denning joined them in the parking lot. "Thanks, guys," he said, sincerity evident in his tone, as he reached out and shook the hands of the four from Timothy House. "This has been a great clinic." Chuckling a bit, he continued, "I've not seen some of my boys work that hard in a long time. Hope you'll come back again next year."

"We'd like that," replied Josh. He walked around the SUV and climbed into the car.

Andy and Davis each raised a hand in farewell and then scrambled into the back seat.

"Just a second, Coach," said Keith before getting into the front seat. He stepped a bit closer to Jackson and lowered his voice. "What can you tell me about DeSean Matthews?"

From the way Jackson seemed to gather his thoughts before speaking, it was obvious there was a story there. "He's a relatively new kid to our school," Jackson began. "He came to us two years ago as a sophomore. He's a loner and doesn't seem to have many friends. He's been in and out of foster care since he was about eight. Max and Edna Smith, his current foster parents, have given him probably the closest thing to a normal family life he's ever known."

As Jackson talked, Keith felt once again, as he had during his lunch with DeSean, that the boy needed help. "He knows his way around a basketball court, that's for sure," said Keith with obvious admiration.

"That he does," concurred the Crockett High coach. "I've tried all sorts of ways to reach out to him but haven't seemed to make much progress. You were kind to go sit with him at lunch today."

Keith shrugged. "I enjoyed getting to know him a little." Glancing at his watch, he realized it was time to head home. "Thanks again, Jackson, for inviting us to be here today. You've got a great group of players."

The older coach smiled at the compliment.

"Keep me posted on DeSean," Keith said as he opened his door.

"I will," Jackson said. "Drive safely."

"Will do," was the reply as Keith hopped in and put the car in reverse.

As the Timothy House coaches and players headed back to Robbin-sonville, Keith tried his best to listen to Josh talk, but for the life of him, he couldn't get DeSean Matthews off his mind. Thankfully, the drive back to campus was short, and it didn't take long to put the equipment back in the storage room of Athlos Court.

As Keith said goodbye to Josh, Andy, and Davis, the afternoon sun streamed through the nearby oak trees. Climbing back into his SUV, he headed down the drive to his cottage. *Lord,* he thought as he pulled up in front of Stone's Throw, *I'm not sure what this was all about today, meeting this kid. Please protect DeSean and bless him. Place in his path people who know You and who will shine Your light into his life. If there's something I'm supposed to do to help him, please make that plain to me.*

As Keith put his key in the front door lock, he already knew the Lord would indeed.

CHAPTER
18

Keith had an important appointment, and he did not want to be late. Try as he might to keep them closed, his dark blue eyes had popped open before the alarm sounded at five forty-five. He made quick work of the shower, and after toweling off, he carefully checked his appearance in the mirror above the bathroom sink as he combed his hair. The barbershop had even been able to schedule a cut yesterday. A can of starch he'd found stuffed underneath his kitchen sink had worked like a charm as he pressed his shirt and slacks with military precision.

Carefully surveying the campus, Keith walked from Stone's Throw, his cottage at Timothy House, to his office in Sanctuary Hall. It was critical that he not cross paths with Abbie this morning. He didn't want to see her until he accomplished the day's mission, whatever the outcome. Keith had finally mustered the courage to attempt one of the final hurdles that stood in the way of their relationship progressing more than it had already. By the end of the day, however, he would know for sure if he'd cleared that barrier or tripped and fallen short of his goal. He only hoped he could survive another heartbreak.

Yesterday, he told Don he would be off campus for a couple of meetings today. Keith tried his best to sound upbeat yet vague. Thankfully Don was preoccupied with several matters and had hardly even raised his head when Keith had stepped into the director's office.

As he slipped behind the wheel of his Explorer, a sense of nervousness washed over him, not unlike that of having to talk to his parents about a difficult subject. *I'm almost fifty-five years old*, Keith thought. *Get over it, man.* He glanced at his watch as he started the ignition. Ten fourteen. *I've got almost an hour before my appointment.* He was torn between staying in the SUV or going back to his office. Unable to stand the tension, Keith shifted into drive. He steered the dark vehicle slowly through the campus, again hoping he would not run into Abbie.

Only after he drove through the stone gates of Timothy House and turned onto the main road did Keith heave a sigh of relief. *One hurdle down, one to go,* he thought. He headed toward Wright's Creek Church but turned off in another direction a few blocks before. The road he was now on led out of town. It was familiar to Keith, as he had traveled down it many times before. A drive in the country always helped him clear his head.

Keith relaxed a little in the warmth of the summer sun shining brightly through his windshield. As he drove, neighborhoods of well-manicured lawns and tidy brick homes slowly gave way to fenced pastures where cattle grazed. Although he had turned the volume down, he thought he heard the faint strains of a song by Journey streaming from an easy-listening radio channel. He worked hard to concentrate on the road before him, but all he could think about was Abbie.

From the first moment he had met her, Abbie Richardson had rocked his world. Although they weren't introduced then, Keith remembered the first time he saw this woman who had captured his heart. It had been last summer in a gift shop in Craggy Bluff, a small town a few hours' drive from Robbinsonville, where Keith had gone with Don on a day trip. They paid a visit to Posie's, an art gallery in the town. The owners, Summer and Elton Tidwell, were potters and had agreed to serve as student mentors for the Tentmaker's Project. Keith hardly spoke on that afternoon drive back to Robbinsonville. All he could think about was the beautiful, dark-haired woman he'd seen at Posie's.

Only a few weeks later, when at the opening session for volunteers at Camp 4Ever, there sat the mysterious woman he'd seen in Craggy Bluff. Keith could hardly believe it. Later that evening, Keith and Abbie met at a get-together in the Fieldings' home. His heart had never been the same since.

The strange thing was that Keith and Abbie had not actually spent much time together. Perhaps at their age and this stage in their lives, they didn't need to. Both were widowed. Both had faced enormous heartache and overcome traumatic circumstances. Their shared suffering was a bridge they had walked over, only to meet each other in the middle. This place where they now stood was a broad plain from which they could glimpse, even though far out in the distance, the possibility of finding genuine, lasting love. *Only*, Keith thought as he turned the SUV around in order to make his appointment on time, *we've still got to find a way to reach love together.*

Swift as a strong rodeo steed, Keith's Explorer made it to Wright's Creek Church in record time. As instructed, he pulled up to the spot and parked. Checking his reflection in the rearview mirror, he said out loud, "Well, pal, it's now or never. Here's to now."

As he watched the tall, slender individual approach his car, Keith said a silent prayer. The two of them had never actually met, though he knew the man from photos he had seen.

Drew Richardson opened the passenger door and climbed inside.

CHAPTER
19

"So," Keith began, once back on the road, "how are you enjoying Robbinsonville?"

"So far, so good," replied Drew as he put on his sunglasses. "McHenry's the only town I've lived in all my life, other than my college years. It's interesting learning about a new place."

"Yeah, Robbinsonville is wonderful. I've only been here about two years myself. Your mother's especially excited that you've come to live here. Your move is all she's been talking about lately."

"I've missed her. She's equally happy about her new opportunity at Timothy House."

Intent on keeping the focus of conversation on Drew, Keith continued, "I hear you're getting settled into your new apartment."

"Yes, sir," replied Drew. "Josh connected me with my landlady, Mrs. Turner. She's already brought me several batches of homemade cookies and a pan of lasagna. At this rate, I'll have to step up my mileage on my morning runs."

Keith smiled as he listened to Abbie's only son banter about his new beginnings on their way to The Market Counter, a new deli-style restaurant in nearby Johnson City. Keith was genuinely interested in this young man. Don, Josh, and Rod Eichman—all men Keith respected—had mentioned what a fine young man Drew was.

As requested, the waitress led the two men to a table in the rear corner of the restaurant. As the men zigzagged through the room, Keith was thankful he'd reserved a table ahead of time, as the lunch crowd was heavy today. After bringing the men something to drink, the waitress scribbled their selections on her small notepad and then headed toward the kitchen to place the orders.

After a long sip of iced tea, Keith asked, "So, Drew, tell me about your job at Wright's Creek."

"Well, Mr. Keith. It's going really well."

Keith held up a hand and smiled at the same time. "Let me interrupt you, son. You're polite, but it's Keith. Please call me by my first name."

Sounding a bit unsure, Drew replied, "The job's going well, Keith."

As the young man used the older one's first name, Keith gave Drew a thumbs-up and flashed a warm smile as any tension vanished.

The delivery of their lunches briefly interrupted the conversation.

After taking a bite of his sandwich, Drew continued, "It will be a challenge to balance my time between Timothy House and Wright's Creek. Mr. Fielding, Josh, and Pastor Rod will be three great men to work with. I've had a dream of attending seminary for a long time, but I'm still not sure about it. Both jobs will allow me to learn more about life in ministry."

"You're smart to take your time in making that decision," Keith concurred. "I'll be praying about that for you."

"Thanks," said Drew, a gleam of sincere appreciation in his eyes. "You probably know the story of what my dad did, at least what we later found out he did."

Keith sat back in his chair and looked steadily at Drew. "Yes, I do. I am so sorry you and your mother have had to deal with the fallout from his crimes throughout these past years."

The change in Drew when he mentioned the subject of his father was noticeable—his body tensed, his eyes narrowed and grew cold, and his voice sounded like he was trying to get a bitter taste out of his mouth.

"Though I can't control how others think of me," Drew continued, "I want people to know that I'm not the man my father was. Honesty and integrity are my guides for building relationships and conducting business. My father talked a good game when it came to God, but I'm not sure he knew Him at all. That's not the walk with the Lord I want to have."

Keith thought for a minute before replying. "Drew, believe me when I say no one will *ever* mistake you for Joe Richardson. I'm only sorry your dad never appreciated what a wonderful young man you are." Wanting to turn the conversation back to a lighter subject, Keith asked, "Tell me more about your responsibilities at Wright's Creek."

As Drew continued talking about his first real job, Keith found himself captivated by the young man's maturity and depth of character. *What a fine son*, he thought. *I can see why Abbie is so proud of him.*

The waitress returned to refill their glasses and take their dessert order. Both men were quiet as they waited politely for her to clear their plates and silverware. Shortly after, she returned with two dessert bowls and a spoon for each—slices of peach pie, the house special.

As the two began sampling the baked treat, Keith prayed silently that the Lord would give him the right words to say and Drew the listening ears to hear them. After a few bites of dessert, Keith put down his spoon and gathered his courage. "I want to talk to you about something."

With that, Drew looked intently at Keith.

"In fact," Keith continued, "it's about someone we both know and love—your mother." After getting out that last part, he exhaled some of the breath he'd been holding. Nervous didn't even describe how he felt.

At the mention of Abbie, Drew lowered his spoon and wiped his mouth with his napkin, his gaze never leaving Keith's face.

"As you know, your mother and I have been seeing each other for some months now. She's an extraordinary lady."

Drew took a sip of his tea.

"Yes, Mom's told me quite a bit about you." Watching Keith's face for a few seconds, Drew finally grinned and said, "All of it's been good."

The smile on Drew's face filled the space in Keith's heart like helium rushing in to fill a balloon. He was elated. "Really?" he asked hesitantly.

"Yes, really." A genuine smile never left Drew's face.

"I'm not sure how to say all of this to you," Keith said, feeling like he was jumping over a huge boulder every time he spoke a word. "I'm sure your mother told you I lost my wife and two children in a car accident almost eight years ago. A drunk driver hit them head-on. They never had a chance."

Keith's voice trailed off and tears pooled in his eyes. Neither he nor Drew spoke for a few minutes. Keith worked to slow the emotional avalanche building inside. Once the feelings had subsided some, he continued.

"After Genny and our kids died, a large part of *me* died. She was a wonderful wife, and we loved each other deeply. Although our marriage had its share of ups and downs, we had worked diligently to make sure it was as strong as it could be. After I lost Genny, I never imagined I could ever love anyone again—that is, until I met Abbie."

Drew surprised Keith by adding to the conversation. "All my life, I've watched my mother suffer silently in a marriage with my father, one that always looked one-sided to me. How awful to have grown up the daughter of an alcoholic mother only to marry a dirtbag like my dad."

Keith noticed the hard glint in Drew's eyes when mentioning his father and describing the pain his mother endured.

"I'm not sure my father ever loved either of us," Drew said sharply. "There were so many things about our family life that never made sense to me while I was growing up, but suddenly they became crystal clear after we learned about the embezzlement and that my college money was gone."

"Your mother told me about that," Keith said, hoping Drew could hear the care and concern in his voice. "I'm so very sorry your father treated you and your mother so poorly. I'm especially sorry that he betrayed your trust. Broken trust is difficult to repair." Keith's eyes held fast to Drew's. "I love your mother. I came to that realization a few months ago. When I did, I made a split-second decision to drive three hours to McHenry and showed up at your house late one night to tell her. She probably told you."

This is more difficult than I imagined, Keith thought.

Drew nodded slightly, trying to suppress a grin. "She did."

"Until that night, I guess I had never considered how destructive your father's actions were not only to your mother, but also to you. Relationships, especially the ones upon which marriages are built on, must be based on trust. Without that solid foundation of confidence—of knowing your spouse will be there for you no matter what—a stable relationship is virtually impossible."

Drew's eyes grew red and moist.

Keith continued, "I love your mother with all my heart, Drew, and although I'm not exactly sure where our relationship is headed, I can tell you that I know where I hope it will go. I'd like to marry Abbie if she'll have me. Just as important, though, is making sure that you and I have a solid relationship. It would mean the world to me to have your blessing, to know that you approve of the relationship between your mother and me. It would be regrettable to gain Abbie as my wife and not you as a son."

Keith let out a long, slow sigh he prayed no one, especially Drew, could hear. He had said what he had come to say.

For a long while, Drew sat silently, looking past Keith into the space beyond.

Keith steeled himself for what was to come.

Finally, Drew's gaze returned to Keith's face, and in his expression, Keith found an openness and sincerity that warmed his heart beyond measure.

"Mr. Keith," Drew began. He immediately realized his mistake. "Keith, I mean. Although we don't know each other very well, you're someone I already admire and respect. Earlier this year, when your name kept popping up more and more in conversations with Mom, I decided to check up on you myself. I hope that doesn't make you mad."

This kid's got chutzpah, Keith thought to himself before replying. "No, Drew, I'm not mad at all. In fact," he said, grinning widely, "I'm impressed that you would work so hard to protect your mother. That tells me a lot about the type of man you are."

Drew instantly relaxed and sat back slightly in his chair.

Reaching for his glass, Keith continued, "What did you find out about me?"

"Well," Drew began slowly, "I learned that you are who you say you are. The people I've talked to say you're one of the finest men they've ever met. They say you're kind and considerate and loyal, and . . ." His voice grew softer. ". . . that you've endured more heartache in one lifetime than most people face in ten."

"The proverbial 'they,' huh?" Keith said with a grin.

The smile breaking across Drew's face lightened the tone of the conversation.

"I'll make you deal," Keith said, leaning forward. "I promise I will keep you informed about every step of the journey your mother and I are on. You mean the world to your mother, and I think you're pretty special, too. Regardless of how this turns out, I want you to know that nothing will stand in the way of your relationship with her."

"Thanks, Keith." Drew's gaze was warm and direct, and his eyes never wavered once in their sincerity.

———

As Keith and Drew got in the truck, the quiet young man Keith first picked up this morning evaporated, and Drew hardly stopped talking.

"What's your favorite college football team?" Drew asked.

Keith chuckled and then said, "That's a hard one." He thought for a few moments before answering. "I would say the Sooners of Oklahoma. I've enjoyed keeping up with Coach Stoops over the years, and the Sooner's quarterback, Jason White, won the Heisman last year. I also like LSU and Coach Saban." Glancing over at Drew, he asked. "Who's yours?"

"I'm an Ohio State man."

"Got it," said Keith, delighted to have found common ground with Drew.

"Next question," said Drew, seemingly enjoying this friendly interrogation. "Tell me a little about getting to play college basketball."

"Wow," replied Keith. "You've been doing your homework."

Now, it was Drew who laughed. "Yes, sir. I have."

For the next few minutes, Keith shared highlights from his glory days. As he did, he flashed back to when his son, David, had asked the same question. Somehow, instead of being sad, the memory lifted Keith's heart with the knowledge that he might once again have the opportunity to serve as a father to another young man.

When it seemed that Keith had finished with his story, Drew broke in. "What's your favorite flavor of ice cream?"

"Oh," said Keith, a smile playing on his face. "Rocky Road, hands down."

"No way!" exclaimed Drew. "That's mine, too."

"We'll have to take your mother for ice cream soon," Keith replied. "I'd like that."

Before Keith knew it, the short car ride had ended, and he was turning the Explorer into the parking lot of Wright's Creek Church.

As Drew unbuckled his seat belt, he turned back to Keith. "Thanks, Keith," he said, "for lunch and for the talk. What means the most is that my opinion matters to you."

Keith looked at Drew intently, hoping the young man was soaking in his every word. "Your opinion will *always* matter to me, Drew. I enjoyed this time with you today. I hope to have more opportunities to get to know you better. You're a delightful young man, and it's easy to see why Abbie's so incredibly proud of you."

Drew beamed with the glow of affirmation.

"Please keep your mother and me in your prayers," continued Keith. "This is uncharted territory for both of us, and we're not exactly spring chickens."

Drew grinned at the use of the dated expression. "I will pray for you and Mom," he said. "Keep me posted."

"One more thing," Keith said in a measured tone. "If you don't mind, don't mention our visit to your mother. I'll tell her about it when the time is right, but I would never want her to think we're plotting behind her back."

Drew gave a mock salute. "Got it!" He extended his hand to Keith, and the men exchanged a long handshake.

After opening the SUV door slightly, Drew turned back to his mother's special friend. With a solemn look reflecting the earnestness of a son totally devoted to his mother, Drew concluded before stepping out of the car, "Since meeting you, my mother's been happier than I've ever known her to be. Though you don't need my permission, I believe you're God's choice for her, and you have my blessing. Only please take good care of my mom."

With that, Drew Richardson turned away from his past and took one step closer to manhood and to the future God was unfolding for him day by day. Although Keith had only partial knowledge of the emotional damage Drew had suffered at the hands of his father, he was certain that Joe Richardson squandered his chance to be a good dad.

"Oh, Lord," Keith prayed as he headed back to campus, "my heart is so full, it feels like it will burst."

Keith's spirits soared with joy as he spoke the words aloud, his hands almost turning white from gripping the steering wheel so tightly.

"Thank you so much for answering my prayers and helping me get through this conversation with Drew today. His positive response to our relationship is more than I could have hoped or dreamed. Bless the friendship developing between us. Keep him close and walk with him in this new season of his life. Continue to guide Abbie and me on this journey. We've both lost so much, and I'm not sure we could recover from a broken heart a second time."

As the traffic light turned green, Keith's Explorer seemed to know that there was only one more block to go before reaching the gates of Timothy House as it surged through the intersection.

Keith finished his petition to his Heavenly Father as the vehicle entered the campus drive. "Please speak to Abbie's heart and restore her ability to trust once again, not just with her head, but also with her heart. Help us both lay the past to rest. Give us courage and hope and help us to trust You for our future, knowing You always have our best interests at heart. Amen."

Reaching the driveway of Stone's Throw, Keith thought as he parked the car, *As long as I have breath in my lungs, neither Abbie nor Drew will ever doubt my love for them.*

CHAPTER
20

Chloe looked more like a china doll than a real-life girl. Her porcelain complexion would have been the envy of any Madame Alexander collection. She was a compliant soul. If not already so when she arrived at the Hendersons', she had learned to be during these never-ending years. She'd lost track of the nights she'd cried herself to sleep.

When she first met Hope and Kevin, Chloe's little heart had swelled with the expectation of actually being a part of a family. Although a taller woman, Hope's angular frame and plain face lent itself to the facade of purity she portrayed to others. She always wore her red, stringy hair in a ponytail at the nape of her neck, giving her the appearance of a postulate, chaste and dedicated. Kevin, about the same height as his wife, was equally as thin. His light, sandy hair fell over the collar of his plaid work shirt, days-old stubble often covering his face. His job in construction always gave him the appearance that he needed a good wash.

"What a pretty little girl you are," was what Hope Henderson had murmured over and over as she patted Chloe's hand as they rode home from the DCS office. Both Mr. and Mrs. Henderson smelled clean— almost too clean. A fragrance not unlike that of mouthwash lingered on both of them. The smell awakened some long-dormant memory in Chloe's tender mind. The thought evaporated amid the process of getting adjusted to yet another household.

Before coming to Timothy House, Chloe had attended a nearby public school. Though sweet and kind, the child had few friends. Perhaps that was due to the fact that Hope Henderson rarely allowed Chloe to invite others over to play. The child lived for the hours between when the bus picked her up across the street from the dirty brown house until the driver dropped her off again. Jane and Emily were her two best friends. Mrs. Henderson had only allowed Chloe to invite the pair to play a few times since the girl had joined the household. Most of Chloe's time after school, rather than dutifully completing her homework, was spent completing a never-ending list of chores for Mrs. Henderson. However, Chloe hadn't seen Jane, Emily, or any other friends much since summer began and was counting the days until Camp 4Ever started.

A kindhearted neighbor, Mrs. Jennings, long a contributor to the program, had dropped off a brochure with Kevin. The matron's influence had paved the way for what would soon be three summers of an all-expenses-paid summer camping experience. Only five more days until Chloe was to return to the campus of Timothy House for the five-day program.

The Hendersons' carefully orchestrated mistreatment of Chloe began shortly after her arrival. Two long periods of being locked in the hall closet assured her compliance when the child first entered their home. Hope and Kevin knew better than to lay a finger on Chloe. However, last year, in a fit of anger, Hope had whipped the child with a wire coat hanger. The end of the wire cut the back of Chloe's left leg and was deep enough to require stitches. A late-afternoon visit to the local emergency room solved the problem. Hope threatened Chloe within an inch of her life about saying anything suspicious to the physician. However, the small scar about three inches above the back of Chloe's left knee remained a silent witness.

Hope and Kevin, who looked like two thin scarecrows, had beaten down Chloe's soul and spirit as surely as they'd knocked her down and kicked her in the stomach. The tall, reedy woman often placed her face within inches of the girl's and spoke to her in a cold, sarcastic tone that haunted the child even in her dreams.

Through these past four years in the Henderson house, Chloe had stuffed her feelings as deep down in her spirit as she had a copy of *Cinderella* under her mattress. The heroine in the fairy tale had become as real to Chloe as Mrs. Dawson, her fifth-grade teacher. Cinderella was now Chloe's role model.

Each night before going to bed, Chloe would reach under the mattress and pull out the borrowed copy of *Cinderella*. The Hendersons, like the make-believe stepmother in the fairy tale, were masters at leaving undetected marks. However, instead of a prince, as Cinderella yearned for, Chloe's little heart ached for the gentle voice and loving embrace of a mother. *Her* mother. Ever since meeting Abbie Richardson at Camp 4Ever, Chloe saw the woman's face in her mind's eye whenever she thought about what a mother would be like. How often the girl had wondered about being part of a family—a *real* family. As carefully as she'd withdrawn the treasured book from between the saggy mattress and squeaky box spring, Chloe returned the tattered edition to its hiding place each night before falling asleep.

The flame of hope, sputtering within Chloe's heart, would surely be extinguished if help didn't arrive soon.

CHAPTER
21

DeSean pulled out of the Smiths' driveway, relieved to have some time to himself. Yesterday morning he'd asked to use the car as he, Max, and Edna finished breakfast. The teen told them he'd been invited to eat dinner with some new friends, which was true, although DeSean really didn't know these guys at all. All day, he'd focused on trying to remember the two guys in the car with C.J. when DeSean saw them in town a few days earlier. For the life of him, his memory refused to cough up their names. DeSean couldn't remember the last time a person his age had extended him an invitation or included him in an outing. Ever since running into C.J. and his pals in Robbinsonville, DeSean had been whistling a happy tune.

The diner on Second Street that C.J. had mentioned was not too hard to find. Even at seven o'clock, the street was not too full, and DeSean found a parking spot in front of a floral shop three doors down. As he pushed through the swinging door of the restaurant and stepped inside, the smell of burned grease and beer wafted past him onto the sidewalk. The room was cavernous and dark. Neon lights displaying the names of several choice ales hung on the wall behind a bar set up in a back corner of the room. Sounds of many conversations, shouts of orders given to kitchen staff, and strains of country music filled the room. After his eyes had adjusted to the dim light, he spotted the trio he was to meet.

DeSean made his way through the jumble of tables to C.J. and his two friends.

"Hi, guys," said DeSean, hoping he sounded confident. Inside, he wasn't so sure.

"Hey, dude," said C.J., looking up at him with dark brown, beady eyes resembling those of a feral animal. "You remember my pals, Ted and Nico," C.J. continued, nodding toward the two as DeSean took a seat at the table.

"Sure," the teen said, trying to sound casual.

DeSean immediately thought of an opossum he'd cornered in the Smiths' backyard one night when it tried to get into their garbage cans. When he'd found it, the thing hissed at him and bared its teeth. *Man, my imagination's working on overdrive tonight,* thought DeSean.

Ted and Nico still had not said a word; they only nodded their heads as they took pulls from their longneck beers. Their eyes didn't look much different than C.J.'s. All three had plates in front of them, and by the looks of it, the food had only recently been served.

A waitress came around and brought a menu to DeSean, waiting for him to place his order. Her pen was poised in mid-air, like a reporter waiting to record the perfect line. He ordered a cheeseburger with fries and a root beer. He could feel the eyes of the three older guys on him as he named his drink. *I'm going to drink what I want to drink,* he thought, again worried he was making too much out of nothing.

"How's work at the auto parts store?" DeSean asked, trying to make conversation.

"It's real good," said C.J., perking up at the personal inquiry. "Mr. Howard—he's the boss—says I'm one of his best workers. Sales are way up since I arrived on the scene." Those eyes again, although this time they glistened with the light of pride.

DeSean asked a few questions about C.J.'s responsibilities at the auto parts store. Like a famous movie actor interviewed on opening night, C.J. took the opportunity to extol more of the many reasons why he was such a valuable employee for Bill Howard.

The arrival of the waitress was a welcome sight for DeSean, as he was trying to figure out common ground with his three table mates. He took a bite of the hot burger while C.J. droned on about work.

Waiting for the chance to congratulate C.J. on his hard work, DeSean seized the perfect opportunity and responded, "Terrific," before taking another bite. Once swallowed, he took a long sip of his root beer, the carbonated liquid stinging the back of his throat.

C.J. and his two friends struck up a conversation about a sports team and a recent playoff. DeSean hadn't eaten since lunch and was focused on the plate before him.

The waitress returned to check on the foursome. "Any of you guys want some pie?"

"What do you have?" C.J. sat back in his chair and looked up at the young woman. By her reaction, DeSean could tell that C.J.'s stare was a little too bold. The girl's cheeks were fire-engine red.

"We . . . we have apple and strawberry pie," she stammered. "Both can be served with a scoop of ice cream." As the blush still burned, the waitress averted C.J.'s gaze and turned her attention to the other three at the table.

"Men?" asked C.J., acting as if he were the lord of a great castle and these were his loyal knights assembled before him.

Ted and Nico both ordered apple pie á la mode. C.J. looked over at DeSean. "You?"

"I'll have the same," answered the teen.

"Make it four slices of apple pie, sweetheart," said C.J., "and make sure you smother them in ice cream."

As the waitress left the table, DeSean felt sorry for her. C.J. gave off some creepy vibes. Although he wasn't quite sure what they were, DeSean hoped he never got on this guy's bad side.

Soon, the waitress served the heaping bowls of apple pie with ice cream melting atop the baked treat. The four dug into the desserts as if it were their last meal.

After a long while, C.J. looked over at DeSean, who was finishing the last of his pie. "Hey, man, how'd you like to make a few extra dollars?"

DeSean perked up at the mention of earning some spending money. "Doing what?"

"Oh, making deliveries of auto parts. From time to time, Mr. Howard has customers here in Jonesborough. Since you live here and know that area, that would really help us out at Howard's Tire and Auto."

Something deep within DeSean responded to this offer of significance. It had been a long time since someone had taken notice of him. To most, he felt invisible. C.J. and these guys seemed like they really got him. Plus, the chance to earn a few dollars of his own hadn't come from any other source.

C.J. grabbed a napkin from the container in the middle of the table. He doubled the thin paper over so it was thicker and pushed it across the table to DeSean. After taking out a pen from the pocket of his dirty jeans, he handed it to the teen. "Write down your phone number. Make sure you put your name with it. The next time we need a delivery, I'll give you a call."

DeSean nodded and did as he was told. He pushed the napkin back across the table toward C.J. and laid the pen on top of it.

"Thanks for thinking of me," said DeSean, now thinking he'd misread C.J. and his friends when he'd first arrived at the diner.

"You're welcome, man," said C.J. as he placed a toothpick in his mouth. "Always glad to help a friend."

All the way home, C.J.'s words rang in DeSean's mind: *Always glad to help a friend.* He couldn't remember many people in his short life that had called him a friend. The fact that these guys were older and wanted to hang around with him was an enormous boost to his ego. He had his eye on a pair of specialty basketball shoes he'd seen in a store window the last time he'd run errands with Max Smith. The price tag had made him gulp.

Now who'll be doing the gulping? he thought. *Just wait till the guys on my team see me in those fancy shoes.* He only hoped the call to make those deliveries would come soon.

CHAPTER
22

Final preparations for Camp 4Ever were underway. The campus of Timothy House was abuzz with summer staff, lawn service crews, and a host of delivery trucks arriving at all hours of the day. As assistant director of the school, Keith's plate had been chock full, but others on the Camp 4Ever staff, especially Josh Hastings, had helped Keith shoulder the load, even taking on several tasks normally assigned to Keith. Even though he was still in his office, Keith was especially grateful that he had little to do this afternoon, as he had a lot on his mind. Looking at his watch, he noticed it was four forty. He and Abbie had been invited to eat dinner with Don and Doris at The Manse, and were due there at six thirty. Although he still needed to run by his cottage and change shirts, he had an important appointment he was determined to keep.

Turning off the light in his office, Keith headed down the hall and out the side door of the administration building. Thankfully, no one was nearby—no yard service personnel, no volunteers from several of the churches in Robbinsonville that had been on campus all week, no one from the school seeking his signature, no one with whom he'd have to interact. It was as if God had placed a cone of invisibility over him. Looking both ways as if crossing the street, Keith headed toward the back of campus and made his way to Peter's Chapel.

Slipping into the cool darkness of the sanctuary, he headed up the aisle to what he now thought of as his pew—second row from the front on the left. Lowering his tall frame onto the bench, he sat for a long while. He leaned back and ran his fingers through his dark hair. *Tonight's dinner will be important, all right,* he thought. When he'd gone to see Don earlier in the week to ask for advice regarding his relationship with Abbie, Don had immediately called Doris. The two of them, his boss had said as he covered the receiver with his hand, would like Keith and Abbie to come for dinner at The Manse. The subject was too personal, and Don's office was too impersonal to discuss it there.

One of the things Keith loved most about this old chapel was the kneeling benches. Folding out from underneath the pew in front of him, the cushioned platform provided a way to kneel and offer one's petitions to the Lord. How many hours Keith had logged on this particular kneeler was anybody's guess. He only knew that this was one spot where he always felt the Lord's presence. Knowing that time was slipping past, Keith unfolded the cushioned rail and lowered himself to his knees, his hands clasped atop the pew before him, his head bowed.

"Oh, dear Lord," Keith began. "My heart is full today knowing that Abbie and I are at this particular point on our journey together. So much has happened in these past few months. I'm especially grateful You are working to open Abbie's heart to the possibility of loving me. Give me the grace and patience to allow her the space in her life to decide if I'm the right man for her. Thank You for the godly counsel of trusted friends like Don and Doris. Speak to Abbie and me tonight as we talk about how to move forward. Because we do work with children, our relationship will be lived out in full view of others. Give us Your guidance for the next steps. All this I ask in Your precious name. Amen."

As Keith walked back to Stone's Throw, he found a peace in believing the Lord had heard his prayer.

———

Abbie and Keith arrived at The Manse at exactly six thirty. This cottage was more expansive than any other on campus. Originally designed for the seminary president, who had lived in it over seventy years before, the massive stone house had heart pine floors and leaded glass windows. Large, wood-burning fireplaces, whose stone chases directed one's eye to the vaulted ceilings, were placed at either end of the large house, one in the living room, the other in a study that served as Don's private office.

Don met his visitors at the front door and brought the two back to the den, a large room facing the rear of the house. Here a third fireplace served as the focal point of the back wall. Oversized leather chairs and plump, upholstered recliners were arranged atop a large Oriental rug. A hand-wrought iron chandelier hung from the center truss of the room, its lights shaped like glowing candles.

"Doris," Don called out as soon as they reached the den, "Abbie and Keith are here."

Turning his attention back to his guests, he gestured toward the large sofa. "Please, have a seat."

Keith sat down, but Abbie turned toward the kitchen.

"Let me see if I can help Doris," said Abbie, who then made her way to the hub of the comfortable home. Doris was standing in front of the stove, stirring something in a large pot. She turned around when she heard the swinging kitchen door open.

"Abbie," she said, delight evident in her voice. Doris reached out to Abbie, who came alongside to hug her. "How wonderful to see you. How's your day been?"

"Not too busy," said Abbie, who then shared with Doris how grateful she was to have time to herself and plan lessons this summer instead of preparing for Camp 4Ever.

"You've had a great deal of change in your life in the last few months," said the older woman, turning back to stir the ingredients of the pot. "I'm delighted you've had some alone time this summer."

Abbie, suddenly a bit shy about getting close to the subject she and Keith had come here to discuss with Don and Doris, offered to fill the glasses with ice and pour the tea. Doris, appreciative of the offer, pointed her in the direction of the dining room.

Before long, dinner was served, and the four friends sat down to enjoy the meal. Doris had prepared a chicken and wild rice casserole, fresh fruit salad, bacon-wrapped bean bundles, and a squash soufflé. Toasted French bread was a perfect accompaniment. During the opening minutes of the meal, Don and Doris regaled Keith and Abbie with stories about funny incidents that had happened at Timothy House throughout the years, and laughter filled the room.

After a few minutes of polite conversation, Keith began. "Don and Doris," he said, "Abbie and I want to thank you for allowing us to visit with you tonight." He turned and looked at Abbie, her green eyes glued to his. He winked, and her gentle smile gave him courage. He reached for her hand before continuing.

"Don, as I've shared privately with you, Abbie and I are committed to seeing where our relationship might lead."

Don nodded, and Doris smiled at them both.

Keith continued, glancing first at Abbie and then back at Doris and Don. "We are taking this one day at a time. One of our greatest concerns is that because we're both on staff at the school, and especially because Abbie will be a house mother, we want to make sure our relationship is God-honoring in every way. We are more than aware that the eyes of our students will be watching our every move."

Doris chimed in, "Don and I are so impressed by your attitude. Not everyone would see this the same way you do."

"Believe me," said Keith, trying to suppress a chuckle, "we're not trying to play the martyrs. Until we get down the road of this relationship a little further to actually know where we're headed, we don't want to do anything that might hinder that process in any way."

Keith now turned his attention to Don's better half. "Doris, you, like Don, know the details of both our stories and that we've each been through challenging circumstances."

Abbie, finding her voice, joined the conversation. "To be fair to Keith, I'm the one having difficulty committing." She looked at Keith for a minute and then back at Doris and Don. "If it weren't for some incredibly faithful and wise friends, I'm not sure I would have survived Joe's betrayal. Since his death, I've had to rebuild the entire foundation of my life."

Don was now the one who spoke up. "Abbie, Keith has told us the details of Joe's financial misdeeds and also the emotional damage you and Drew suffered at the hands of your former husband. You are one courageous lady, is all I've got to say."

Abbie smiled softly at the unexpected compliment. She turned to Keith as if encouraging him to continue. "Believe me," he said, "we're also aware that we are, in some ways, walking a tightrope. On the one hand, the clock is ticking. It's not like we're eighteen and twenty and have our whole lives ahead of us. We're middle-aged and have both been married before. This won't be a years-long process.

"On the other hand, we don't want to succumb to temptation and sample the fruits God prepared for our enjoyment solely in the context of marriage simply because we wouldn't practice a little self-control. We realize this will cause many people to wonder, as a great deal of the world thinks this is a ridiculous way to live. Nevertheless, we believe this is God's best plan for us going forward, and we don't want to do anything to spoil that."

Keith gently squeezed Abbie's hand, as he had said what he'd come to say. She looked at him intently, her eyes glistening with tears.

For a few minutes, no one said a word.

Don was the first to break the silence. "I have to say," he began, looking over at the younger couple, "you both inspire me beyond telling."

Abbie covered her mouth as she tried to suppress a giggle. "What is inspirational about us?"

"The fact, my dear," said Don, sincerity and admiration evident in his every word, "that you have counted the cost of dating in this unique situation and yet are willing to move forward in your relationship."

Keith was anxious to know just how unique their case was. "In all the years you've been at the helm of Timothy House, have you ever had other faculty or staff members date one another?"

Don and Doris looked at one another as if they might help the other recollect something from an earlier time.

Suddenly, Doris held up a finger and said, "Why don't we put a pause in the conversation? Let's move to the den, where we'll be more comfortable, and we can have our dessert there."

The dinner party guests rose and made their way to the den of The Manse.

While Keith and Abbie settled onto the large sofa and Don sat in his recliner, Doris brought in a platter containing thick slices of sour cream pound cake and placed it on the hunt table that doubled as a sideboard as it nestled against the back of one of the large sofas. Before returning to the kitchen, Doris asked for her husband's help. He rose from his chair and followed his wife. Soon, the couple returned to the den—Don carrying a tray containing four cups of coffee and containers of cream and sugar and Doris ferrying a second tray filled with plates, napkins, forks, and a bowl of whipped cream.

Keith and Abbie, although full, didn't have to be told twice to sample Doris's mother's recipe and headed toward the sideboard. This cake recipe was a legend among the faculty and staff of Timothy House. The coffee smelled heavenly, and both brought a cup back to where they were seated on the couch. As Keith looked around the handsome room and over at Don and Doris, who had become such trusted friends throughout the past eighteen months, he said a silent prayer of thanks. He also asked the Lord, as he took two more bites of cake, to bless the conversation they were all about to share.

After a long sip of coffee, Doris said, "Now, where were we?" Looking at Keith, she continued, "Keith, I believe you asked if we'd ever had this type of situation with other staff members. The answer is yes. We've had two other couples in the past ten years or so in a similar situation. One of the couples broke up. The young lady resigned at the end of the semester and left town. She stayed in touch for a while, but it's been a few years since we've talked with her. Her former boyfriend taught another year and then left education to pursue a career in another field."

Don added thoughts of his own. "Teaching, as a profession, is rewarding but incredibly demanding. However, teaching in a residential setting requires a special type of individual. Throughout the years, Doris and I have come to realize that some people have to try on the shoe, so to speak. For those who find this particular footwear doesn't fit, we do all in our power to help them find another job that will be fulfilling, even if it's in another profession. Timothy House is committed to cultivating relationships that last, not merely building them for the sake of convenience. We're talking about people's lives, especially those of the children entrusted to us, and we take that seriously."

"Doris, you mentioned you'd known two couples who began dating while working here," Abbie said. "Who was the other couple?"

"Tim and Taylor Nunley," Doris replied.

"Really?" said Abbie, incredulity on her face.

"Really," said Doris, a bright smile dawning. "You'll have to get them to tell you that story sometime."

"In fact," Don interjected, "I bet they'd be happy to share some of the lessons they learned in their early years at Timothy House."

Turning to look at each other, Keith and Abbie said almost in unison, "We will."

Keith looked back across the room at these two wonderful people whom he had come to love and admire. "Thank you both for your hospitality. The dinner tonight was delicious!" he said. "We especially thank you for your support and your wise counsel. What we need, going forward, are your prayers."

"You've got them," Don said. "In fact, would you mind if I prayed for you two right now?"

"Oh, that would be wonderful," Abbie exclaimed.

"Terrific," said Don, slapping his knees. "Let's pray."

As the four friends bowed their heads, Keith reached out to take Abbie's hand in his. How right and natural it felt.

"Dear Father," Don began, "we thank You for this evening and this opportunity to share food and fellowship with Abbie and Keith. We thank You for bringing both of them to Timothy House. We thank You especially for this new journey they're on. Protect and guide them. Give them grace and patience with one another. Bind up old wounds which may hinder them from realizing Your will for their lives. Equip their spirits with courage and strength.

"Most of all, Lord, we ask that You confirm for them the direction they are to take, especially Abbie. Fill Keith and Abbie with Your love and give them wonder and excitement for the gift of relationship they have with each other and with You. We ask that You do incredibly more than all they could ever ask or think. We believe You to be the Way, the Truth, and the Life. Help each of us to represent You well in this dark world. All this we ask in the powerful name of Jesus. Amen."

As heads lifted, every eye was filled with tears. A few of them had made their way down Abbie's beautiful face in silent rivers. Keith leaned over and wiped them away gently, then kissed her lightly on the forehead and pulled her close. She leaned into his embrace. His heart was so full of the fierce love he had for the woman beside him, and tonight's visit with these dear friends had only strengthened those feelings.

Don and Doris made their way over, and each gave Keith and Abbie a hug before walking their guests to the door. From the front porch, the Fieldings watched as Keith and Abbie made their way back to his SUV and then drove toward the front of campus. As Don and Doris walked back into The Manse, the director of Timothy House turned to his wife and said, with a twinkle in his eye, "I'll give them until Christmas to make their decision. If the wedding date is not set by December twenty-fifth, I'll owe you a steak dinner."

"You've got yourself a deal, buster," said Doris, smiling brightly.

Keith parked the Explorer in front of Mistletoe Cottage and turned off the motor. He and Abbie had said little on the short ride. Keith couldn't believe how well the evening had gone. How grateful he was for Don and Doris's advice and support. He was especially touched by how responsive Abbie was during the evening. Dare he hope?

He turned to Abbie and pulled her close. He stroked her hair as he held her against his chest. "I love you, dear Abbie," he said, his voice barely above a whisper. "Don't you ever forget that."

She pulled away from him and looked into his eyes with an intensity he'd never experienced before. Finally, she said, "I know you do, Keith, and I hope to soon tell you the same."

Once he and Abbie reached the front door of Mistletoe, he bent down and kissed her softly on the cheek.

"Good night, sweet Abbie."

"Good night."

Keith stood on the porch as Abbie stepped inside, and he waited until he heard the lock turn in the door. As he headed back to his car, Keith whispered aloud, "Lord, I surrender my love for Abbie to You. Do with it what You will."

As he glanced up at the full moon gleaming in the night sky above, Keith felt a presence and a peace only God Himself could convey.

CHAPTER
23

The bright summer sun was high in the sky on that July morning as Abbie crossed the Timothy House campus toward Covenant Kitchen. The first full day of Camp 4Ever was underway. As a new member of the school's faculty, Abbie was excused from any camp duties. This transition to a new way of life had not been as difficult as Abbie had imagined. Still, she savored these extra free days and time spent as she pleased as opposed to the organized chaos of camp.

As she stepped through the doorway into the dining hall, a cacophony of voices and excited conversation greeted her. Winding through the crowded room, she slid into the empty seat her best friend had saved for her. Lane Wyatt and her husband, Eric, drove in five days before so they could spend time with Abbie ahead of Sunday's Camp 4Ever volunteer orientation session.

The trio had sat up talking until late into the night and laughing until their sides hurt. They reminisced about hurtful seasons of the past and spoke hopefully about what the future might hold. Abbie had missed her dear friends, and even though Robbinsonville was only a three-hour drive from McHenry, Abbie knew she would see Lane and Eric every month as Eric was a member of the board of directors for Timothy House. He came to campus for the board meetings held on the first Thursday of every month.

Toward the end of lunch, Lane leaned over to Abbie. "Sorry this is last minute, but I need to attend a volunteer meeting tonight and wondered if you'd mind leading share time with the girls before bedtime.

Becky Carter is the other volunteer counselor in Cabin Seven, but this is her first time at Camp 4Ever, and she's still learning the routine."

"Glad to, Lane." Abbie smiled, knowing she could visit with Chloe Minton, who was housed in Cabin Seven. Chloe had been one of the campers in Abbie's cabin last summer, and the two had become quite close. The child now attended the school on a partial scholarship. Throughout visits to Timothy House the past year, Abbie had furthered the relationship with the girl.

"Thanks," said Lane as they pushed their chairs back to the table. "I should be back right after lights-out. Becky will meet the girls when the buses bring campers back from tonight's program at Wright's Creek Church. She'll be looking for you at the cabin. I can't wait to hear how everything goes."

———

Abbie arrived at Cabin Seven fifteen minutes prior to the time Lane had given her. She laid her Bible and notepad on the small table in the middle of the bunkroom and then headed back outside to sit on the front steps. The evening was cool. Bright stars twinkled across the night sky like diamonds shimmering on black velvet atop a jeweler's counter. Abbie heard the campers long before she saw them. As the group came into view, one of them broke away and ran toward her.

"Miss Abbie, Miss Abbie!" Chloe Minton dove into Abbie's outstretched arms. "I'm so glad you're here!"

"Hey, Chloe!" said Abbie, hugging the ten-year-old tightly, suddenly overcome with a wave of emotions. "I'm so glad to see you." Abbie held Chloe out from her to get a better look. "You have gotten so tall!"

The crunch of footsteps on the path in front of Cabin Seven drew Abbie's attention. Looking past Chloe into the faint glow cast by the cabin's exterior security lights, Abbie saw a group of campers accompanied by a lady she presumed was the other volunteer counselor.

"Hello, Abbie," the lady called out in a friendly voice as she stepped in front of the group of girls. She extended a hand. "I'm Becky Carter. It's nice to meet you. Lane has told me so much about you. Thanks for leading share time tonight."

Abbie shook Becky's hand. "I'm delighted to help."

Moving up the stairs to the cabin's threshold, Abbie held open the screen door as the girls and their counselor came inside. The campers, still chattering, made their way to their bunks.

Becky walked to the center of the room and clapped her hands twice. Displaying a bright smile, she said, "Ladies, we have a special treat tonight. Miss Abbie Richardson is here to lead our share time. You have five minutes to get ready for bed and be back on your bunks."

The two women shared light conversation while the girls washed their faces, brushed their teeth, and changed into their pajamas. As the campers reappeared, the fresh scents of soap and toothpaste accompanied them. Finally, when each bed was occupied, Abbie sat down at a small table in the middle of the room.

"Hey, girls," Abbie began, "I'm Miss Abbie, and I'm so happy to be here with you tonight. Miss Lane is my best friend, and she invited me to come see you. She and I were counselors in Cabin Five last summer at Camp 4Ever."

"Miss Abbie and Miss Lane were my counselors last year," chirped Chloe's cheery voice.

"That's right." Abbie smiled at the dark-haired girl as a quiet hush settled over the cabin.

Making sure she looked directly into each pair of young eyes staring back at her, Abbie continued, "Now that you've been at Camp 4Ever three days, you have discovered that share time is a special way to end each day.

"The verse I want to share with you tonight is from Joshua 1:5." Picking up her Bible, Abbie opened it and began reading, "'I won't give up on you; I won't leave you' (The Message). The book of Joshua is in the Old Testament, the part of the Bible written before Jesus was born and came to live on earth as a man. Although he was a grown-up, Joshua was still a younger man when he was tasked with leading the Israelites into Canaan, the land God promised He would give to His chosen people.

"Never forget: God is *always* with you and *nothing* . . . no difficult circumstance, no problem, *nothing* you will ever go through will prevent God from being right by your side.

"Do any of you want to share something you've learned this week at camp about God's promise to *never* leave you?"

Before Abbie finished speaking, several hands shot up into the air. "I do, I do," was the collective response.

Abbie laughed with delight at the campers' enthusiasm.

Looking around at the various bunks, she pointed to a little girl with curly red hair and a dusting of nutmeg-colored sprinkles across her plump cheeks and the bridge of her nose. "I've learned that God is with me and will help me, even in school subjects that are hard for me."

"That's a great answer!"

Abbie selected another camper to share her testimony, this one a tow-headed blond girl with turquoise eyes. "My parents are getting a divorce, and even though my dad has left us, God will not leave me."

All Abbie could offer was a nod as the lump in her throat prevented her from speaking. Thankfully, Becky was paying careful attention to the conversation and selected the next camper who would share.

"My dog died last week," said a girl with horn-rimmed glasses and light brown hair. "I was so sad I didn't want to come to camp, but once I got here, I wasn't sad anymore. Mr. Don has taught me this week that God is always with me, especially when I'm sad."

"Wonderful answer, Sarah!" said Becky, pride evident in her voice.

While Becky responded, Abbie checked her watch. It was almost time for lights-out.

She took charge of share time once more. "We've got time for one more person to share. Who'd like to go next?"

Abbie scanned the bunks one more time. When her eyes settled on Chloe's raised hand, she smiled brightly at this precious child. "Chloe, what do you want to share?"

Chloe was silent for a moment, like she was figuring out what to say. Swallowing hard, she began, "I've learned that God is always with me, even when my foster parents are mean to me." Once she'd made this declaration, Chloe scooted back into the shadow of the bunk above her, only her small feet sticking out into the light.

For a moment, no one said a word.

Realizing this time meant to encourage these girls had suddenly taken a serious turn, Abbie said, "Thanks, Chloe, for finding the courage to share that with us." A quick glance at Becky told Abbie the counselor was relieved this moment was over.

"I want all of you to crawl into your sleeping bags," Abbie continued. For the next few minutes, all she heard was the creaking of the wooden bunks and the metallic sounds of zippers being pulled along their tracks.

"Let me pray for you and then it's bedtime."

"Dear Lord," Abbie prayed softly, "how thankful we are for Camp 4Ever and for all the volunteers and counselors who are here to make sure this is a great week. I thank You, especially, for these precious girls. Please protect them and bless them. Allow them to feel Your presence and experience Your love. When the time is right, I pray each of these girls would ask You to live in her heart forever. Send your angels to watch over these dear girls of Yours tonight. In Jesus's name. Amen."

A few of the girls repeated, "Amen."

"Good night, sweet girls," Abbie called out.

"Good night, Miss Abbie," the Cabin Seven girls called out.

Becky turned off the light, immersing the room in darkness. A faint glow of the nightlight in the bathroom cast a blue sheen across the floor.

"Abbie, thank you so much for what you did tonight," whispered Becky as she held the cabin's screen door open.

"You're welcome," replied Abbie. "It was a special time. I'll see you tomorrow."

"Be careful walking back to your cottage." Becky stood on the cabin's porch and watched Abbie disappear into the darkness beyond the exterior lights.

———

By the time Abbie walked back to Mistletoe Cottage and got ready for bed, it was nearly midnight. Despite the fact that she was tired, both physically and emotionally, she could not go to sleep. Chloe's comment about her foster parents kept Abbie tossing and turning.

As she lay in the dark, Abbie wondered if she had misunderstood what Chloe had said, but after replaying the conversation dozens of times in her mind, she knew she had heard the girl correctly. Something fishy was going on in that household.

Abbie's thoughts wandered back to a segment of last summer's Camp 4Ever counselor orientation that had life or death importance. Don Fielding's tone had become noticeably serious when he reached that portion of the training session. "No matter how insignificant you may believe a comment to be, you are legally and duty bound to report any comments made to you by a camper that implies that camper might harm either him or herself or that someone else might harm them."

Duty bound.

Abbie's inner warning system was suddenly on high alert.

More of Don's words from the dinner she had shared with Don and Doris last fall burst to the surface of Abbie's memory. "I just hope they're helping Chloe for the right reasons." He was referring to Hope and Kevin Henderson, Chloe's foster parents. What was it he had said? "More than a few times, people have overheard Hope bragging about the money she and Kevin make from fostering."

Clang. Clang. Clang.

Abbie's instincts that Chloe might be in real danger were now calling out loudly to her.

"Oh, dear Lord," Abbie whispered aloud. "Chloe is facing something dark and evil. I just know it. Please protect her. Send Your angels to guard and guide her. Give me the courage to speak up for Chloe. Help us to help her while she's here this week at camp. Amen."

A mental reminder to talk with Don first thing in the morning was her last thought before sleep overtook her.

CHAPTER
24

After Abbie left the cabin, Miss Becky said a prayer with all the girls, made sure they were tucked into their bunks, and then slipped under the covers of her own bed. It wasn't too much later that Chloe heard the creak of the screened front door as it opened. Backlit by the porch lights, she could just make out Miss Lane's shape as she slipped quietly into the cabin. After a few minutes, the light went on in the bathroom and Chloe heard the sound of water running in the sink. Soon after, the light turned off, and Miss Lane settled into bed.

Pretending to be asleep, Chloe kept her eyes closed until she heard the breathing of both counselors slow to that of deep sleep. The girl's eyes popped open again as she lay awake in the dark cabin, the sounds of the summer night humming outside the screened windows. A gentle breeze blew softly. An owl called into the night, somewhere out in the woods beyond the cabin. The distant, mournful call of a whistle blowing miles away marked the journey of a freight train as it rocked its way through the countryside.

Chloe's attendance last summer at Camp 4Ever had marked an almost imperceptible turn in the road of her life toward a hopeful future, although she could have never imagined how. Meeting Miss Abbie had been one of those markers. Having her as a counselor that first summer on the Timothy House campus had been the highlight of last year's camp session. Miss Lane was also a sweet lady who had been encouraging.

Chloe had come to camp wearing the protective cloak she often drew tightly around her bruised heart. She had taught herself to rebuff most acts of kindness extended by others. It was a form of self-preservation. Chloe had hoped that coming into the Henderson household four years ago would provide her with the family she had always dreamed of. Life with the Hendersons, however, had turned out to be a living nightmare. The scar on the back of Chloe's left leg was yet another reminder of her terrifying existence within the Henderson house.

Until tonight's share time, Chloe never mustered the courage to speak up about her situation. Chloe had no working knowledge of what a truly happy family should look like, but her wounded heart and instinct, deep within her soul, told her it was *not* supposed to be like the Hansel and Gretel existence she endured.

How delighted Chloe had been when Miss Lane had told the girls that Miss Abbie would be coming to the cabin to lead share time. Chloe had seen Abbie several times since camp began on Monday, but reveled in being in her presence tonight for the short devotional time. Although Chloe could not fully comprehend the psychological implications of what she was suffering at the hands of Hope and Kevin Henderson, she only knew she felt safe and genuinely loved when she was in Abbie's presence.

When Miss Abbie asked the girls to share what God had been teaching them about His never-ending love for them, Chloe had felt a nudge within her, almost as if someone had pushed her gently from behind, encouraging her to speak up. Her heart, in fact, still pounded wildly, even as she lay in her bunk, thinking about the declaration she had blurted out about the Hendersons.

Having been removed from her mother at the age of three, Chloe had been shuffled in and out of foster homes for almost seven years. Although it was not something she totally understood, Chloe felt her spirit crumbling within her. The Henderson household had by far been the worst of the homes in which she had lived, and the darkness within Hope and Kevin Henderson had all but extinguished any flicker of hope within the precious girl.

The human spirit, however, is hard-wired for survival, and the fact that Abbie Richardson was present tonight with Chloe provided the courage the little girl needed in order to cry out for help. Although she could not comprehend the firestorm unleashed by what she had told the group tonight, Chloe only knew she felt like the weight of the world had been lifted from her shoulders.

What was that verse Miss Abbie taught us? Chloe thought to herself as sleep began to overtake her. *God has promised He will never leave me or abandon me.*

Sweet peace, the kind that only comes from God Himself, blanketed the child as she slept.

CHAPTER
25

Abbie was closing the front door of Mistletoe Cottage when the breakfast bell sounded. The sky was dark and gloomy, its ominous clouds matching Abbie's troubled spirit. As Abbie made her way across campus, she mentally rehearsed how she would share with Don what Chloe had repeated to her and the girls of Cabin Seven in last night's share time. Abbie knew she wanted Keith sitting beside her when she completed this difficult task.

The sound of chairs being pulled back across a polished wood floor greeted her as she wound through the crowded dining room toward the staff table. Doris waved a greeting and pointed out an empty seat next to her. Abbie nodded and smiled a greeting of her own. She took her seat as Don stood to bless the food. Just before she closed her eyes to pray, she caught a glimpse of Keith's gentle, indigo eyes smiling at her from across the table.

This morning's meal was another testimony to Charmaine Jenkins' culinary talents—breakfast casserole, fresh fruit salad, grits, and home-made biscuits with butter and jelly. Glasses filled with milk and orange juice stood on the nearby beverage table. One by one, in the order they followed at every meal, diners at each table stood and approached the serving line. Finally, it was the head staff table's turn.

Keith managed to stand next to Abbie as they inched closer to the delicious-smelling breakfast offerings. "Hey, you," he said.

"Good morning," Abbie replied, the lack of enthusiasm and dark circles under her eyes telegraphed to Keith that this morning was anything but good.

"Are you okay?" Concern was evident in his voice.

"Not really," replied Abbie, trying to choke down the clammy fear rising within her. "I need to talk to you and Don once breakfast is over. Last night, I helped out with share time in Cabin Seven. Chloe Minton said something to the group that I can't get out of my mind. Didn't get much sleep thinking about it."

Now the circles under Abbie's eyes made perfect sense to Keith.

"I'll hang back once breakfast is over and let him know you need to talk with us," Keith said, his calm tone reassuring. "We can probably talk in Don's office. I'll meet you there."

"Thanks, Keith," Abbie said while picking up a plate, cutlery, and napkin from the serving line. Even though she didn't feel much like eating, the sausage, cheese, and egg casserole smelled appealing. She put a biscuit on her plate as well.

The noise level in the dining hall had lessened as campers and counselors alike gobbled down their breakfast. Abbie remembered last summer at Camp 4Ever and how surprised she'd been at the appetite the camp activity schedule produced. Even though she wasn't working at camp this summer in an official capacity, Abbie had nevertheless found herself practically starving by each meal time. Thinking about the potential threat Chloe might be facing, however, had put a serious dent in her hopes to enjoy this morning's meal.

———

Don closed the door to his office and nodded to Abbie and Keith to find a place in the sitting area near the windows. Abbie fondly remembered last summer when she and Don had discussed the possibility of her joining the Timothy House family. Today's conversation would be considerably more serious. Dealing with the possible endangerment of a child was not something she had any experience with.

No one said a word for a long while after Abbie finished recounting share time in Cabin Seven.

Finally, Don spoke. "Abbie, thank you for telling us about Chloe's statement. I wish I could tell you I'm surprised, but unfortunately, I am not. For some time, I've heard rumors in the Robbinsonville community about Hope and Kevin Henderson and that they might not be serving as foster parents for the right reasons. I've been around children and parents long enough that God's developed a sort of sixth sense within me about these matters. Ever since Chloe's first session at Camp 4Ever, something didn't square with me about this couple. What you've just told us has confirmed those suspicions."

Tremendous relief washed over Abbie, like she'd been holding her breath for some time.

"Trent Lockhart recently told me about a new investigator with the Department of Children's Services. Her first name starts with an H. Maybe Hannah or Harriet. I can't quite remember. I'll call Trent and get her number. Once I know something more, I'll be back in touch.

"I'll find Lane and fill her in on the situation. Camper schedules are in the front office. Loren can help you with that. Doris is in her office. Let her know I need her to go with you. Once you know where Chloe is, I want the two of you to find her. Tell her you need her to collect wildflowers for a special flower arrangement for the dining room. Take her on a walk before lunch. Don't prompt the child, but see if you can find out any more information about the Hendersons from her.

"Afterward, I want you to write down exactly what you've told me and every detail you can remember of what I hope Chloe will tell you. That will be of great help to the investigator."

Don turned to Keith. "Tell Loren I asked you to go over the notes for Cabin Five from last year's Camp 4Ever session. Read through the file and see if there's any mention of either Chloe or the Hendersons." Keith nodded his assent.

Glancing back at both of his trusted colleagues, Don said, "Let's plan to meet back here tomorrow morning at the same time. Abbie, bring the document I've asked you to prepare with you. And don't breathe a word of this to anyone. If the Hendersons are involved in something nefarious, we don't want to tip our hand. The last thing we want is to expose Chloe to any more danger than she may already be in."

Abbie glanced at her watch on the way back to the cottage. It wasn't even nine o'clock, and this had already turned out to be a complicated day.

CHAPTER
26

As soon as she left Don's office, she went straight to Don's assistant, Loren Davis. Ever since meeting her last summer while at Camp 4Ever, Abbie had always found the young woman pleasant, courteous, and extremely helpful.

"Good morning, Abbie," Loren chirped.

"Good morning, yourself," Abbie replied. "How's this week of camp going?"

"Busy, but good."

"Glad to hear." Abbie tried to look nonchalant but wasn't sure she pulled it off. "Don asked me to check on one of the campers for him— Chloe Minton. Could you tell me which class she's in?" She glanced at her watch. "If I hurry, I think I can catch up with her before Class Two begins."

"Got it." Loren reached for a bright orange file folder on her desk and opened it. Looking through several documents, she selected one. She repeated Chloe's name as she ran her finger down a column of class schedules. Finally, her finger stopped on one particular listing.

"Here it is," the assistant announced. "You'll find Chloe in the needle arts class. Becky Carter is the volunteer teaching the campers this morning."

"Thanks so much, Loren," Abbie said, still working to appear nonplussed and calm.

"You're welcome," the young woman answered. "Glad I could help."

In less than three minutes, Abbie was walking into the crafts building, a long, cabin-like structure containing several classrooms, each located off a common hallway and devoted to a separate art form. Becky's needle arts group was meeting in the third room down the hall.

Knocking gently on the door frame, Abbie announced her presence. Becky was about to begin her comments to the group assembled but walked over to see Abbie instead. Abbie stepped out into the hall and motioned for Becky to follow.

Lowering her voice, Abbie said, "Becky, I'm sorry to interrupt class, but I've not been able to shake what Chloe said last night."

"Me, either."

"I talked with Don this morning, and he asked me to spend some time with Chloe to see if she'll divulge more about how the Hendersons were mean to her."

"Oh, I hope she will," replied Becky.

"Would you mind asking Chloe to step out into the hall?"

"Not at all," said Becky, her eyes filled with the same concern mirrored in Abbie's.

Abbie watched as the counselor went back into the classroom and motioned for Chloe to follow her.

Chloe's face lit up like the Fourth of July when she saw Abbie waiting in the hallway. "Oh, hi, Miss Abbie!" the child exclaimed. "I'm so glad to see you."

The girl's winsome smile had a way of endearing her to all who knew her.

"Hey, Chloe," said Abbie, as she gently patted Chloe's shoulder. "It's great to see you. Miss Doris asked me to come find you. She is making a special flower arrangement for the dining hall beverage table. She wants you to help us pick a few wildflowers. Do you think you could do that?"

"Sure, Miss Abbie," the girl said delightedly. "I love flowers."

As Abbie and Chloe walked toward the path to Shelter Lake, the child chattered nonstop about all that had been taking place this week at Camp 4Ever. A few yards down the sidewalk, Abbie and Chloe saw Doris waiting for them, a flat-bottomed wicker basket in one hand.

"Hello, dear Chloe," said the older woman, wrapping Chloe in a bear hug. "I'm so glad you can help me and Abbie find some special flowers. Some of the prettiest ones grow on the banks of Shelter Lake."

The trio walked the path to the lake, Chloe between the two women. As the camper continued more of her cheerful banter, Doris and Abbie exchanged knowing glances.

Abbie uttered a silent prayer and asked the Lord to help her find the right words to say to the child.

"Chloe, I've been thinking about what you shared last night. It was special to hear you explain how God is teaching you things about Himself this week at camp. Miss Doris was so excited to hear you learned that God will never leave you. Would you tell Miss Doris what you told us at share time last night?" Abbie looked directly into the girl's dark eyes, glistening like the button centers of a black-eyed Susan.

"Sure, Miss Abbie," said Chloe as she bent down and picked a weed that also held a bloom. After gathering the plant, she stood and turned to face Doris. "My foster parents, the Hendersons, say mean things to me sometimes. But it's okay. God is with me."

Doris carefully chose her words. "I'm sorry to hear that, Chloe. Do you think that sometimes they've had a bad day at work and maybe that's why they sound mean?"

Chloe continued in a matter-of-fact tone. "No, ma'am. Mr. Keith goes to work, but Miss Hope sits around the house all day reading magazines and watching soap operas. They both say ugly things to me, but they also say them to each other."

By now the two women and the girl had reached a landscaped flower bed near the lake's shoreline. Bright blooms of a variety of flowers were waiting for them.

Abbie ventured a turn in the conversation as she leaned down to pick a flower. "What sort of ugly things do they say, Chloe?"

Suddenly, Chloe's attention seemed captivated by the brightly colored flowers. For a second, Abbie was worried that this attempt at learning more about Chloe's troubling home life would fail. The look on Doris's face showed she was thinking the same thing. The two women waited quietly, watching the girl's amazement and delight at the beautiful blooms as she stood looking at the flower bed.

The camper turned back to Abbie and Doris. "Miss Hope calls me stupid and dumb sometimes, but I know I'm not." Chloe's bottom lip quivered a bit.

After a moment, she continued. "One time, Miss Henderson told me she was going to take me to an orphanage. After that, she shoved me into a closet and left me there for a long time. It was dark, and I was scared." Looking up at Abbie as a drowning swimmer might look desperately for a life ring, Chloe blinked back unshed tears and said softly, "I really am a good kid."

Abbie knelt beside the child and drew her close, wrapping her in a tight hug. "I'm sorry, Chloe," she said as she stroked the girl's hair.

Chloe continued, her voice now barely above a whisper. "Once, Miss Hope even hit me with a wire coat hanger." Reaching down to rub the back of one leg, she said, "Here, Miss Abbie, you can see where it cut my leg."

A thin, jagged scar could be seen several inches above the back of Chloe's left knee.

Abbie hardly had words for what she was witnessing. "Oh, dear," was all she could manage.

Pulling away so she could see Abbie's face, Chloe said bravely, "It's okay, Miss Abbie. God has protected me, and He's the one that makes me strong."

After the shocking revelation, Chloe didn't say another word for a long while, but instead turned her attention to the flowering weed she held in her hand. Finally, she looked up at Abbie and asked tentatively, "Is it okay if I step in and pick a few flowers?" Apprehension and fear were written across her face.

"Certainly, it is," Abbie reassured her. She offered Chloe her brightest smile. "The flowers you're selecting will be the prettiest ones in Miss Doris's arrangement. Won't they, Doris?"

"They certainly will." Doris could barely get the words out for fear she'd shed tears of her own. Although she had heard rumblings about the Hendersons for years, this confirmation of neglect and emotional and physical abuse was almost more than she could process. Working to maintain a calm, pleasant tone, Doris laid the wicker basket on the ground outside the flower bed. "Chloe, when you've gathered the flowers you want, you can put them in this basket."

The camper stepped gingerly across a low berm of variegated monkey grass that served as the protective edge of the landscaped area. Once across the barrier, Chloe made quick work of picking several stalks from a blooming hydrangea, a few Gerber daisies, and a bunch of yellow snapdragons. Turning back to the women, she held out the flowers like she was making an offering at the altar.

"Here you go, Miss Doris," Chloe said, the pride and accomplishment at the success of her task evident in her voice. "Thanks for letting me pick these. Miss Hope never lets me pick any flowers from our yard."

Abbie and Doris clapped their hands and exclaimed their delight at Chloe's selections as the girl stepped back over the monkey grass border and placed the blooms carefully, almost reverently, in the wicker basket.

As she bent down to pick up the woven carrier, now brimming with the blooms of summer, Doris said in a sincere, cheerful tone, "Dear Chloe, you are welcome to pick as many flowers as you want while you're here at Timothy House. Our yard is your yard."

Chloe beamed as if she'd been awarded first place in the school talent contest.

As the three began their walk back to the main part of campus, a throng of campers and staff appeared as if on cue. Several counselors called out to Chloe to come and join them as it was now time for lakefront activities. Several of the girls from her cabin ran up to greet her.

"Bye, Miss Abbie," Chloe said, offering her best smile. "Bye, Miss Doris. Thanks for letting me pick flowers with you."

Both women returned the greeting. Doris reminded Chloe to look for the flower arrangement when she came for lunch in the dining hall.

Saying her goodbye to Abbie, Doris headed back to Covenant Kitchen to arrange the freshly picked blooms for the upcoming display.

Abbie stood for a minute and watched the campers along the waterfront. Sounds of splashing and gleeful squeals of laughter filled the air.

As she headed up the pathway to her cabin, Abbie prayed with all her might that Chloe had given them enough information to prevent the Hendersons from abusing any other child *ever* again.

CHAPTER
27

Don grabbed the phone receiver and punched in the number for the Robbinsonville Police Department as his blood pressure built. It had been a long time since he'd been this angry. After identifying himself, he waited on hold for the chief of police.

"Don?" Trent Lockhart's voice boomed over the line.

"Hey, Trent," Don replied. "Thanks for taking my call."

"Long time, no see. How are things at Timothy House?"

"Things at the school are going well. This past school year was one of our best." Don paused a minute, choking back his angry tone. "Things at Camp 4Ever, however, have been better. I need to come talk with you about a matter concerning a family here in town. Is now a good time? I can be at your office in ten minutes."

Even to himself, Don's tone sounded sharp and snippy. Not his usual, laid-back version.

"Sure," said Trent. "Today's been a light day so far. The troublemakers must be waiting until later in the day to start their shenanigans."

"Thanks. See you in ten."

Don practically slammed the phone into the receiver. His heart was pounding in his chest, the anger within about to spill over. Even though Don had no children of his own, the news that any child might have suffered physical or psychological harm sent him into a state of near rage. The fact that Chloe, a Camp 4Ever camper, was under the watchful care of Timothy House made him feel responsible for her wellbeing.

Pushing back from his desk, he bowed his head. He would need a special measure of the Lord's help to deal with this present threat to the welfare of one of his campers.

"Lord," he prayed quietly, "please forgive my anger. Calm me down. Protect sweet Chloe. Guide me in how best to protect this child from further harm. Bind the Hendersons from doing any more damage to this child or any other. Empower law enforcement officials to bring swift and certain justice and resolve this situation. Amen."

Don sat for a few more minutes at his desk until he was certain he had control of his emotions. He wouldn't be much help to anyone if he let them run away with him. Don was a man who felt deeply about the central issues of life—faith, family, and fellowship with others. He had now walked with the Lord for almost sixty years but still struggled in this area of his personal life, his anger too easily stoked. Learning to allow the Lord to contain it was the constant "thorn in his side." Once he felt his pulse slow, he made his way to the door of his office.

As Don headed past Loren's desk, he told her, "I'm headed off campus for a meeting. May not be back until after lunch. If anyone needs something, send them to Keith. He can handle it."

As promised, the director of Timothy House was soon in the waiting room of Trent Lockhart, the town's chief of police. Although younger than Don, Trent and the school director had now known each other for almost twenty years and had mutual respect and affection for one another. Don's strong sense of justice was curbed by Trent's level-headed approach to law enforcement. "Truth wins out" was the mantra Trent lived by, professionally and personally.

Once seated at Trent's desk, Don proceeded to tell him all that he knew about Chloe Minton's disturbing revelation made in the presence of Abbie Richardson. Don also shared his suspicions about Chloe's foster parents, concerns based on rumors around town that seemed to only get worse each time he heard a new one. "Where there's smoke, there's fire" was a credo Don had found reliable.

Like Don, Trent was alarmed and believed there was probable cause based on what Don had shared.

The chief of police leaned back in his chair. "Unfortunately, Don, this child is probably telling your counselor the truth, or at least a version that's pretty close to it." Generally, Don thought of Trent as more level-headed than himself. However, the older man could see the anger flashing like shards of flint in Trent's gray eyes, which were now a shade more akin to the uniform the police chief wore. "We need to move fast, Don. Today's Wednesday. Isn't camp over on Friday?"

The police chief looked at the camp director for confirmation, and Don nodded.

"When will your staff member have her write-up ready? Abbie, did you say?"

"Yes," replied Don. "Abbie Richardson. She was a counselor last summer at Camp 4Ever and, in fact, was one of Chloe's counselors. She's one of the most impressive ladies I've met in many years, if ever. She would not make this up. Keith was also present in my office this morning when Abbie told me about Chloe."

Before calling Trent, Don had already considered the fact that Trent and Keith had become good friends in the short time Keith had been at Timothy House. In that same span of time, Keith had also become a trusted and respected member of the Robbinsonville community.

"After we finished talking with Abbie, I asked Doris to go with her and take Chloe for a walk in hopes of bringing up last night's conversation," Don said. "I figured that another witness to any statements the girl made would make a stronger case."

He reached up to run his hair over his pewter-colored, short-cut hair. Some days Don looked more like a mature Marine than a school administrator. "Although I'm not sure of the gist of it, Doris did confirm that Abbie's concerns were validated by some additional comments Chloe made this morning. Abbie went back to Mistletoe to write down her account of what Chloe has told her. I can have her bring it to you later this afternoon, if you'd like."

Trent pulled his desk calendar closer. Don noticed only one notation on the space for today's date.

"Don," Trent said carefully, "we need to move as quickly as possible. I only have one meeting this afternoon, and I can send my assistant chief of police in my stead. Let me see if I can work this out."

As Don had done earlier in his own office, Trent reached for the phone receiver and punched in the office extension of his ACP. Don could hear a man's voice over the line.

"Chief?"

"Gordon, I need a favor," Trent said. "I need you to take that one-thirty meeting with the Kiwanis Club Safety Council for me. Something's come up. They're meeting in the board room at First Bank and Trust on Main. I'll fill you in later."

"Roger," came the reply on the other end of the line.

Trent put the phone down and leaned back in his chair. He laced his fingers together and placed his hands behind his head, as if concentrating on some unseen point on the ceiling. After a few minutes of thought, he turned his gaze to Don.

"I don't want to do anything to raise any kind of alarm that might spook the Hendersons. Because of that, I think it would be better if we met here in my office. See if you, Doris, Abbie, and Keith can be back here at two o'clock. Between then and now, I'm going to make a few calls.

"There's an investigator in this part of the state that I've worked with before. She's an expert on child welfare situations. Her investigative work is some of the best I've ever seen. Name's Hayley Collins. Let me see if I can grab her for this meeting. Chloe Minton does not need to go back to the Henderson home ever again. Not if I can help it."

Warm reassurance swept over Don—now an entire team of protectors had Chloe's back.

"Once I get back to campus, I'll call you within the hour to confirm the meeting at two."

As he stood to leave, Don extended his hand to Trent Lockhart. The chief's handshake was firm and sure. Trent was a man who could be trusted.

As Don drove through the stone gates of Timothy House, he thought about a quote that was carved into a truss in the vast vault of the dining hall at Covenant Kitchen. Borrowed from a respected colleague in the Christian camping community, the proverb seemed the perfect guide for this mission in which Don, Doris, Keith, and Abbie were now engaged: "Words are so powerful they should only be used to bless, to heal, to prosper."

Chloe Minton was in harm's way, and no more unseemly words, uttered from the mouths of either Hope or Kevin Henderson, would ever injure the heart and soul of this precious girl.

Don Fielding would see to that.

All requested parties were present at the two o'clock meeting in Chief Lockhart's office. The four from Timothy House—Don, Doris, Keith, and Abbie—rode together in Don's car. As soon as they arrived at the chief's office, the official's assistant invited them in. As the group approached, Trent Lockhart's office door opened.

The chief's imposing six-foot-four-inch frame filled the doorway. He stepped back so the Timothy House foursome could enter his office. As the men crossed the threshold, Trent shook Keith's hand and clasped a reassuring grip on Don's shoulder. Trent smiled broadly at Doris and Abbie and motioned toward a small sitting area.

"Hayley's running late," the chief explained. "She'll be here shortly."

As the group took their seats, Trent closed the door, then sat next to Don.

Turning his attention to Abbie, Trent ventured, "You must be Abbie Richardson." His manner was direct, yet friendly.

Seated close by, Abbie stood slightly and extended her hand. "It's nice to meet you, Trent."

"You, too," said Trent, reaching out and shaking the hand offered.

The group in Chief Lockhart's office exchanged pleasantries until a knock at the door interrupted their conversation. The door opened slightly, and Trent's secretary popped her head in.

"Ms. Collins is here, Chief. You said to bring her in when she arrived."

"Thanks. Please show her in."

Trent stood as Hayley Collins entered his office. She was as small and diminutive as the chief was large and imposing. He walked over and shook her hand and then led her to where the others were seated.

"Folks," began Trent, "this is investigator Hayley Collins. She's with the Tennessee Department of Children's Services. As I'm sure, from what you've told me," the chief continued, looking over at Don, "that some physical abuse has taken place, I felt it best to call Hayley. She is the perfect person to help us get to the bottom of this disturbing matter with Chloe Minton.

"I've filled Hayley in on the details concerning Chloe. However," he said, turning to look at the newest member of the Timothy House faculty, "Abbie has had direct interaction with the child. Why don't you tell Hayley all you've learned in the past two days?"

Abbie nodded slightly and began. "I first met Chloe last summer while a counselor at Camp 4Ever. She was one of the girls in my cabin. From the start, we bonded. I don't remember her saying anything last year that made me suspicious of her foster parents, the Hendersons. Although looking back, I do remember a few comments made by other counselors and volunteers that live in Robbinsonville. I probably should have paid closer attention." Abbie sat silently for a minute, looking as if she was struggling with guilt.

Hayley spoke up. "Sounds to me like you did exactly the right thing. You acted as a safe, friendly adult in Chloe's life and helped shape a positive experience for her. From what you've just said, she did nothing last summer to raise a red flag." Hayley gave Abbie a reassuring look. "Please continue."

"This past Tuesday evening, I was asked to lead share time in Chloe's cabin, when campers explain how a featured Bible verse has impacted their life during the camp week." Abbie swallowed and brushed back a strand of hair behind her ear. She looked over at Doris, who smiled brightly and gave her a reassuring nod. "I could hardly believe what I heard her say—'I have learned that God is always with me even when my foster parents, the Hendersons, are mean to me.'"

The group in Trent's office stayed silent for a few minutes. Although, over the years, Don and his staff had dealt with many problems faced by students at Timothy House, this was the first case of possible abuse Don and his team had ever encountered. None of them wanted to let Chloe down.

The Timothy House director took over the conversation for a minute. "Yesterday, after Abbie told Keith and me about what Chloe had said, I asked her to spend a little more time with Chloe to see if the girl might offer any more incriminating comments about Hope and Kevin Henderson." Turning to look at his wife, Don continued, "I asked Doris to go with Abbie to see if Chloe might repeat some of what she said from the night before."

Husband and wife looked at each other for a long moment before Don continued, "I have had situations in the past where an allegation turned into a 'he said, she said,' and I didn't want that to happen in this case."

"I need to have the four of you come to work with me," said Hayley brightly as she looked with admiration at the group from Timothy House seated across from her. "Please continue, Abbie."

Abbie's attention was drawn to Keith. Finding courage in the kind expression in his eyes, Abbie proceeded with her story. "As Don said, Doris and I took Chloe with us yesterday on a flower-picking walk. During our time with her, Chloe shared more about how the Hendersons have mistreated her."

Reaching into her purse, Abbie pulled out a handwritten sheet of paper. Extending it to Hayley, she explained, "I've written down everything about my two encounters at Camp 4Ever this week with Chloe, as Don asked me. I also included my recollections from the time I spent with her last summer."

Pointing to the paper Hayley now held, Abbie explained, "Unfortunately, this is not the first time in my teaching career when I had to report suspicions of child abuse. I wrote several similar accounts in the years I taught at Kent Academy. One was for a child being physically abused by a step-parent and another by a babysitter. I've dated and signed the document for you. I hope this will help." Abbie settled against the back of the chair in which she sat, relieved that her difficult task was now over.

The group sat silently as Hayley read over the document. Looking up, she addressed Trent Lockhart first. "As you and I discussed, tomorrow we'll be using the conference room in the building next door where another member of our department will interview Chloe. The room is small and a bit private. I want her as comfortable as possible."

"Will you be the person talking to Chloe?" Abbie continued.

"No, but I'm hoping to enlist the aid of one of the best forensic investigators in this part of the country. I still have a few calls to make," Hayley told Abbie, "but will be back in touch later today to let you know exactly with whom Chloe will be visiting."

Abbie was silent for long minutes. Finally, she said, "Hayley, how does this work?"

"That's a great question, Abbie," Hayley said, noticing Abbie's obvious concern for the child, "and I'm glad you asked it. Chloe will be a little unsure of the two of us, but she certainly won't be of you. We'll need you to play a big role in this investigation."

"Me?" Abbie looked around the group quizzically and slumped in her chair. "I don't have a clue about child endangerment."

Hayley looked at Abbie for a long while before she spoke again in a gentle tone. "You may not have experience helping other children, but I have a pretty strong suspicion you have experience from your own childhood that has given you a special awareness of the pain others may be suffering."

Abbie's face paled. She looked over at Don and at Keith, doubt and suspicion in her eyes. Slowly, Abbie turned back to Hayley. "How did you know?"

"I didn't know—not exactly," said Hayley. She reached over to cover Abbie's hand reassuringly with her own. "Not until now."

Abbie's eyes grew hard and she inched back in her seat.

"I've been in this business long enough to sense when someone, like you, has a kind and sincere heart, one borne out of deep pain and suffering. Everyone gives off clues. Most people miss them completely, but I've been trained to look for them. Clues like the look in your eyes. An inflection in your voice when you talk about Chloe. A protective nature you exude. You don't have to tell me the details of your childhood, but your difficulties have allowed you to recognize life-threatening situations in Chloe's life."

As Hayley continued talking, Abbie wrestled with something to tell her. Finally, she spoke up in a voice barely above a whisper. "My mother was an alcoholic. Once my dad died, I had to pretty much fend for myself. Although the circumstances are different, I've been where Chloe has been. My heart breaks for her."

"I know it does," Hayley said. "The fact that you found the courage to voice your concerns to Don may have well saved this girl's life. Thank you, Abbie." The investigator offered Abbie a bright smile.

Finally, Abbie relaxed a little.

"Before we leave each other," said Hayley, "let's go over how this will play out. Abbie, I'll begin with you since your role is critical to the success of this mission. You'll get Chloe from camp tomorrow before rest time. That way, her absence will be least noticeable. I'll meet the two of you at one thirty at the Child Advocacy Center next door to the police department. You and I will wait together while Chloe's in the interview."

Hayley scribbled a few notes to herself on a lined pad she held before continuing. "Once I leave here, I'll head back to my office and begin making various calls. One of the most important will be to determine the names of several local families who have volunteered to take in children removed from their foster homes during an investigation. Chloe will need a place to live, at least for the short term. We can determine the child's future living arrangements later."

Turning toward Trent, Hayley said, "Trent, I need you to call the county hospital and check to see if you might be able to determine when Hope Henderson took Chloe in for those stitches."

"I'll see what I can do," the chief replied.

Looking over at Don and Keith, Hayley explained more of the plan. "You two must make calls to the school's board members. From what you've told me, Don, you developed an accountability plan years ago that stipulated the Board of Trustees were to be made aware of any threats to the integrity of the school. I'd say this constitutes such a threat."

Every eye in the room was on Hayley. The investigator gave one final word of instruction. "Remember that confidentiality is of the utmost importance. Please don't mention a word of this to anyone. We don't want to do anything to tip our hand or warn the Hendersons that we're aware of their little scheme."

When the meeting ended, Doris and Abbie walked out with Hayley. Don and Keith stayed behind with Trent.

"What do you think, Trent?" ventured Keith.

Trent ran his hand over his close-shaved head. "I'm not sure, Keith, but I do believe we have a real shot at stopping the Hendersons from ever hurting another child."

"Will you let us know what you find out?" Don asked.

"Definitely," replied Trent. "I'll spend the rest of this afternoon finding out all I can about Hope and Kevin Henderson. My assistant chief, Gordon Sanders, will be able to help me. I'll be back in touch with both of you by ten o'clock tonight."

"Sounds like a plan," said Keith, extending his hand to Trent.

"That'll be great," offered Don, also shaking the chief's hand. "We'll look forward to hearing from you."

By the time Don, Doris, Abbie, and Keith arrived back at Timothy House, they had all reached the same conclusion. Chloe would never return to live with Hope and Kevin Henderson.

Not if they could help it.

CHAPTER
29

The call from Trent Lockhart had seemed normal enough. The situation he described was, unfortunately, one that was happening to thousands of children in scores of locations every day. Hayley Collins, however, wasn't satisfied with a "that's just the way it is" mentality where child abuse or neglect of a minor was concerned. In her opinion, one case was one too many.

The meeting, which had ended a short time ago, gave her food for thought. As she drove back to her office in Johnson City, she knew she had little time. It was already pushing four o'clock. Hayley had less than forty-eight hours to ensure the safety and welfare of Chloe Minton, and she was determined to do it.

Since moving to this side of the state from the Memphis area seven years ago, Hayley had made a name for herself as a trusted advocate and defender of mistreated or abused children. Well-proportioned and trim, the investigator had an olive complexion, giving her the appearance that she spent time in the sun. Her long, dark hair was pulled back in a ponytail. Black eyes, an upturned nose, and a delicate mouth completed her competent, confident appearance. She would not know, however, whether this investigation would take the case to youth court or into the circuit court of Robbinsonville. The fact-finding evaluation Hayley hoped to conduct with Chloe tomorrow morning would provide the clues needed to make that determination.

After reaching for a plump folder on a table beside her desk, Hayley thumbed through its contents until she found what she was looking for.

Bart Pulaski—that was the name she needed. Placing her finger underneath his contact information, she reached for her office phone and punched the number. He answered after two rings.

"Department of Children's Services. Foster Care Division. Bart speaking." The tone was professional and measured.

"Bart," Hayley began, "Hayley Collins."

"Hayley," Bart's tone immediately grew warmer and friendlier. "Long time no see. How are you? How are things in your little corner of the state?

Hayley smiled as she listened to his reference to her placement in the Department of Children's Services Johnson City office—a frontier outpost by any agency standard.

"Good, Bart. Staying busy. You?"

"Swamped. If I didn't care so much about these kids, my heart would turn to stone." Bart's voice had now taken on a serious tone. For all his bluster, Bart Pulaski was a tender-hearted man. "It still defies all logic to learn about some of the awful things folks will do to children. Evil is still present in this world, and don't you forget it."

"I know. It's sickening. I'm seeing the same thing here," Hayley replied. "That's why I'm calling you. Trent Lockhart, Robbinsonville's chief of police, brought me in on a potential case of a ten-year-old female who may have suffered abuse from her foster parents. She's been in their home now for four years. The child's name is Chloe Minton.

"That name's familiar to me. Let me see if I can find the name of her case worker."

Hayley heard clicking on a keyboard and shuffling papers for a few minutes.

"Found it," said Bart at last. "The contact's name is Constance Jones."

As Bart talked, Hayley wrote down the phone number.

"I'm going to get in touch with her immediately, as we don't have much time," said Hayley. "This girl is at a summer camp at Timothy House, a local residential school. Parents collect their children on Friday morning. I have less than forty-two hours to determine whether or not her foster parents will be allowed to take her home. I've also got to contact Monica Forster to conduct a forensic interview with the girl early tomorrow afternoon. If the child's story is credible, I need a safe spot to send her. Do you have the names of any potential foster parents you'd recommend?"

"Not sure right off the top of my head. Can you give me about ten minutes?" Bart asked. "Let me check the database. I also have a file with several inquiry forms for potential foster parents that couples have filled out, but our staff has not yet placed the information in the system. Might find a name or two there."

"That would be great, Bart," Hayley replied hopefully. "I'll be right here at my desk."

"Will call you back in a few." Bart clicked off the line.

Even before the call with Bart ended, Hayley initiated a database search of her own. Finding the info she needed, she clicked on the bio for Chloe's case worker.

Some job you're doing, thought Hayley as she dialed the woman's number. On the second ring, the case manager answered.

"Constance Jones, how may I help you?"

"Constance, this is Hayley Collins with DCS. I'm calling about one of the foster children in your caseload—Chloe Minton."

A few seconds of silence followed.

"Minton? Chloe? Let me look through my files."

At this apparent lack of concern, more awareness of the dire nature of Chloe's situation sent Hayley's temper sky-high. She swallowed hard and worked to control her anger.

"Yes, Constance," said Hayley, her voice cold and hard. "The girl's name is Chloe Isabella Minton, and she's ten years old. Her foster parents are Hope and Kevin Henderson. They live in Robbinsonville."

"Sure, I know the case," replied the caseworker in a tone as legit as a three-dollar bill.

"Look," broke in Hayley, "I think you and I know you probably haven't checked on Chloe in a while. She may be in physical danger, and I don't have much time."

Hayley could almost hear the imperious attitude deflate within the woman on the other end of the line. When Constance didn't answer right away, Hayley peppered her again.

"I need to know *exactly* when you last made phone contact or conducted a home check.

Constance sounded like a second-grader being called on by her teacher. "Listen," she began and then choked back a sob. "I'm so overworked. I'm handling dozens of cases, and somehow Chloe's fell through the cracks. Are you going to report me to my supervisor?" Hayley could hear the woman, now crying in earnest.

"I'll worry about that later," said Hayley, disdain for the woman's incompetence evident in her voice. "Tell me the date of your last foster placement interview with the family."

"Two years ago in two thousand and two," Constance replied, slightly above a whisper.

"Oh, goodness," Hayley said as politely as possible. "You *are* out of touch with your caseload."

Before the case worker could reply, Haley said, "Thanks for your help," and ended the call. After putting down the phone, she made a note in the file to call the case manager's supervisor sooner than later.

As Hayley had not yet heard from Bart, she accessed the DCS database once again, locating the contact she needed—Monica Forster. Hayley knew of the woman only by her excellent reputation. She crossed her fingers as she dialed the phone, hoping the forensic investigator could conduct the interview on such short notice. Although considered a criminal investigator, forensic interviews weren't in Hayley's wheelhouse. Her tender heart, where children were concerned, perfectly equipped her with the passion to expose and bring to justice adults who abused and mistreated those already vulnerable simply due to their placement in the foster care system.

A woman's voice answered on the third ring. "Monica Forster."

"Monica, this is Hayley Collins, an investigator in the Johnson City office."

"Hello, Hayley. What can I do for you?"

Crossing her fingers, Hayley continued, "I'm hoping you can meet me in Robbinsonville in the morning to interview a potential abuse victim—a ten-year-old female foster child. She's made incriminating statements to staff at a summer camp. She's supposed to be picked up by the foster parents on Friday morning, and we're hoping to prevent that until we can get to the bottom of the allegations."

"Give me a second. Let me check my schedule."

Hayley heard a click followed by soft strains of elevator music. She twirled the pen she held back and forth like a seesaw in her fingers.

Monica's voice interrupted the music. "Hayley, it looks like you're in luck. What time's the interview scheduled for?"

"One thirty." Hayley crossed her fingers once more.

"That'll work," said Monica. "I'll leave Knoxville by eleven. Is Trent Lockhart still the police chief in Robbinsonville?"

"He is," said Hayley brightly.

"Good to know. I'll give him a call."

The two talked a few minutes more as Monica recorded name and address information for Chloe and the Hendersons.

I need to cross my fingers more often, thought Hayley as she listened to the investigator confirm the appointment and end the call.

Afterward, Hayley began to fill out the preliminary paperwork to set into motion an official investigation into the welfare and safety of Chloe Minton. She used the notes from the meeting earlier that afternoon at Trent's office to complete the portions of the document for which she had answers. Reaching into her desk drawer, Hayley pulled out a small pad of yellow sticky notes. Placing several at various places on the face of the paper, she scribbled notes to herself that would later serve as guides when completing the form.

The phone on her desk buzzed, and she answered immediately.

"Department of Children's Services. Hayley speaking."

"Hayley, Bart here," her colleague replied. "Were you able to reach Chloe's caseworker?

The investigator snorted under her breath. "Some help she was."

Bart seemed incredulous as Hayley recalled her phone call with Constance Jones.

"Someone, somewhere, must be looking out for this kid," said Bart after Hayley's comments. "This girl better be thankful she has you in her corner."

"Thanks, Bart," said Hayley, the storm within her now subsided.

Bart continued, "There are three couples in your part of the state that might be a match. They've already filled out the appropriate paperwork and been vetted."

The investigator had her pen poised over the surface of the notepad open on her desk. "I'm ready."

"The names of the first couple are Henry and Patricia Wilson." Bart waited a few seconds before continuing. "They live in Watauga and have two children—an eleven-year-old daughter, and a fourteen-year-old son. The Wilsons have served in this capacity three times."

The scratch of Hayley's pen filled the silence on the line.

"Got it," said Hayley. "Ready for the next."

"Ben and Cindy Freeman. They live in Limestone. The couple has one biological child, a daughter, who's a high school senior, and they've taken in only one other child in an emergency like Chloe's."

Again, Bart gave Hayley time to write down the information.

"Ready for the third one?" he asked.

"Ready."

"Get this," said Bart excitedly as he introduced the third selection. "This couple, Tim and Taylor Nunley, live in Robbinsonville. They're both teachers. Guess where they work?"

Hayley could almost hear the excitement crackle through the phone line. "At the post office?" she replied, mainly to tease her long-time colleague. Instinctively, she already knew the answer to Bart's question.

"No, silly," Bart replied. "They're on the faculty of Timothy House."

Silence hung between them; the significance of this possible development regarding the welfare of this innocent young girl was not lost on either of them.

"I would say this is more than a coincidence," Hayley ventured.

"Sounds like it to me."

After ensuring she had the correct phone numbers for all three couples, Hayley ended the call with a promise to keep Bart informed of the case's progress. Next, she called Don Fielding and the call went straight to his voicemail.

"Don, this is Hayley Collins. I've checked on families in this area who might provide a safe shelter for Chloe if we have to remove her from the Henderson home. One of these couples is Tim and Taylor Nunley. I want to ask you about them. Call me at your earliest convenience."

More than mere coincidence seemed to be at play. Time would be the teller.

CHAPTER
30

The Chloe Minton file developed quickly, absorbing Hayley's attention once she finished talking with Bart. Time was immaterial. She discovered, however, when she finally looked up, that the sun was slowly descending out her window, and the office building was as quiet as a tomb. Glancing at her watch, she was amazed to discover it was seven forty-five.

It's time to head home, Hayley thought. For another ten minutes, the investigator gathered a stack of files and documents related to Chloe's case and stuffed them into her worn leather briefcase. After punching in the security code beside the back entrance, she left the building, pulling the door tightly behind her.

As she placed the key in the ignition of her car, she rummaged mentally through the dinner options available in her refrigerator. One partially consumed half-gallon of skim milk. Three marbled cheese sticks. Part of a roasted turkey and Swiss sandwich leftover from lunch two days ago. Four small containers of strawberry yogurt. As she pulled out of the parking lot, she already knew the answer for tonight's menu option. Dairy Queen.

After picking up a loaded cheeseburger, French fries, a hot fudge sundae, and a soft drink, Hayley headed home. Her townhouse was one of six in a small development near Buffalo Mountain Park. Hayley's home was the last one on the right. Although the front entrance was attractive enough, the rear side of each unit was where the treasure lay, as here, residents were offered a spectacular view of Buffalo Mountain. The park surrounding the mountain contained over seven hundred acres, offering hikers and nature lovers alike myriad opportunities to enjoy the outdoors.

The summer sun's golden rays had draped a luminescent glow over the scene before her. Hayley closed the sliding glass door behind her and stepped out onto her patio to enjoy the last moments of this beautiful day. Brushing off the glass-topped table with the arm of her blouse, she settled down to unpack and eat her dinner. She had just taken a bite of her cheeseburger when her phone rang. Hayley hoped it might be Don Fielding, as the area code was that of Robbinsonville.

After gulping down the rest of the bite, Hayley answered.

"Hey, Hayley, this is Don Fielding," said the Timothy House director.

"Hi, Don," said Hayley, wiping her mouth with a napkin. From the look of the condiments smeared inside the foil wrapper around the burger, she might well have a ketchup and mustard goatee. "Thanks for calling me back."

"Sorry to be calling so late. I went with our campers off campus to the night program. Once I heard your message, though, I headed back to my office. Fill me in on the Nunleys."

Hayley explained the process of what she thought might happen in the next two days regarding the investigation into Chloe's possible abuse at the hands of the Hendersons.

"Monica Forster, one of our best forensic investigators, will interview Chloe early tomorrow afternoon. She'll determine the facts of the case and whether she thinks we have reason to remove Chloe from the Henderson home. I'll be there with Abbie and Chloe for moral support.

"If Monica confirms what I think she will, I'll then place a call to DCS. A social worker will be sent to the Henderson home to inform them that a complaint had been filed against them and that Chloe will be removed from their home pending the outcome of the investigation."

"All this can happen before Friday morning?" Don asked, sounding a bit perplexed.

"Yes, sir, it can."

Hayley continued her explanation. "Up until this point, Chloe has only inferred emotional and physical abuse. If Monica can corroborate the allegations, then the investigation would be turned over to a child advocate in the Washington County Youth Court system. If Chloe tells Monica specifics about either physical or sexual abuse, then this will automatically become a criminal investigation. I'll be the lead DCS investigator and will work with law enforcement officials to bring the case to trial."

For a few seconds, neither said a word. From years of experience, Hayley surmised Don's silence was because he wasn't someone acquainted with the intricacies of child abuse investigations.

"Regardless," Hayley continued, "Chloe will be removed from the Henderson home at least until after the investigation. She will live in a temporary foster home with a couple who has received special training for this type of situation.

"I spoke this afternoon with my colleague Bart Pulaski, who works in the Knoxville DCS office. He gave me the names of three couples in this area who might provide a temporary safe haven for Chloe, should we need it. All three have been thoroughly investigated and approved by our department. Because Tim and Taylor Nunley are already a part of the Timothy House family, and because Abbie told me Chloe has attended Camp 4Ever and various school functions open to the community, this couple might already know Chloe, which might make the transition easier for her."

For a minute, Hayley thought the connection might have been lost. Listening carefully, though, she thought she heard Don breathing on the other end of the line.

"Hayley," he said carefully, "Tim is the chair of our math department, and Taylor teaches computer science in the lower grades. They are some of the finest young people I've been around in all my years at Timothy House. What I'm about to share is confidential." Don paused for a minute.

"I certainly understand," replied Hayley. "This information will stay with me."

"This couple has struggled for many years with infertility issues. That journey has been one of the great heartaches of their lives. I'd have to look at their files, but if my memory serves me right, they're in their mid-thirties. And yes, they might know Chloe—at least Taylor would, as she has served on the Camp 4Ever staff for the years Chloe has attended."

Hayley listened as Don continued filling in more background on the Nunleys. More coincidences and dots being connected in the lives of the people in this case.

"Could you do me a favor, Don, and contact the Nunleys?" Hayley asked hopefully. "Tim and Taylor may be more amenable to this idea if the suggestion comes from you. As you know, until my interview tomorrow with Chloe, the Nunleys' involvement is a moot point. If Chloe does offer more information while talking with Monica, I would need to meet with the Nunleys tomorrow afternoon. Would a four o'clock appointment in your office be a possibility? I would want you privy to all that is said."

"Certainly, Hayley," Don replied. "Your plan sounds like a good one."

Hayley thought she heard a broad smile as Don ended their conversation.

"Hayley, God works in mysterious ways. Not sure if you believe that, but I do. I'll wait for your call tomorrow morning."

CHAPTER
31

As soon as Don ended his call with Hayley Collins, he thumbed through his phone contacts until he found Tim and Taylor Nunley's number. Glancing down at his watch, he saw it was already nine twenty. Realizing the late hour but weighing it against the critical nature of the matter, Don punched in Tim's cell number. He answered after the first ring.

"Evening, Don," the young man said.

"Hey, Tim," Don replied. "Look, I apologize for calling you so late, but there is an urgent matter I need to talk to you and Taylor about, and I don't think it can wait until tomorrow."

"Taylor's sitting right here beside me," Tim said. "Would you like me to put the phone on speaker?"

"Tim, I'd rather come to your house. I could be there in ten minutes. This won't take long, but I'd rather share what I've got to say in person."

"We'll be looking for you. See you soon." Tim Nunley sounded apprehensive, but Don couldn't be sure.

Don was already in his car before he ended the call with Tim. *Poor guy,* he thought. *I bet he thinks he and Taylor are about to lose their jobs. They have no idea they may be about to gain one of the chief desires of their hearts.*

Looking up at the stars twinkling above, Don said aloud, "God, what are You up to?"

Although Don knew, from his many years of walking with the Lord, that one didn't always get an answer to such a question, he knew with absolute certainty that God's plans are always the best.

———

As Don pulled into the driveway of the Nunley home, he caught a glimpse of Taylor peering out through the living room curtains. Walking up to the front door, he felt a bit chagrined about his insistence on seeing them in person at such a late hour. Still, Chloe's safety was hanging in the balance, and he wasn't about to take a chance with that.

Tim's warm welcome gave Don hope that the information he had to share might be a win-win for them. After shaking Tim's hand, Don headed into the living room, where Taylor was seated, as Tim closed the door. The young computer science teacher rose as her head of school entered the room. Don walked near and gave her a hug. At Taylor's bidding, Don took a seat across from her. Tim sat beside his wife on the couch.

Don leaned forward in his seat and rested his arms on top of his knees. Clasping his hands before him, he began. "First, thank you for allowing me to come over at this late hour. I would not have done so had this not been a matter of the highest importance."

Tim and Taylor were sitting near the edge of the sofa, like two elementary students who had been called into the principal's office.

"Second, what I'm about to tell you is highly confidential and involves the safety and welfare of one of our Camp 4Ever students— Chloe Minton."

At the mention of Chloe's name, Taylor's facial expression changed. "What's wrong with Chloe?" she blurted out. After her outburst, she sat back a little on the sofa, looking like she was holding her breath. What she didn't know was that what Don was about to say might actually take it away.

"Well," continued Don, "to be honest, I'm not quite sure. However, it appears that she may have suffered emotional and possibly physical abuse while in the home of her foster parents, Hope and Kevin Henderson." He ran through the details of share time, the flower walk with Doris, and the meeting with the chief of police and DCS investigator.

"As you already know," Don said, looking first at Tim and then at Taylor, "when an investigation into a foster home takes place, the child at risk is removed from that home until the investigation is complete. I spoke less than thirty minutes ago with Hayley Collins, the DCS investigator. The agency returned a list of individuals willing to care for a foster child in an emergency situation, and your names were on it."

Tim looked longingly at Taylor and then back at Don. "We filled out that paperwork several years ago."

Don looked at both of them, a grave expression on his face. "Chloe is now in an emergency situation."

As Don shared this vital bit of information, Taylor's eyes filled with tears. She looked at Tim. He leaned over and hugged his wife gently. Taking his arm from around his wife's shoulders, Tim clasped his hands together, looking at them for a long while as if trying to decide what to say. When he looked up, he was also blinking back tears.

"Taylor and I have longed for a child of our own. Although we know God loves us, He has not chosen, for some reason, to answer that prayer." Tim reached up and wiped his nose with the back of his hand. The young man looked over at his wife for encouragement. Her affirmation shone in her bright eyes. "As time has passed, however, we've thought more and more about the possibility of fostering or even adopting a child. The thought that Chloe may be in danger is unsettling. When would we have to give you our decision?"

Don hesitated for a moment and then told them, "Hayley has to know something by early tomorrow morning."

Both their eyes widened at this revelation.

"The interview with Chloe is at one thirty. If the child says what Hayley suspects she will say, Chloe won't return to the Henderson home. She might come here to live with you tomorrow night. That is," Don hesitated, "if you agree to keep her."

The young couple looked at each other for what seemed the longest time. Don felt as if he were witness to a sacred moment. Slowly, they turned back to face Don.

Taking one of Taylor's hands in both of his, Tim spoke quietly. "We need to talk about this and pray. Regardless of whichever decision we make, our lives will be forever changed. We believe God will tell us what to do. I'll call you at seven tomorrow morning with our answer."

"That sounds fair enough to me," said Don, relieved that this difficult task was over.

As the threesome stood to end their conversation, Tim's face suddenly lit up, and between wide grins he said, "Although this is a serious matter, Taylor and I are relieved to know we still have our jobs." He heaved a sigh of relief before continuing. "We thought we were getting fired."

Don laughed loudly and clapped the young man heartily on the back. "Are you kidding me? You're two of the best teachers we've ever had. If we can't manage to keep you and Taylor happy at Timothy House, then I'm the one who might need to be fired."

As Tim opened the front door, Don turned and stopped. Reaching out, he took one of their hands in each of his. Squeezing them gently, he said, "Know that I'll be praying with you this night. You two have to do what you believe is right for your family. If, for any reason, you have a hitch in your spirit about bringing Chloe into your home, then don't do it. There's your answer. God will confirm for you, in a manner you recognize and in a language you understand, His will for your life."

Soft tears pooled in both Tim's and Taylor's eyes as they nodded at Don, too moved to speak.

He raised a hand in farewell and then turned toward his car.

——— — ———

After cranking the engine, Don searched his phone for Hayley Collins's number. The digital glow of the cell phone showed ten fifty-five. After putting the car in reverse, he eased to the end of the driveway. As he dialed her number, he hoped Hayley was still awake.

She answered on the second ring. "Hello."

"Hey, Hayley, this is Don Fielding. I am so sorry to be calling you so late."

"Oh, hi, Don. That isn't a problem at all," said the investigator. "I've had mounds of paperwork to get through. Can't ever seem to get it done at the office, so I brought a stack home tonight." Don could hear the fatigue in Hayley's voice. "Your call is a welcome interruption."

"I'm just leaving the Nunleys' home. They're thinking over the possibility of taking in Chloe. Tim promised to call me in the morning. I'll call you as soon as I hear from him."

"That's great, Don," replied Hayley. "I'll look forward to receiving their answer. If they decide not to take her, we've still got two other solid families. I give you my word—I'll take care of Chloe."

Don ended the call, knowing that Chloe Minton had found a worthy advocate in Hayley Collins.

He said a silent prayer for Tim and Taylor Nunley.

At least they didn't say no, Lord, Don thought as he pulled through the gates of Timothy House. *We will wait to see what You deliver.*

CHAPTER
32

Tim closed the front door and turned to face his wife. He took her hands in his and stared into her soft hazel eyes for the longest time. Tears streamed down her face, and her lips quivered. As he drew her close, Tim's own eyes were brimming. Husband and wife held each other tightly, too overcome with emotion for words.

After a few minutes, Tim still held his wife in his arms. Whispering to her, he asked, "Did Don just say what I think he said?"

Drawing back from her husband, Taylor looked into his handsome face, his dark brown eyes glistening. "I think he did. Do you think God may be answering our prayers?"

"I'm not sure. I honestly don't know what to think."

Tim led his wife across the room, and they settled on the sofa, still holding each other's hands.

Although this young couple held fast to their faith, they were still hard-pressed some days to understand God's seeming disregard for their ceaseless prayers. The candle of hope, lit many years ago in their hearts, the possibility of ever having a child under any circumstance, had almost burned out, its wick dwindling to a nub barely able to hold a flicker, let alone a flame.

An unexpected invitation to attend a marriage enrichment seminar a year ago had breathed new life into their relationship. The weekend retreat, although intense and painful at times, brought Tim and Taylor face-to-face with the fact that their marriage might actually be in jeopardy. Through the conference sessions and personalized counseling—both as a couple and individually—the Nunleys came to grips with the reality of the pain they both endured when suffering two miscarriages within the past seven years. They realized how close they had come to losing each other simply because they had taken the brutal heartache of infertility and stuffed it deep inside rather than addressing the dilemma constructively.

Before leaving the retreat center when the conference was over, Tim and Taylor knelt by the side of the bed in their cabin and rededicated their lives not only to their Lord, but to each other. They asked God's forgiveness for believing the lie that He had abandoned them. They also asked His help in developing with them, individually and as a couple, the patience to wait for the perfect timing for His plan to unfold and the discernment to recognize it when it did. They told God they were willing to accept His plan for their lives, even if it meant never having a child. As hard as those words were to say, Tim and Taylor each experienced a peace beyond telling after voicing their prayer.

Neither spoke for a few minutes once they settled in the living room. Tim gently squeezed Taylor's had. The mantel clock struck the hour—forty-five minutes past midnight. Time seemed to stand still, not only in this night, but in the lives of this young couple. After years of ceaseless, lengthy, and often teary petitions made to the Lord, Don Fielding had appeared tonight and, like an angel of the Lord, brought with him a word seemingly from Heaven itself.

True, not long after the marriage enrichment seminar, Tim and Taylor had filled out the paperwork to become potential foster parents, but they had also filled out documents stating they would provide aid and comfort on a short-term basis to a child facing a potentially life-threatening situation and would do so without advance notice.

Tim and Taylor had come to know and love Chloe in the time that she had been enrolled in Timothy House or Camp 4Ever. The summer camp counselor experiences allowed the husband and wife to care for others' children despite the pain of not having their own. Last year, Taylor's experience serving as a cabin "mother" for second-grade girls had been as close to picture-perfect as possible. Tim had worked with Josh Hastings to coordinate outdoor skills activities. Both had seen quite a lot of the girl during that week.

During this past school year, Chloe had been in Taylor's first-period basic computer skills class. The teacher was amazed at the girl's intellect and ability to figure out more complex technical issues that would baffle most other students her age. Tim, as chairman of the math department, had gotten to know Chloe through a math skills class. Both had discovered the child had a sweet spirit, a willing heart, and determination that knew no bounds.

Tim turned to sit sideways on the couch to see his wife's face. "Tay," he said softly, "Chloe's in trouble. What do you want to do?"

"Oh, Tim," his wife said after releasing a long sigh. "Years ago, when we first married, I couldn't imagine bringing someone else's child into our home. I wanted one of our own so badly."

The pain in her eyes was evident, but Tim sat silently, his eyes never leaving hers, as he allowed Taylor the opportunity to put into words all that was in her heart. She was quiet for a moment, working to calm the emotion bouncing around inside.

"After the conference, though, it's like God has changed my heart." Taylor looked back up at her husband, her eyes shining brightly with a light of hope. "Do you remember that counselor who talked with us about parenting?"

Tim nodded.

"She said to us that being the right parent is more about being the right kind of person that a child needs and less about biology."

Tim chimed in, "Think about the details of some of the family situations we're privy to here at Timothy House. Just because someone produces a child does not necessarily make them a good parent."

"The counselor also said," Taylor continued, "that God may be silent about our own desires to have a child because He is waiting for the right time to share with us His plan for our family, one that is greater and more wonderful than anything we could imagine."

Tim looked back at his wife, a silly grin dawning across his face. "Chloe Minton needs a home and a momma and daddy who will love her unconditionally. We desperately want to have a child to love and nurture. Maybe God is answering both our prayers."

For the next three hours, the couple poured out their hearts to one another. Once Tim found the courage and voiced the words about the hopes and dreams he'd packed away and placed high on the shelf of his heart, Taylor couldn't speak fast enough to utter more words of the same, her thoughts poured out, like water that had been slowly building up pressure along the weak side of a dam and now finding a crack in the wall. In a candid and forthright conversation that was both terrifying and invigorating, the Nunleys talked about the possibility of taking in Chloe as a foster child at first but with the full intention of adopting her as their daughter as soon as the legal system would allow. They spoke aloud fears long harbored, ones borne from the dark places where doubt and discouragement had whispered to their hearts that God had forgotten all about them and could not possibly have "a future and a hope" prepared for them to enjoy.

Once Tim and Taylor were both spent, with no more words to say, a great peace filled their hearts, its sweet ointment a soothing balm to their souls, like a salve to heal a deep wound. At almost the same time, they moved to the edge of the couch and knelt side by side. Tim reached for his wife's hand, and they bowed their heads before Heaven's throne.

"Dear Lord," Tim began, "before we even begin this prayer to You, we want to thank You for who You are and for Your unfailing love for us. We know that in this last year, You have saved our marriage, and for that, we are incredibly thankful." He gently squeezed Taylor's hand as he spoke.

"Although Don's visit caught us by surprise tonight, it did not catch You off guard. We acknowledge that You are our Lord and sovereign of every aspect of our lives, individually and as husband and wife, even though we don't often understand how You work. We ask You to forgive us for thinking that simply having a child would complete us. Thank You for bringing us to the realization that we will only find our true peace and our highest joy and purpose in You, Lord, and in You alone."

The room was silent as the impact of what the Nunleys were praying about sunk in.

"Taylor and I don't know what to think," Tim continued after a few minutes. "We did take a step of faith last fall when we filled out the paperwork at the Department of Children's Services. Are You leading us to bring Chloe into our home and possibly to adopt her?"

Once more, the gentle breathing of this man and wife and the ticking of the mantel clock were the only sounds in the living room.

"Lord," Taylor's voice implored, "You are our Creator and our Heavenly Father. Tim and I are asking You to make Your way clear to us. As much as we would love to have a child, we also realize that bringing someone of Chloe's age into our lives will bring its own set of unique parenting needs we may not be equipped to handle. This precious girl has already been through so much heartache. The last thing we want to do is to add to it.

"You tell us, Lord, in Your Word, that if we have faith as little as a mustard seed, that You can use that as a starting point for what You want to do in our lives. Tim and I have no idea how this might work. What will adjusting to the addition of a ten-year-old girl in our home look like? What if we get into this relationship and decide we can't do this? What if Chloe comes to live with us and decides she doesn't like us? What if our hearts get broken?"

Tears prevented Taylor from speaking. Tim waited patiently while he wiped away tears of his own.

Finally, Tim finished the prayer Taylor had begun, their hearts and words now united as one. "Here's our mustard seed, Lord. We surrender to You our hopes and dreams of what we think a family—our family—should look like and trust that You will do more than we can ask or comprehend. Be our Shepherd and our Guide. Give us courage and strength, and equip us for the days ahead. All this we ask in the strong and precious name of Jesus. Amen."

A holy hush filled the room as the realization that something more wonderful than words could describe had just occurred between them and the Lord. As the mantel clock struck six, the first rays of the new day shone bright and golden through the trees outside their window.

Ten minutes later, Tim dialed Don's cell phone.

"Hey, Don," said Tim. "Sorry to call you so early, but Taylor and I have been up all night praying and talking about Chloe's situation."

On the other end of the line, Don sat waiting with bated breath, praying for what Tim might say next.

"Our answer is yes!"

CHAPTER
33

Don stared at his cell phone long after Tim Nunley had ended the call. Tim had assured his trusted friend and boss that he and Taylor would be in Don's office that afternoon. *Thank You, Lord,* was the only thought running through Don's mind while recalling the past twenty-four hours' fantastic, even miraculous, events. As badly as he wanted to get on his knees and offer proper thanks to God, time was of the essence. For Chloe's sake.

Don's first call was to Trent Lockhart to update him on Chloe's case. Next, Don connected with Hayley to confirm that Tim and Taylor Nunley agreed to offer Chloe safe refuge in their home.

The last call was to Abbie, an integral player in this plan. As had the Nunleys, Abbie had assured her boss she was on board to protect Chloe and would pick her up from Timothy House and bring her to meet Hayley.

Don looked at his watch—five minutes after seven. "Mission: Save Chloe" had commenced.

———

Abbie made sure she was in the dining hall early to watch as the campers filed in. Girls and boys tried hard not to run as they jockeyed for the perfect place at the tables. When Charmaine's kitchen staff placed lunch on the serving line, Abbie was among the first to eat. While she ate, she watched Chloe, who was sitting with the other girls in her cabin. Abbie could also see Lane and Becky at the table.

One of the hardest things about this ordeal was not being able to share any of the information about Chloe with Laney. Her best friend. Her chief confidante. Although Becky had probably told Lane what Chloe had said during share time, it may not have caught either counselor's attention. Abbie had not seen Lane or Becky since Tuesday nor talked with either of them about the incident. *Boy,* thought Abbie, *I'll have a lot to tell Lane and Eric when this is all through.*

As soon as Abbie saw Chloe and her friends take their trays to the kitchen window, she excused herself from her table. Uttering a silent prayer for wisdom and guidance, she followed Chloe out of the dining hall.

"Chloe," Abbie called out as the girl bounced down the steps of Covenant Kitchen.

"Miss Abbie," came the excited reply as Chloe turned and came over to where Abbie stood on the porch.

"Hey, you," said Abbie, reaching out to hug the girl.

"Camp has been so much fun this week," Chloe began. Abbie listened as the girl told her about the week's activities.

"I'm so glad you've had a good week." Motioning with her hand, Abbie led Chloe down the steps. "Let's go for a walk."

After the two were far enough from the dining hall to avoid being overheard by others, Abbie suggested they sit on a bench just ahead. Once seated, Abbie patiently listened as Chloe chatted excitedly about the new friends she had made during the week.

Taking a deep breath, Abbie interrupted the girl. "Listen, Chloe," she began, momentarily hesitating as she worked to find the right words. "Do you remember what you told me during share time at the cabin and when we picked flowers with Miss Doris?"

The fact that Chloe did not respond at first made Abbie think the girl had forgotten the shocking revelation she had made. Chloe's next words, however, let Abbie know that the child precisely remembered what she had disclosed. "You mean what I told you about all the bad things the Hendersons say to me? And what I said about being locked in the dark place?"

Abbie slowly nodded in agreement, "That's right, Chloe. I'm sorry." She looked down at the child's innocent face—porcelain skin like that of a china doll.

"That's all right, Miss Abbie," said Chloe brightly, her brave spirit shining through every word.

"No, Chloe," continued Abbie, this time using a more serious tone. "It's not all right. Mr. Don and I have two special friends we want you to meet this afternoon. One is Miss Hayley, and her job is to protect children from foster parents, like the Hendersons, when they act mean or hurtful. The other is Miss Monica, who gathers information for Hayley."

Looking deep into Chloe's dark eyes, Abbie prayed silently that the child would come willingly to the interview. If she would not, all of this would have been in vain.

"Chloe, through these last few days, you were so brave to share with me and several other adults about some of the ugly things the Hendersons have said to you."

"Yes, ma'am," said Chloe solemnly, her eyes never leaving Abbie's.

"I need you to brave one more time," said Abbie, gently brushing Chloe's dark hair from where it had fallen around her face. "Can you do that for me?"

Chloe nodded her answer, her eyes clear and bright.

As the pair made their way to Mistletoe Cottage, Abbie recited another silent prayer that God would give Chloe the courage required to find her voice and bring into the light all the darkness she had struggled against.

———

The Robbinsonville Child Advocacy Center was located next to the police department. Although the two buildings shared a common wall, the newly purchased one had a different façade, looking more like a storefront than an institutional building. The Center contained administrative offices on the first and second floors and a series of more private meeting rooms on the third floor. It would be in one of these rooms that Monica's visit with Chloe would take place. The entry door, on a side street, gave the building the appearance of having no connection whatsoever with the Robbinsonville Police Department.

Before the two got out of the car, Abbie reached into the back seat and grabbed a brightly colored gift bag. Handing it to the child, she said, "This is for you, Chloe!"

Wideyed, Chloe took the gift from Abbie and pulled away several sheets of tissue paper that filled its opening. Delight shone in the child's eyes as she drew out a stuffed ivory bunny, a pink satin bow tied smartly around its neck. "Oh, I love it," exclaimed Chloe, hugging the cuddly toy tightly as if it were a long-lost friend.

In the next instant, she held the soft, stuffed bunny out in front of her in order to get a better look at it. "I think I'll call you Maisie," Chloe said, as if talking to herself.

"Maisie's a wonderful name," Abbie told her. "I thought you might like a friend with you when you visit with Miss Monica."

Chloe nodded wordlessly, hugging the stuffed animal to her once more. The smile on the girl's face told Abbie all she needed to know.

Once Abbie and Chloe entered the building's lobby, they walked to the nearby bank of elevators. The interior hallways were painted a light gray that appeared soft blue, depending on the lighting. Framed prints of pastoral scenes hung on the walls every few feet down the long hall, giving the space less of an institutional feeling. Though only ten, Chloe seemed to sense the magnitude of this meeting—she hadn't let go of Abbie's hand since they left the car.

Abbie and Chloe found Hayley Collins and Monica Forster waiting in the hall when the elevator doors opened on the third floor.

Once Abbie and Chloe reached them, Abbie bent down close to the child's face. "Chloe," she said, "these are my friends—Miss Hayley and Miss Monica."

As if on cue, Chloe said brightly, "Hi, ladies." She even waved at the investigators.

"Hey, Chloe," said Hayley, waving at the child.

"Hello, Chloe," said Monica, suppressing a giggle. "It is so nice to meet you." Looking over at Abbie, the investigator continued, "You must be Abbie Richardson."

The two women exchanged a handshake.

Abbie, unsure of whether this process would work, asked, "Where would you like Hayley and me to go?"

The investigator nodded to her left. "There's a waiting room at the end of the hall."

"Thanks," said Abbie. She gave Chloe a quick hug and then headed with Hayley toward the seating area. Nearing the end of the hallway, Abbie turned back, her eyes filled with tears as she caught one more glimpse of this courageous child with Maisie the stuffed bunny tucked tightly under one arm. Only God knew what had happened to Chloe while living under the Hendersons' roof. As she sat down, Abbie prayed that Chloe would reveal that information to Monica Forster.

———

Monica quickly turned her attention to the girl. She knelt beside her and asked, "Chloe, is it okay if you and I visit for a minute?"

"Yes, ma'am."

"Good girl," continued Monica. "What's your friend's name?" the investigator asked, pointing to the stuffed animal.

"Her name's Maisie," said Chloe brightly. "Miss Abbie said she could come with me."

"She certainly can," Monica said as she stood. She pointed to a door across the hall from where they were standing. "We can talk in this room." She walked over to open the door. When Monica turned on the switch, the light revealed a simple wooden table with a chair on either side. A large, white dry-erase board stood atop an easel nearby. Several colored markers lay on its tray.

Chloe took a seat as Monica closed the door to the interview room.

———

Monica was amazed at how comfortable Chloe seemed during the interview, as if the child truly understood the Hendersons could harm her no longer. The investigator took notes as Chloe answered the questions.

"Chloe, the other night you told Miss Abbie that the Hendersons had been mean to you. Can you tell me about that?"

The child nodded seriously before answering, her dark eyes glistening. "When I first got to their house, Miss Hope locked me in a closet. She didn't let me out for a long time. When she finally opened the door, she told me she'd hurt me if I ever told anyone."

"Did she ever put you in the closet again?" Monica asked.

Chloe nodded.

"Did the Hendersons ever hit you?"

Chloe's eyes became hard and cold, and she gripped Maisie tightly to her. "Yes, ma'am. One night after dinner, Mrs. Henderson got angry with me, though I'm not sure why. She brought in a wire coat hanger and opened it like you do when you roast marshmallows. She whipped me on the back of my legs."

Shifting in her chair, Chloe pointed to the two-inch scar on the back of her left leg. "The cut wouldn't stop bleeding, so Miss Hope took me to the hospital. Before we got out of the car, she got in my face and said, 'Now, you listen here. You know where bad little girls go. Straight to the orphanage. If you tell the doctor anything other than you cut your leg falling off the swing set, that's where you'll be headed.'"

Monica was amazed at how calm Chloe seemed while recalling this terrible experience. "Did you tell the doctor what Mrs. Henderson told you to say?"

"Yes, ma'am."

Monica took a few minutes to record more information from the interview. While she did, Chloe stroked the bunny's soft fur.

Soon, the girl shared a few more stories of how both Hope and Kevin Henderson yelled at her. "Miss Hope thinks I'm stupid."

Monica sat silently for a few moments, totally unprepared for this statement. "Why would you say that?"

"Because, late one night, when they thought I was asleep, I crept into the hallway. The Hendersons were talking really loud in the living room. Miss Hope was saying how smart she was to have written a plan for fooling the government."

The investigator leaned forward. "What kind of a plan?"

"Like a diary, I think. That night, I heard Miss Hope say she put the plan in a file folder and kept it hidden on top of the bookcase in the living room. Two days later, when she was out in the backyard, I dragged a chair over, looked on top, and saw the folder. It's really thick. She almost caught me, but I put the chair back when I heard her coming up the porch steps."

Monica continued writing furiously. "What else did the Hendersons say that night when you were listening to them?"

"Mr. Kevin talked about all the drinks he bought with the money they were supposed to be using to take care of me."

"Soft drinks?" asked Monica.

"No, ma'am. I think he was talking about alcohol."

"Did you ever see the Hendersons drink alcohol in front of you?

"No, ma'am, but that night, Mr. Kevin talked about his special hiding place down in the basement where he kept all the bottles. Just like with the bookcase, I found the bottles behind the freezer one morning while Miss Hope went to the post office to mail some letters. It's dark and scary down there. Lots of spider webs and shadows." Chloe hugged the toy to her after making this last admission.

———

Fifty minutes later, when Abbie and Hayley heard the interview room door open and saw Monica and Chloe approaching, the expression on the investigator's face let them know that their worst fears had been confirmed.

CHAPTER
34

The tension in the room was so palpable one could almost cut it with a knife. All but one of those seated in Don Fielding's office were nervous, as they had encountered a situation such as this one before. Abbie, though she had been through similar scenarios several other times, still felt a few butterflies in her stomach, as there were many details of this complicated case yet to unravel. The atmosphere in this administrator's office, however uncertain, contained an air of expectation and excitement, like that shared by those waiting to see a comet pass overhead or glimpse shooting stars streaking across the night sky.

Tim and Taylor Nunley sat together on a loveseat in Don's office. They held hands and whispered to each other.

Don Fielding, Keith Haliday, and Abbie Richardson were around a nearby small, round table. Like the Nunleys, they also spoke in low tones.

An empty club chair was near the Nunleys.

At exactly four o'clock, the five assembled looked up as Don's office door opened. Five pairs of curious eyes watched as criminal investigator Hayley Collins entered.

"Hello, everyone," Hayley said as she looked into the faces of those assembled. As if on cue, she sat in the club chair.

Every eye in the room was on the investigator.

Don spoke up. "Hayley, thanks so much for meeting with us today." Looking toward the young couple seated across from her, Don continued, "Let me introduce you to Tim and Taylor Nunley."

Hayley nodded in the couple's direction.

"We are eager to hear about your visit with Chloe," Don continued, concern evident in his voice. "What were you able to learn?"

Hayley, bound by strict rules of confidentiality, measured her words. "I can tell you that what Chloe said to Abbie and Becky was indeed true. Furthermore, the allegations the child made in the presence of Abbie and Doris were repeated to Monica Forster. Surprisingly, Chloe also offered new details during the interview.

"Yesterday afternoon, after Monica's visit with Chloe, I went to Chief Lockhart's office. Combined with what we already know, I'll be working with his office to launch a criminal investigation into Hope and Kevin Henderson. A case worker from DCS went to the Henderson home at seven thirty this morning to tell them that, due to a complaint lodged against them, Chloe would not be returning to their home. Monica felt Chloe offered testimony that could land Hope and Kevin in jail, but we'll have to wait until Trent's detectives complete the investigation."

Looking over at Tim and Taylor, Hayley said, "Chloe will *never* go back to the Henderson home, and that's where you come in."

At this, the couple turned to look at one another and then gazed back at the investigator.

"Don called me this morning to tell me you're willing to bring Chloe into your home," Hayley continued. "Thank you," the investigator said quietly.

The Nunleys' rapt attention and the gleam in their eyes let Hayley know they were eager to help the girl in any way possible.

Tim spoke up. "I would be less than honest, Hayley, if I said we aren't a little scared. But all that fear fades quickly when thinking about how much Chloe needs our help."

At this point, Taylor reached over to take Tim's hand. Looking at Hayley, Taylor said softly, "We believe God will show us the next steps."

Hayley sat forward in her chair. "We're ready for you to take one of those next steps now. Chloe is outside in the hall with Doris, and I'd like to have her come in here. Don has told me that she knows both of you, so the idea of her staying with you for a few days probably won't be hard for her to grasp." The investigator sat silently for a few moments as she allowed the gravity of her words to sink in.

Taylor spoke first. "We'd love to see her."

Hayley was more than a little surprised by the excitement shining in the other woman's eyes. Looking back at Don, Hayley said, "Let Doris bring her in."

With that, Don left the office. As he did, Hayley glanced over to glimpse the Nunleys, who seemed to be holding both a collective breath and each other's hands tightly. A few minutes later, the investigator watched the couple's shoulders relax as if they had received a soothing massage.

Chloe stood beside Don, her delicate hand in his strong one, an ivory colored stuffed bunny in her other hand. All heads turned to see them.

Abbie spoke first. "Hey, Chloe!" She hugged the girl, then she looked over at the investigator and said, "You remember Miss Hayley that you met earlier this afternoon?"

Chloe's eyes immediately fixed on Hayley's face. "Hey, Miss Hayley," she said, hugging her new stuffed bunny.

"Hello, Chloe," said Hayley. She lowered herself to Chloe's height. "You remember when we met that I told you the Hendersons would never hurt you again?"

The girl nodded slowly, her eyes fixed intently on Hayley's.

Hayley straightened and continued, "Two of your teachers, Mr. and Mrs. Nunley, have told me how much they've enjoyed getting to know you in their classes and how much they like you. They've invited you to stay with them for a while. Would you like that?"

Chloe then turned her attention from Hayley to Tim and Taylor and said, as a big smile broke across her face, "I'd love to come to your house." Lifting the new stuffed animal Abbie had given her, she asked, "Can Maisie come with me?"

The nervous tension Tim and Taylor had been trying to suppress broke out in peals of laughter.

"Of course, Maisie can," said Tim, his eyes moist with emotion.

He and Taylor stood and opened their arms. Without any hesitation, the girl walked over and pressed herself into this circle of love that had now enveloped her. For the longest time, Tim and Taylor held Chloe close.

As the arms of the Nunleys wrapped around Chloe, all the others standing nearby worked hard to contain tears of joy over what was happening. None of them doubted for a second that they were witnessing a miracle.

A miracle of love.

CHAPTER
35

The "dog days" of summer were about to end, and soon DeSean would begin his senior year at David Crockett High. How he had survived his sophomore and junior years, he wasn't quite sure. He had finished the last year with Cs and Ds but knew he'd have to step it up. The start of school, however, was the furthest thing from his mind. DeSean's thoughts were in a tailspin as he replayed the events that had led up to this day.

Two days ago, when the phone at the Smith house rang, Edna called from the kitchen and told DeSean that someone was calling for him. How surprised and pleased he was to hear C.J.'s voice on the other end. The older guy had told DeSean to meet him in the parking lot of the Jonesborough Community Center at ten o'clock on a Wednesday morning, so here he sat.

DeSean noticed C.J. was nine minutes late. He looked up from his watch to see a late-model tan sedan cruising to a stop next to his car. DeSean's first thought was to get out of the car, but before he could, C.J. pulled up so close to Mr. Smith's car that opening the door was impossible. Feeling more like he was in a drive-through burger joint, DeSean found himself sitting across from C.J., their drivers' side windows adjacent to one another.

"Hey, man, thanks for helping me with this delivery today," C.J. said. Turning toward the interior of his car, he picked up a cardboard box, a little bigger than that for athletic shoes, and handed it through the window to DeSean. The carefully sealed package had the words "Auto Parts" stamped in black letters across the top of it. Although not terribly heavy, the contents jiggled a bit inside.

"Bill at Wilson's Body Shop over on Tenth Street will be looking for this," C.J. instructed as DeSean placed the box on the car seat beside him. "He's expecting you."

"I'll head that way right now," said the teen. Pride swelled within DeSean as he looked back at C.J. Delivering car parts probably wasn't the glitziest job, but it felt good to have someone give him responsibility and show faith in him.

"Terrific. Mr. Howard appreciates your help," C.J. said as he slid a fifty-dollar bill to DeSean across the space between them.

Although DeSean had seen one before, he had never held a bill of this denomination in his hand. The paper was crisp and cool against his fingers.

"Wow," said the teen. "Thanks."

The morning sun was rising in the sky, and DeSean had to shield his eyes from it as he peered over at C.J. A fleeting thought about C.J.'s animal-like expression raced through his mind as it had before. The older guy's dark, beady eyes stared through the car window at him.

"So . . ." continued C.J., giving DeSean a thumbs-up. "I'll be in touch the next time Mr. Howard needs a delivery made here in town." Following his announcement, the car's electric window hummed, and before DeSean could say a word, C.J.'s car was pulling away toward the main road.

———

The mechanic's shop was easy to find. Funny, though, that the garage door was down and only one car was in the parking lot. DeSean got out and headed for what looked like the office door.

A few minutes after he knocked, the door opened to reveal a tall, slender fellow in tattered jeans and a T-shirt that looked like it hadn't been washed in centuries. DeSean supposed this was Bill. "Yeah?"

DeSean stammered as Bill's steely gray eyes looked coldly into his own. Thrusting the package forward, DeSean said, "Delivery from Howard's Tire and Auto. C.J. sent me."

Although the eyes grew no warmer, a slight smile played around the corners of the fellow's mouth as he took the box. "Yeah," he said dryly, "C.J. told me you might be stopping by."

Without another word, the mechanic stepped back into the darkened space and slammed the door shut. DeSean heard the click of the lock on the other side.

Feeling a bit foolish, DeSean walked back to Mr. Smith's car and climbed inside. Although the exchange at the mechanic shop had been awkward, the thought of the extra cash in his pocket quickly erased those feelings. DeSean started the car and headed for home.

Back inside Wilson's Body Shop, Bill picked up a small knife from the workbench and slit open the box. He tore open the cardboard container to find a collection of small, black radiator hoses inside. He inspected them, one by one, until he found the one he was searching for. Holding the short rubber tubing in one hand, he picked up a long set of tweezers with the other. Skillfully, he inserted their pointed tips deep inside the rubber hose and withdrew a small plastic bag hidden deep inside. Thirty small pills of a greenish hue, no bigger than aspirin tablets.

Bill smiled a wicked grin as he stuffed the plastic bag into the pocket of his jeans. The hook was set.

———

DeSean sat for a few minutes in the Smiths' driveway before getting out of the car. Opening his wallet, he peered inside to look once again at the fifty-dollar bill. A rush of accomplishment filled him. It felt good to be needed.

What the teen had no way of knowing was that he had just walked right into a trap.

A mule trap.

CHAPTER
36

Keith and Abbie were on their way to dinner with Portia Dockery, who lived about twenty miles west of Robbinsonville. As Keith drove, Abbie was mesmerized by the beautiful scenery. Cattle grazed on green fields, and rolling hills rose up behind the farmland, tidy farmhouses with wide front porches and barns and silos nearby.

"So, tell me again, how long have you known Portia?" Abbie asked.

"I met her last year shortly after I arrived at Timothy House," said Keith, glancing briefly at Abbie. "A few weeks after that, she invited me to dinner one day after a board meeting. Ever since, Mama Dee calls and invites me to dinner from time to time. You'll really like her."

"How long has she been on the school's board?"

"I think about ten years."

"How old is she?" Abbie asked.

"I'm not sure," Keith replied, pausing a minute to calculate Mama Dee's age. "Probably in her early seventies. She's had a lot of loss in her life, like I have, so we had much in common when we met. You'll see. She's someone you feel like you've known all your life."

"After what you told me she said to you after the June board meeting, I hope I pass muster with her."

Keith laughed. "You'll do fine. She's going to love you, just like I do."

At this Abbie blushed and her questions ceased.

———

When the front door to the modest brick ranch house opened, Portia Dockery greeted Keith and Abbie with a bright smile and a hug.

A starched, floral-patterned apron covered her blouse and the top of her slacks. Tantalizing smells of the dinner she was preparing filled the home's foyer.

After saying hello, Mama Dee led her two guests back to her kitchen. As they followed behind, Abbie was instantly struck by how much this older woman reminded her of her dear friend Audry MacDonald, the loss of whom Abbie was still recovering from.

Once the three were seated at Portia's dining room table and the plates served, easy conversation followed. *Keith was right*, thought Abbie as she listened to the comfortable banter between Mama Dee and Keith. *I do feel like I've known her all my life.*

As the older woman passed a cloth-covered dish of rolls to Abbie, she said softly, "So, Abbie, did Keith tell you my story?"

For a minute, the direct nature of the question caught Abbie off guard. She glanced over at Keith for encouragement. His warm smile was exactly what she needed.

Looking into this gentile lady's deep, blue eyes, Abbie said, "He told me a little of it, but I'd like to hear it in your own words."

"Well then, dear," said Mama Dee, "you shall."

Abbie sat quietly while this new friend gathered her thoughts.

"Thomas and I thought we had a wonderful life," Mama Dee began, "until one day we didn't. Much to our dismay, we discovered that our college-age daughter, Cindy, was struggling with depression. We tried to help her in every way possible. Professional counselors. Appointments with a psychiatrist. Appropriate medications. Bringing her home to live with us for a semester. Thomas and I even took her to visit other colleges, thinking perhaps it was her school environment."

Abbie felt as if she were the only person in the room as Mama Dee opened up a part of herself not often shared with others.

"I can still remember the phone call we received from the school's president, who had called to tell us that Cindy was gone. The poor man tried his best to hold it together but practically fell apart on the phone as he told me the terrible news that our daughter had taken her own life."

Mama Dee reached in the pocket of her slacks for a tissue and dabbed at her eyes.

Abbie blinked back tears of her own.

Bravely, the older woman continued her sad story. "Poor Thomas . . . For weeks after Cindy's funeral, he would cry for hours on end. I'd never seen another person grieve this way." She brushed away an errant tear. "Now, don't get me wrong . . . as her mother, I was also in a horrible state, trying to make sense out of such a senseless act. Yet, somehow, I dealt with the pain in my heart in a different way.

"One day, not even six months after we lost Cindy, I came home to find Thomas sitting in his chair in the den with a blank expression on his face. I couldn't get him to speak to me or even focus on my face. After several hours of this, I grew worried and called our neighbor and good friend, who was also our family physician. Larry came right over and helped me take Thomas to the hospital. Four days later, after a thorough psychological evaluation, my dear husband was admitted to a psychiatric hospital. Losing his precious daughter caused him to literally lose his mind. Afterward, I visited him twice a week. Twelve years ago, he contracted pneumonia and died at age fifty-six."

Tears glistened in Abbie's eyes as Mama Dee finished her story. Working hard to control her emotions, she took a sip of tea and dabbed her mouth with her napkin. *And I thought the trials I slogged through with my mother and Joe were hard to handle,* she thought, gazing back with newfound respect at this dear lady.

Over coffee and dessert, Keith and Mama Dee discussed the progress of the Tentmaker's Project. While they visited, Abbie worked up the courage to ask Mama Dee a question, one which Abbie had been mulling over in her mind for months. Until now, she had not known who might lead her to the answer. *Lord,* she thought, as she took a sip of coffee, *I think Mama Dee will know.*

"Mama Dee," Abbie said, finding a break in the conversation, "would you mind if I asked you a question?"

"Certainly not," replied the older woman, delight evident in her voice. "I'm happy to tell you anything you would like to know."

Across the table, Keith winked at Abbie when she glanced at him. His dark blue eyes urged her to find the answer she was searching for.

"Before I met Keith," Abbie began slowly, as if searching for the right words, "I felt as if I was the only person who had ever walked through dark valleys for many years. I have felt so alone and abandoned by God." Despite her best efforts, tears sprung up in the corners of her eyes. Abbie sat quietly until the small storm within her passed.

"Last summer, after volunteering at Camp 4Ever, I realized that adults aren't the only ones who go through or survive terrible circumstances. That may sound silly," Abbie said as she brushed back a strand of hair that had fallen near her face, "as I know full well how much my son, Drew, has suffered. Somehow, though, meeting several younger children in similar circumstances, like Chloe Minton, helped me understand my situation was not unique."

As a board member, Portia was well aware of the details of Chloe's case, as Don had contacted the board members via a conference call once the Hendersons were notified that Chloe was being removed from their home. The older woman continued to listen as the younger one opened her heart, the words spilling over each other like water tumbling over small boulders in a river.

"My coming to Camp 4Ever last summer was perhaps the first time in my life when I'd been around a larger group of individuals—children specifically—who had suffered terrible tragedies. Witnessing their resilient spirits and seeing their bright smiles was like a tonic for my soul.

"I also met Keith last summer as well. The fact that he lost his entire family in one cataclysmic moment suddenly made me feel that what Joe had done to Drew and me was somehow not quite as horrible as I'd made it out to be."

"Abbie, if I may?" Keith interjected. "What Joe did to you and Drew is no less a tragedy than my loss of Genny and our children or Mama Dee's loss of Cindy and Thomas . . . only different. Each of these tragedies was horrific in its own way for each of us."

The three sat silently for a few moments.

Finally, Abbie seemed ready to put her query into words. "Sorry I've rambled on so, but until recently, I couldn't see how God was connecting the dots between the heartache of my past and the suffering in the lives of others that He has allowed me to see."

Keith and Mama Dee both sat silently as Abbie worked to voice her question.

Looking intently into Mama Dee's soft eyes, Abbie continued, "How have you found the courage in your life, in the years since your daughter and husband died, to keep getting up each day and not be bitter about what's happened to you?"

Portia Dockery reached over and took hold of Abbie's right hand atop the table. "With God's help, Abbie," said Mama Dee as she squeezed the hand held within her own. "Do you know the Twenty-third Psalm?"

Abbie nodded, her eyes intent on Mama Dee's face.

"Years ago," the older woman continued, "a Bible study teacher opened my eyes, just as yours have been opened, to the simple yet profound truth found in verse four of that psalm: 'Even if I walk through a very dark valley, I will not be afraid because you are with me. Your rod and your shepherd's staff comfort me' (ICB).

"After Cindy's suicide, and then years later after Thomas was gone, all I could focus on when reading that verse was the first part, 'through a very dark valley.' It seemed I had lived in that sad, gloomy place for most of my married life. My grief and my pain were so all-consuming that I couldn't see past them.

"Finally, in a tiny step of faith, I tried to work on following another phrase in that verse, 'I will not be afraid.' I'd try to be bold and courageous, but I failed every time. Do you know why?"

Abbie shook her head.

"I was trying to muster that courage using my own strength. What I didn't seem to realize at that time was that I didn't have any bravery of my own. Oh, I could bluster and bluff like the best of them, but at the end of the day, human strength can only take you so far. When I reached the end of my puny resources, I found myself back in that same dark valley."

"How did you get out of it?" Abbie asked tentatively, as if she wasn't quite sure she wanted to hear the answer.

"I changed my focus," Mama Dee said, her eyes shining brightly with hope and encouragement. "The third part of that verse says, 'because you are with me.' *Because* Jesus is always with me, He will supply all I need. *Because* He is always with me, He will be brave and courageous for me through the mighty power of His Holy Spirit working through me. *Because* Jesus is always with me, I don't have to figure life out on my own.

Because Jesus is always with me, the glorious light of His presence is the lantern that led me out of my dark valley and keeps leading me through the others I've wandered into since learning the key to this verse.

"I have found that when I keep the eyes of my heart focused on Him and not on myself, He takes all the hard feelings away. It's not that they don't come back from time to time. I would not be honest with you if I didn't tell you that I still struggle with bitterness. However, I exercise the gift of free will that my Lord has given me, and I choose to be thankful for *all* things and to take Jesus at His word—He has promised He will always be with me.

"Jesus promises He will do the same for you, Abbie," said Mama Dee as she gently squeezed Abbie's hand and then released it.

Overcome with emotion, Abbie reached over and hugged the older woman, clinging to her as if to a life raft. Mama Dee hugged her back, and as she did, she winked at Keith, who was watching them both.

———

As Keith's Explorer reached the end of Mama Dee's driveway, the touch of Abbie's hand on his shoulder caused him to put on the brakes. "Are you okay?"

He could hear, more than see, her smile due to the car's dark interior. "I'm fine," she said. "I only want to give you a hug." After unbuckling her seat belt, she leaned over as far as the console between them would allow. Abbie wrapped her arms tightly around his neck and laid her head on Keith's shoulder. Returning the embrace, he pulled her close.

After a few moments, he gently kissed the top of her head. "We'd better head home," he said, "or Mama Dee's going to wonder what we're doing in the car."

Giggling, Abbie moved back into her seat and refastened her seat belt as Keith backed into the street. As the pair drove back to campus, Keith and Abbie said little to each other. An air of wonder filled them both.

Abbie felt a peace and calm envelope her, a sense of being safe and protected she'd never experienced before. Thinking back over the evening, she knew, without a shadow of a doubt, that God had used Mama Dee's testimony of simple yet powerful faith to shed light on how Abbie was to live now.

Keith pulled up in front of Mistletoe Cottage. It was almost ten o'clock, and for a minute, he thought Abbie might have fallen asleep. He put the car in park as gently as possible and sat for a long minute in the silent night. Her voice, low and soft, surprised him.

"Can I tell you something?" Abbie sat forward in her seat, turning sideways to face him. The blue glow of the dashboard played against her face, and the security light mounted high on the post nearby cast a bright glare into the front seat.

Although not sure what her declaration would be, something within Keith told him he must not miss a word of what Abbie was to say.

Abbie clasped her hands in her lap and gazed down at them for a long time. Slowly, she raised her head and looked straight into Keith's dark blue eyes. "I love you, Keith Haliday," she said without hesitation or doubt.

Keith drew in a slow, deep breath.

"I'm scared, Keith," she said, her voice barely above a whisper. "Terrified, actually." A laugh caught in her voice. "But what scares me the most is losing you," she declared as she took hold of his hand once more.

"I know," said Keith, drawing her closer to him. Tears trailed slowly down Abbie's face. "Sweet Abbie," he said gently, reaching up to wipe them away. "I told you in April, when we talked in the chapel, that there's no pressure and that I'm willing to wait as long as it takes to see where this relationship goes."

Abbie nodded, working hard to control emotions that had lain dormant for far too long.

Cocking his head to one side, Keith looked at Abbie curiously. "What exactly was it that Mama Dee said tonight?"

"I'm not really sure," said Abbie as she tried to sort through a symphony of thoughts, each clamoring to be heard. "Perhaps . . . that she, like me, has been through a dark valley. It was encouraging to hear how her choice to thank God *in spite of* the terrible loss in her life has given her a fresh perspective. What touched my heart the most was her reminder that God is *always* with me.

"Even though I'm terrified of failing at a relationship with you, God's given me a tremendous sense of His presence tonight, His assurance that He will be with us each and every step of this new journey we're on. Because the Lord is with us, I am *not* going to let fear rule my life anymore."

Keith sat silently, soaking in the joy and wonder of this moment. Reaching out to take her face in his hands, he kissed her tenderly, his lips lingering on hers.

Once the kiss was over, he opened his door. "It's time to get you home," he said, his voice thick and husky with emotion. After walking around to the passenger side, Keith opened Abbie's door, and she climbed out.

With arms around each other, the two made their way up the stone steps and to the door of Mistletoe Cottage.

As they turned to say good night, Keith spoke first. "From this moment on, Abbie, any move, any step, any decision we make will be done with God's help."

Abbie nodded, and as she did, she reached out gently, placing two fingers across Keith's lips. "Amen."

CHAPTER
37

Peter's Chapel was filled with faculty, old and new, and the buzz of conversation. The opening convocation for Timothy House staff would soon begin. Beautiful hymn selections filled the room, softly played by Celeste Daniels, the school's choir director. *This is really happening,* Abbie thought, still in disbelief at all God had accomplished in her life throughout the past few months. A shiver of excitement ran over Abbie as she slid into the seat Keith had saved for her. His strong, tall frame made her feel safe and protected as she sat in its shadow beside him. He grinned at her, and she returned the smile with one of her own.

"I was scared I'd be late," Abbie said.

"Well, you'll be glad you weren't," Keith answered, trying to sound like a crotchety school official. "If you had been, Don would have made you recite the school's three guiding principles and the main Scripture verses upon which Timothy House is founded."

Abbie's eyes widened like saucers. "Are you serious?"

"No, silly," Keith said. Then he laughed while he nudged her slightly. "Just trying to welcome you the same way I was welcomed last year when I joined the team."

"You're in trouble, mister," Abbie said, trying to suppress a smile she couldn't quite seem to wipe off her face.

She leaned forward slightly to look past Keith and greet Evelyn Benson and Tim and Taylor Nunley, who were seated toward the middle of the same pew. They each returned the acknowledgment with a "Hello," a "Welcome," a wave, or a smile.

Suddenly remembering that Drew was also here, she turned to look behind her. It wasn't long before she was delighted to see her son seated next to Josh Hastings. Although he had not seen her, Abbie's heart brimmed with thankfulness that both she and Drew would be working together at the school. She turned around and settled against the firm, worn back of the pew, still a little awestruck by this moment.

As more and more of the faculty took their seats and as Don and Doris Fielding entered the front row pew, the sound of voices chattering in the old chapel diminished. Shafts of sunlight glowed through the multicolored panes of the stained-glass windows of the chapel, reminding Abbie in a strange way of balloons at a child's birthday party. *This is a celebration*, she thought as she smiled to herself. *A new school year, a new start.*

Soon, the music stopped and the room became quiet and still. After a few more seconds, Don Fielding climbed the platform steps to the chapel's lectern. "Good morning, folks," the school's director said warmly.

A collective and hearty "Good morning" followed.

"Doris and I are delighted this day is finally here. It always seems to be the same way at the end of each school year—none of us can even stomach thinking about getting back into the classroom. However, through God's grace, we all return each fall with refreshed spirits and a renewed commitment to give our very best to our kids. Bow with me for a word of prayer.

"Our gracious Heavenly Father, we give You thanks for this new school year and for this fine group of men and women assembled here today. We thank You especially for the children that will be with us this year, both our day students and our boarders. Lord, You are aware of the great needs of these young people. Only You have what these students really need. Use us as agents of Your grace. As a faculty, give us unity, perseverance, and courage to complete the task before us: that of educating not only the minds but also the hearts of our students. We can only do that if You are with us. Empower us to be the men and women You have created us to be. We ask all of this in the name of Jesus. Amen."

A murmur of "Amen" ricocheted around the chapel until the sound disappeared altogether.

Don adjusted his reading glasses. "Before we get started, I want to introduce all of you to the hostess of Timothy House, the one who is truly the heart and soul of this school, my better half, Doris Fielding." Don extended one hand forward to encourage his wife to stand. Thunderous applause for Doris followed, as well as a few hoots and hollers.

Don's lovely wife grinned from ear to ear, looking for all the world like she had just won the Kentucky Derby. She turned and waved, her bright smile and teary eyes evidence of how touched she was by the faculty's warm reception before retaking her seat.

Don continued with his remarks. "This year marks the sixty-first year that Timothy House has been educating young people in this part of eastern Tennessee. As you know, my uncle and aunt, Roger and Marie Stevenson, founded this school in 1942. It was a different time back then. The world was at war, and many worried that civilization as they knew it would end. History, however, has proved that the lessons learned from those who fought in World War II have helped us—not only here in the United States, but across the globe—build a better, stronger world.

"Roger and Marie planted the seeds of their educational dream in the era of the forties. No technology. No instantaneous communication. No fast food. No space travel. Even though the circumstances of the times were different, people are basically the same today as they were in 1942. They love; they hate. They're happy; they're scared. They need to learn how to make their way in this world, be it through education, learning a trade, or military enlistment."

A wide grin broke across Don's face as he made his next remark. "Oh, how Roger and Marie would love to see the Timothy House of today. Although the school they founded has morphed and changed, it has nonetheless stayed true to its core values and founding principles. To the faculty who have been with us for many years and to those of you who are joining us for the first time, thank you for picking up the torch of excellence in Christian education lit by Roger and Marie all those years ago."

Hearty applause rang out across the pews of the chapel. Keith looked over at Abbie. Totally unaware that he was watching her, she sat mesmerized by the electric atmosphere in the room. He could also feel it, a sense of purpose and shared community that now settled over this group like a warm mantle. This was something only the Lord could establish within an organization.

As before, the clapping died down after a few minutes. Once it did, Don continued, "Now, I'd like to introduce our new faculty. As I call your name, please stand as I share a little of your bio.

"First, please give a warm Timothy House welcome to Bonnie Dalton."

A small, stocky woman with short blond hair that framed an attractive face stood a few rows behind where Abbie sat. The two had met a few weeks ago when Bonnie was on campus for meetings with Don and Keith. Abbie caught the woman's eye and smiled at her. Bonnie, looking grateful to see a friendly face, returned the expression.

"Bonnie has recently moved to this area from Cincinnati, Ohio, where she served as the foreign language department chair at a large public high school. Bonnie brings with her a wealth of language experience gleaned from serving as a volunteer interpreter at a local multicultural community center and from various mission trips to Central and South America. Bonnie will be teaching our Spanish classes and will also serve as the sponsor for the foreign language club. Please give a warm Timothy House welcome to Bonnie Dalton." The same boisterous applause heard earlier was now repeated. Bonnie looked around the chapel, gave a quick wave, and sat down.

"Next," Don shared, "I'd like to introduce you to Celeste Daniels."

The lady who had been playing the piano in the minutes prior to the opening of the convocation rose from her seat. Abbie immediately recognized the woman from the Timothy House's Christmas Pageant held last December. Chloe had been in that program.

"Celeste is no stranger to Timothy House, as she has been here on a temporary basis for almost a year. She comes to us from Chattanooga, where she previously served on the music faculty of a local community college. As many of you will remember, our choral director, Holt Thomas, had to leave us unexpectedly due to health problems soon after the school year began last year. It was our good fortune that Celeste could step in. I am especially pleased that she is joining us as a permanent member of the Timothy House faculty. Welcome, Celeste!"

The tall, slender woman blushed slightly and waved gingerly at those on either side of her. Just as Bonnie had done, Celeste sat down quickly after her introduction was completed.

Don introduced new faculty members joining the math and science departments. Abbie was impressed with the accomplishments of this august body she was joining. As this faculty group was not large in number, she knew Don must be almost finished with his comments.

"This year we have the privilege of having not one but two members of the same distinguished family," said Don, as he looked out over the devoted faculty and staff of Timothy House. Like an electric shock, a tingle streaked down Abbie's spine; she and Drew were about to be introduced.

"First, I'm extremely pleased to introduce Drew Richardson to you."

Abbie's heart swelled with pride as she turned to watch her now-grown son stand as his name was called. Drew stood quietly, straight as an arrow and handsome as could be. She could hardly believe they were both this far down life's road after all the pain and heartache they had endured over the years.

"Drew is a talented young man who will be working part-time with Josh Hastings, our outdoor skills instructor, as Josh and I direct several special sports camps offered throughout this school year. Over the past eighteen months or so, Josh and I have been developing ideas for specialized experiences. Now that Drew has joined us, those plans will become a reality.

"Drew will also be partnering with Josh in a youth mentoring program at Wright's Creek Church. This program, developed by Rod Eichman, is another dream becoming a reality due to Drew's presence in our community. Please give a hearty welcome to Drew Richardson."

It may have been motherly pride, but Abbie thought Drew's introduction garnered louder applause and more cheers and whistles, especially from many of the young men on the faculty, than other introductions. Drew's eyes locked on his mother as he took his seat. How long she had waited to see the confidence and contentment reflected in her son's countenance.

Thank You, Lord, she said, within her heart. *Thank You for loving my Drew and for bringing us both to this hope-filled place.*

Looking down from the simple platform at the front of Peter's Chapel, Don glanced at Abbie and gave her a gentle nod.

"Lastly, but certainly not because she's the least, I'd like to introduce you to Abbie Richardson."

Abbie rose from the pew and faced this small sea of new colleagues. She only hoped her face looked calm and serene because inside, she felt like that proverbial picture of a duck who appears to be floating lazily upon the water's surface but underwater is paddling frantically. She managed a smile and listened as Don continued.

"Abbie comes to us from Kent Academy in McHenry, Tennessee, three hours southwest. She was a well-respected member of that school's faculty, having served on it for twelve years as a junior high English teacher."

Abbie felt a blush start to make its way slowly up her cheeks. Looking down, she became aware of Keith's steady gaze. He winked at her and smiled, simple acts of encouragement that steadied her nerves. Abbie turned slightly to face Don.

"Abbie's principal, Arthur Patterson, a greatly admired administrator in Tennessee educational circles, just retired. His departure helped me convince Abbie that the time was right to join us. As all of you are aware, Timothy House is still on the hunt for house parents—a couple—for the seventh-grade girls. Until we find one, Abbie has graciously agreed to serve as the house mother for Mistletoe Cottage. Abbie will also teach English to our students in grades seven through nine.

"Please join me in welcoming Abbie Richardson to the Timothy House family."

As if she had been the only new faculty member introduced, the applause was loud and strong and continued for several minutes. Abbie wasn't sure, but she thought she heard her son whistle and whoop when her name was called. Turning back to face the group seated in the pews, Abbie grinned broadly and waved slightly before sitting down next to Keith.

CHAPTER
38

Abbie's introduction concluded the presentation of the new faculty members. Afterward, Don moved to the next item on the agenda: discussing several matters related to the school calendar. As he spoke, faculty and staff pulled out the requisite paperwork from a large, white packet they had picked up before the meeting began. Abbie's mind raced, trying to take in all the new information regarding the upcoming school year.

While walking into Peter's Chapel this morning, she felt confident about the many hours she'd devoted to lesson plans and preparations for her various classes. Now, as she rifled through the thick packet, she wasn't so sure. Suddenly, the wise advice of her dear friend Winnie Jeffers, Kent Academy's junior high guidance counselor, came to mind, "Aim small; don't miss at all." Winnie's Target Plan had enabled Abbie to soar above her difficult mental hurdles. Although she still felt a bit overwhelmed, a sense of calm settled over her now that she remembered one trusted way to keep the chaos of uncertainty at bay.

"I'm about to run into our allotted time for a break," Don said, looking at his watch. "Charmaine and her fine staff from Covenant Kitchen have some refreshments prepared for all of us. You'll find them waiting under the tents just outside the chapel. Let's plan to meet back in here in forty-five minutes. Thanks for your kind attention."

The assembled group rose en masse. No one had to be told to head to the food tables. It was as if someone had turned on a noisy outdoor spigot, and faculty and staff members gushed out of Peter's Chapel, flowing toward the tents, the sound of their happy chattering like rushing water.

Abbie filled her plate with several of Charmaine's homemade baked treats—two chocolate chip cookies, several cheese straws, and a bar of almond biscotti. She'd also selected several cubes of cheddar cheese and a small bunch of red grapes to offset the sugary confections. After taking a glass of lemonade from one of the Covenant Kitchen staff, she left the tent and found Evelyn Benson waiting for her.

"Hello, Abbie," her department chair said. "This has been a busy morning." Evelyn looked like she was doing the same thing Abbie was— trying to juggle a small plate of food and a beverage glass.

Abbie smiled and lifted her glass in a mock toast. "Oh, hi, Evelyn! I'm sorry we didn't get to visit inside this morning. The walk across campus took longer than I thought, and I guess I was nervous about this first meeting with the faculty and staff." She still hadn't figured out how she would eat and drink without spilling the refreshments.

In preparation for this morning's meeting, Timothy House staff had set out white folding chairs, and almost one hundred dotted the lawn surrounding Peter's Chapel. Evelyn nodded in the direction of several nearby that were empty. "Care to join me?"

"I'd like that," said Abbie, genuinely glad to have the opportunity to visit with Evelyn.

The two women chatted easily as they savored the cookies and treats Charmaine and her fine team prepared. Both emptied their glasses. Abbie returned to the food tent for more lemonade, which she and Evelyn were enjoying.

After setting down her glass, Evelyn looked at the new faculty member. "So, tell me, are you overwhelmed by all you heard this morning?" Her eyes, the color of honey, glowed with warmth and sincerity.

"More than I thought I'd be," replied Abbie, trying to stifle a laugh. She blotted the remains of a chocolate chip cookie on her face with her napkin. "All I could think about as Don ended this morning's session is that I'm not ready for my students."

"If you don't mind me saying so," Evelyn said, "you're sometimes your worst enemy. You're among the most earnest and hard-working ladies I've ever met."

Abbie blushed slightly at the unexpected compliment.

"You've also set incredibly high standards for yourself," continued Evelyn, "which, from what I can tell, you meet most of the time. Sometimes, though, you need to give yourself a little grace. You have more than exceeded the glowing recommendations Don gave about you. What a marvelous addition to our department you are. I only want you to relax and enjoy the journey more."

"I'm not sure I recognize that woman you're describing," replied Abbie, a look of doubt creasing her brow.

The older woman laughed softly. "Oh, Abbie," she said, "you're going to be just fine."

"Thank you, Evelyn, for that encouragement," Abbie said, her smile returning. "I pray God will use me to make a positive difference in the lives of my students and that they will see glimpses of Him in my own imperfect life."

"I'm confident that both prayers will be answered," concurred Evelyn before taking one last sip of her lemonade.

Josh Hastings' voice, booming over the loudspeaker, interrupted their conversation, announcing that the faculty meeting was about to resume.

"Well," said Abbie as she gathered the remains of her refreshments, "I think that's my cue. I'll look for you at lunch, Evelyn. Have a good morning."

"You, too, Abbie." The older woman, still seated in the lawn chair, looked up at her. "I've got to pick up something from my office before heading to the chapel. See you soon."

As Abbie threw away the paper dinnerware, she found Drew headed her way.

"Hey, Mom!"

"Hey, yourself," said Abbie, reaching out to put her arm around her son's waist. He returned the greeting.

"May I escort you, madam?" Drew asked, employing a British accent.

"You certainly may, kind sir," came his mother's reply.

As they walked, Abbie thought to herself, *God, how like You to have brought us both to this same place. Thank You for this blessing and this opportunity to work with Drew. Bless us both in this new season.*

They headed toward the chapel, walking past various groups of faculty members gathered on the lawn. Abbie beamed at Drew as he looked down at her. A new sense of belonging was in the air for them both. She could feel it. Squeezing her son's arm, Abbie signaled her readiness to take their seats. Following his mother's cue, Drew led her up the stone steps and into the welcoming shelter of the stone sanctuary.

CHAPTER
39

This second day of faculty meetings was reserved for the new faculty members' orientation. The group of nine sat scattered across three pews near the front of the chapel. Don sat on one of the pews, a notebook and various papers nearby. Already, Abbie felt much more relaxed. It was especially meaningful to share the experience with Drew.

Looking around at the faces of his new faculty members, Don began, "Well, folks, let's get started. As I said yesterday, all of us on the Timothy House team are excited and honored to have each of you join us."

As Don spoke, shy smiles and nods gave evidence that the new additions felt the same way.

"This morning, I thought I'd offer some backstory about the founding of the school and our purposes for life at Timothy House."

Several of those seated, including Abbie, took out a pen and paper and began making notes as Don spoke.

"As you know, the school's founders, Roger and Marie Stevenson, were my maternal aunt and uncle. My mother, Sadie, was Marie's younger sister. As a young man, Roger joined his father in what was already a successful business venture, Stevenson Timber Company. Roger's dad unexpectedly died when Roger was a young man, requiring of him a leadership role he might not have assumed until years later.

"Roger was bright and had a mind like a steel trap when it came to business. During his tenure, Stevenson Timber became the second-largest lumber supply company in the southeastern United States. Roger and Marie were never able to have children of their own. So, instead of spending his well-earned dollars on himself and Marie or fancy cars or houses, Uncle Roger and Aunt Marie decided to invest in the future of other people's children."

Looks of amazement and admiration were evident in the expressions of the new faculty.

"The motto of Timothy House is 'Establishing a Foundation of Faithfulness.' That is our goal: to undergird all we do, say, think, and teach with the strong, unshakeable foundation of God's faithfulness and His love. Although all our faculty members sign a statement of faith to say they are professing and practicing Christians, not all of our students are believers. Many, especially the small portion of the student body that comes from dysfunctional situations, may find it nearly impossible to believe that God is good and could actually love them.

"Although some of you have vast experiences in teaching children and youth, you may not have come face to face with some of the awful situations from which some of these children come. One of my prayers for each of you is that God would protect your hearts and keep them soft and tender toward such students. Believe me, the danger of becoming jaded is a serious temptation when working with troubled children."

Stuart Lassiter, the new high school science teacher for biology and anatomy and physiology, raised his hand.

"Yes, Stuart?" Don asked.

"Can you elaborate on the three main purposes of Timothy House?" Although the man's tanned face and tall, slender build made him look younger, the flecks of gray sprinkled throughout his wiry, dark hair let one know he was no spring chicken. He certainly came across as earnest and thoughtful.

"Great question, Stuart," replied the director. "Let's talk about each of these three principles. The first: To build up solid young men and women in Christ and to equip them for His purpose in the world. One of our main prayers for each of our students is that they will come to a saving knowledge of Jesus Christ as their Lord and Savior. That's the most important decision any of these young people will make in their entire lives. We try to be as faithful as we can, through all we do, to plant the right seeds, but only God can change a heart. However, as you well know, God also gives each of us a wonderful gift called free will, and that decision to follow Him, or turn our backs and walk away from Him, is still an individual choice.

"Timothy House takes its name from the New Testament Bible character Timothy, whom the Apostle Paul referred to in 1 Timothy 1:2 as 'my true son in the faith' (GNT). Uncle Roger was first introduced to stories of young Timothy by a Sunday School teacher, and they fascinated him. Timothy quickly became my uncle's favorite Bible character. As a result, Roger incorporated many of Paul's instructions to and encouragements of Timothy into the foundation of this school."

The small group seated in the pews listened intently to Don's every word.

"The second purpose of Timothy House is to provide an excellent education, equipping students for the wider world. As God always gives us His best, Roger and Marie wanted to provide an academic setting where children in this part of the state, which in many ways is more rural, receive excellence in all aspects of their education. Raising up generations of young people committed to giving their best efforts and then leaving the results up to God is, in many ways, a revolutionary concept.

"The third purpose of this school is to bind up the wounds of mind, body, and soul that might hinder our students, in any way, from realizing their full potential in Jesus Christ. Although most of our student body go home each night to a safe, welcoming home and loving parents, our boarders are usually the ones for which the term 'home' is a dream, at best. As you will discover, a portion of our student body has suffered greatly in their short lives, experiencing more heartache in their childhoods than some people suffer in a lifetime.

"Within your first year at the school, each of you will attend a three-week-long counseling course at a seminary in Nashville. Our school maintains a long list of qualified subs that will fill in for you. We also have two wonderful counselors on our staff—Marcy Graham, who ministers to our female students, and David Cooper, who takes care of the emotional needs of our male students. They are also available to help you at any time."

Abbie and a few others were now on their third page of notes.

Stuart raised his hand again. "Though it's helpful to understand the purposes of Timothy House, it's quite a challenge to uphold these tenets in the midst of this crazy, self-centered, twenty-first-century world. My last school didn't do such a great job of supporting faculty. What's your advice?" Relief was evident on the teacher's face, as if he'd finally completed a difficult assignment.

A few heads nodded.

"Another astute question, Stuart," said Don warmly. "My best advice is to stay true to the Word of God. The first purpose for Timothy House is based on 1 Timothy 1:5, which says, 'But the goal of our instruction is love from a pure heart and a good conscience and a sincere faith' (NASB 1995). These are the qualities we seek to cultivate in our young men and women: pure hearts, good consciences, and sincere faith.

"The second purpose, focused on excellence in education, is based on Paul's advice to Timothy found in 2 Timothy 2:15, 'Be diligent to present yourself approved to God as a worker who does not need to be ashamed, accurately handling the word of truth' (NASB). Keeping our eyes on Jesus rather than on what the world considers to be important, and encouraging our students to do the same, will go a long way in building up a new, strong generation of believers.

"The third purpose, however, is the one that may be the most difficult of all to realize, as it deals with the intangibles: the wounds of mind, body, and soul that are often invisible. The promise we claim for undergirding this purpose is Psalm 147:3, 'He heals the broken-hearted and bandages their wounds' (GNT). We serve the Great Physician, who has the power and ability to heal what we, in our own strength, cannot. Although we are committed to educating the minds of our students, we are also committed as much or more to making sure their hearts and spirits are strong and healthy."

Abbie's face had a quizzical look on it that Don noticed. "Did you have a question, Abbie?"

"I do," she began. "What do you do when you discover a child has needs too great to be met by Timothy House?"

"That's a question for which there's no easy answer." Don spread his hands before him and gestured as he spoke. "We do, however, have a protocol we follow. First, Marcy or David, with input from a student's teachers, makes an assessment. Oftentimes, our counselors and a student's academic team offer the best insight into a student's difficulties. Next, we meet with the student's family, such as the one you've described, to determine if moving back into the home might be a viable possibility. Extended family members are also contacted, as they are often able and willing to bring a student into their home. Sometimes these first two steps bear fruit; sometimes they do not."

Drew piped up. "Do kids sometimes act out simply because they want to go home?"

Don grinned and said, "They do, and that's why the family conference is such an important part of the puzzle. We've had several situations in the past school year that fit that description, and I'm happy to report that all those students are settled and readjusting nicely to life at home."

Stuart chimed in. "What if a child is uncontrollable or has serious mental health issues?"

"If it is determined that there may be a serious emotional or psychiatric problem," Don continued, "we make the necessary connections and schedule an appointment with the student and closest adult family member with one of several pediatric and adolescent specialists throughout the state. Based on the findings of that professional's evaluation, we then contact other residential schools who can provide the level of care for this student that we cannot."

The faces of the nine new faculty members reflected the seriousness of the situations just described.

"Look, guys," said Don, readjusting on the pew, "it's easy to sit here and get all worked up about something that may never happen. We'll cross those bridges together when we reach them. Doris, Marcy, David, and I are here to help you. The counselor training you will all receive will also provide you with helpful tools for use in the classroom." Looking down at his watch, he said, "It's time for lunch. This afternoon, we're meeting in the conference room in Sanctuary Hall. I'll see you all there at one thirty."

With that, the meeting ended.

As Abbie and Drew headed toward Covenant Kitchen, Drew broke the silence between them. "I'm not sure I'm equipped to handle this job." Uncertainty and doubt laced his every word.

Abbie noticed a slump in her son's shoulders. Reaching up, she patted him on the back.

"Drew," she said, hoping to encourage him as much as herself, "you'll be great! Don would not have hired you if he didn't think you could handle this job. Besides, your interaction with the students will be different from that of a teacher like me, who will see them every day in a classroom. These kids, especially the guys, will love you!"

Drew's mood brightened. "Thanks, Mom," he said, smiling at her. "I'll try to take Mr. Don's advice to heart: don't worry before I have to."

"Sounds good to me, son." She gave him another pat on the back.

They had now reached Covenant Kitchen, where a long line snaked out the door of the dining hall and down the steps. Abbie and Drew joined the hungry diners.

"There's Josh," Drew said as he waved at someone ahead. "Would you mind if I ate with him?" Excitement crackled in Drew's voice.

"Not at all. Tell Josh I said hi."

Drew scampered up the steps and disappeared into the crowded throng.

Abbie's spirits soared as she watched with pride this son who had endured so much emotional anguish because of his father. How good of God to allow her to watch this part of Drew's entry into manhood and be alongside him here at Timothy House.

As she joined the others in the food line, Abbie prayed the Lord would also be with her.

CHAPTER

40

The towering hardwoods dotting the campus of Timothy House offered shade from the bright summer sun as Abbie walked to Sanctuary Hall for the last session of the new-faculty orientation. A gentle breeze ruffled her hair, and as it did, she brushed a few errant strands behind one ear. Hearing footsteps behind her, she turned to find Keith approaching. She stopped to wait for him, and as he drew near, a smile broke across both their faces.

Abbie brought one hand up to shield her eyes from the midday sun and looked adoringly at him.

"I was hoping to find you," Keith continued. "Sorry I haven't been able to see much of you. These first days of faculty meetings are always so busy."

"No need to explain," Abbie said as they turned to continue down the path.

Reaching the building, Keith stepped forward and opened the heavy paneled door for Abbie. He asked, "How about dinner at Gravlee's tonight?"

Beaming with delight, Abbie stopped and turned to him. "You've got yourself a date, mister."

"Pick you up at six thirty," was the reply.

The sunlight streaming through the open doorway was so bright that Keith's features were obscured. All Abbie could see was his strong, towering frame silhouetted before her. *How protected and safe he makes me feel,* Abbie thought. *I never want to lose that feeling.*

As Keith closed the door behind them, Abbie realized with startling clarity that her heart had taken a definite turn in a new direction.

———

When the buildings of what was now Timothy House were designed in the late 1930s, Sanctuary Hall served as the administration building of what was a bustling seminary at the time. Each of the building's three floors contained a number of comfortable-sized offices, as well as storage closets and a sizeable conference room in which to conduct the Lord's business. Timothy House personnel still used these meeting spaces to do the same.

As one of the school's administrators, Keith had a key role to play in the meeting. Rounding the corner of the hallway, Abbie and Keith could see other attendees already heading through the open door into the room. Lively conversation filtered out into the hall. Through the open doorway, the high ceilings gave one the feeling of being in the drawing room of a large estate rather than in a space used to conduct the business of a school. The attention to detail and special design elements the architects incorporated into the original buildings of the seminary campus were part of what drew Roger and Marie Stevenson to purchase the buildings and the acreage surrounding it all those years ago.

As they neared the conference room, Keith gently squeezed Abbie's elbow, causing her to stop and turn to him.

"Later," he said, almost in a whisper. His conspiratorial wink exhilarated her.

With a nod of her head, she turned and headed in to take her seat. Keith came through the doorway a few minutes later. Doris, already at the table, patted the seat of the chair next to her as she caught Abbie's eye. Once Abbie joined her, grateful for the gesture, the two made small talk.

Movement across the table drew her attention to Keith, who had stood up to greet Stuart, the new science teacher. As she watched Keith, Abbie thought about how the friendship she shared with him had deepened and grown since her arrival at Timothy House. Throughout the summer, God had somehow torn down the hedge of distrust and wariness that had grown up around her heart due to the wounds of Joe's betrayal. Watching Keith nearby, Abbie knew, beyond a shadow of a doubt, that God had been answering her prayers to make her heart soft and pliable once more.

Keith suddenly turned to look at her, as if he sensed she had been watching him closely. For the longest time, their eyes held fast. For the first time since they had met, Abbie did not want to be the one to look away. However, Don's voice, calling the meeting to order, made her realize she must look like a teenage girl crushing on a handsome classmate. Feeling a warm flush run over her, Abbie looked away, hoping no one else in the room had noticed. Keith took his seat, and Abbie looked attentively at the school director.

"Welcome," Don began. "Hope all of you had a good lunch. How blessed we are to have Charmaine Jenkins and the ladies who serve with her to provide such delicious meals for us."

Heads nodded and murmurs of approval filled the room.

"Before we jump into this afternoon's agenda, I want to go back to a question Abbie posed in our morning session."

All heads turned to look at Abbie, who grinned shyly at her new colleagues.

Don continued, "Abbie, you asked a most insightful question: What if we can't meet the needs of a Timothy House student? Truth be told, none of us around this table or any of our other faculty are equipped to offer to these children what they need most: love and healing from their Heavenly Father. We are, though, vessels He can use to pour out His grace and mercy and restoration into the lives of the children we teach each day.

"I want to remind you of encouragement from Paul's second letter he wrote to Timothy, his young partner in the ministry—2 Timothy 1:7 and 2 Timothy 1:12. The first verse is one Uncle Roger taught me the summer I first came to work here at the school. 'For God has not given us a spirit of fear and timidity, but of power, love, and self-discipline' (NLT). It was 1953, and I was fourteen years old. I was eager to help him and to work hard, but there was also a great deal I did not know.

"When I got discouraged, Roger would walk me into the dining hall, where we'd head straight for the kitchen. I can still hear those swinging doors flapping closed behind us. He'd pull open the door of that huge cooler and pull out a cold bottle of Nehi Grape soda for each of us. After popping off the cap with a bottle opener, he'd hand me my bottle and say, 'A cold grape soda always helps make problems seem smaller.' We'd then go sit on the steps of Covenant Kitchen and talk about whatever was bothering me. While we did, we'd sip on our Nehis, and Roger would talk about how to apply that Bible verse to my problem."

One of the new teachers piped up, "Do you still keep Nehi sodas in the Covenant Kitchen fridge?"

Everyone laughed at the question.

"No," said Don, still chuckling. "But, if you'll look on the back porch of the kitchen, there's a white refrigerator you'll find stocked with several different brands of soft drinks. It's near the door to the storeroom. Those drinks are there for you to enjoy. Any time you need an object lesson with one of your students, feel free to reach in and grab a cold soda. You can't believe the times I've been able to help a kid feel less threatened about some difficult issue. There's something natural and easy about sharing a soft drink together."

The smiles and thoughtful expressions on the faces of the teachers gathered around the conference room seemed to suggest they'd just been made privy to one of the secrets of the universe.

Don continued, "The second verse my uncle taught me that summer has helped me, ever since then, to keep my eye on who is really the *only* One able to meet our students' needs: Jesus. 2 Timothy 1:12 says, in part, '. . . for I know whom I have believed and I am convinced that He is able to guard what I have entrusted to Him until that day' (NASB 1995). All the work we accomplish here at Timothy House is done in Jesus's name and through His power. However, just as with faith, we are only the farmers. Some of our students' needs will not be met until years after they've left this campus. God will be the One to bring to completion the potential and possibility within the lives of our students. Do your best work, as unto the Lord, and leave the results up to Him."

Don sat back in his chair and seemed to relax against its padded back. "Now, I'm going to turn it over to Keith Haliday, our second-in-command here at Timothy House."

As the group was small and the table large enough that all seated around it could see him, Keith moved forward a little in his chair rather than standing. "Thanks, Don, although second-in-command sounds like a military position."

Laughs erupted around the table. Don's expression looked sheepish.

Seizing the opportunity to rib his boss good naturedly, Keith continued with his tongue-in-cheek monologue. "Sometimes running a school can feel a little like overseeing new recruits at boot camp."

Keith stood up, smiled brightly at Don, and then offered a military-style salute. His boss returned the gesture and then waved his hand toward Keith as if swatting at a fly.

"I don't know what I'm going to do with this guy," said Don, friendship and respect obvious in the older man's voice. "I think, however, that we'll keep you."

A few around the table clapped their approval.

"Oh," said Don, remembering one other important fact, "don't forget: Keith is also our boys' basketball coach. This man wears many hats."

Several clapped again.

Keith sat and faced the group assembled. "Seriously," he said, "my main function is to assist Don in the administration of the school. That includes everything from making sure we're financially sound to ensuring that the IT needs of Timothy House are met. Many of you probably have a personal laptop. We are working on a plan that will provide one for each faculty member, but that is still a year or so away.

"There is a faculty computer lounge on the third floor of this building, a room about twice the size of this one. There you will find cubicles and a desktop computer in each. There are ten stations, so at least during some part of each day, each of you should be able to access the internet. The lounge also has two printers—one at each end of the room. Cabinets containing extra paper and ink are also nearby. Hopefully, you'll have all you need."

Bonnie Dalton, the new Spanish teacher, raised her hand. "Where do students have access to computers?"

"The library is located on the ground floor of Timothy Hall," Keith said, "which you know to be our classroom building. Bethany Bronson is our librarian. You'll find in her a willing colleague. Bethany has a real servant's heart.

"In a setup not unlike our faculty computer lounge, students have access to twenty-five desktop computers. The number of computers we have available to both our teachers and students is due, in part, to the generosity of an IT firm in eastern Tennessee that read an article about the good work we're doing here at Timothy House and wanted to partner with us. Don's Uncle Roger also left an endowment which funds the school's operating expenses."

"Thank you," said Bonnie, amazement evident on her face. "That's a remarkable story. I'm not used to being in a community so supportive."

Doris Fielding, who had been silent until now, joined the conversation. "Bonnie," she said brightly, "business partnerships with our school won't be the only significant aspect of life in Robbinsonville. Don and I hope you will find a nurturing environment, both here at Timothy House and in town. We are glad you are here, as well as the rest of you."

"Well, that's the perfect way to segue to our last portion of this afternoon's meeting," Keith said, as he closed the notebook in front of him. "Doris is going to share some encouraging words for your new jobs."

With that, Doris picked up a small notepad and leafed through several pages of its yellow lined paper until she found the one she wanted, then rolled the excess pages over the top of the pad.

Doris looked back at Keith and smiled warmly at him, pausing a moment before she spoke. "Before I get started," she said, "I want to take this opportunity to tell Keith, in front of these new friends, how very glad Don and I are that you are with us at Timothy House."

A slight flush rose on Keith's cheeks as Doris's kind words caught him off guard. He looked down at the table for a moment.

Doris continued, "I know each of you will find in Keith Haliday a genuine and supportive colleague. You'll be hard-pressed to find a finer man."

The flush on Keith's face deepened slightly in color. Abbie, touched by Doris's sincere praise for Keith, caught his eye and grinned.

Doris looked down and moved her fingers softly across the lined surface of the memo pad. "I know it's been a long day, but I wanted to leave you with a few thoughts. Teaching, as you know, is a demanding profession. The hours are long, the duties constant, and the rewards often appear fleeting at best. You certainly don't become a teacher for the pay."

Smiles and a few laughs broke out among the group.

"The opportunity, however, to leave your thumbprint and that of the Lord on the hearts and minds of the young people you teach is one not to be taken lightly. We have talked a lot today about the portion of our student body that may be facing more difficult circumstances, but remember that all of our students bring troubles with them to school each day. It's typical teenage behavior to stuff whatever's bothering you down deep inside and look as if you don't have a care in the world. You and I both know better.

"The many truths found in Paul's writings to Timothy are what Roger and Marie and Don and I have tried to include in the godly legacy Timothy House seeks to impart. One of my favorite portions comes from 1 Timothy 1:13-14. To paraphrase Paul's words, grace covers the ignorance of unbelief. Ask the Lord to use you as a vessel of His grace. Employ His words and your own to bring hope and healing into each encounter you have with a student. Think back to your childhood and the teachers who looked beyond the twelve- or thirteen-year-old you were at that time to the possibility that lay within you. Look for that promise in each of your students and help them to believe in it."

As Doris glanced around the table, she saw tears glistening in some of the teachers' eyes.

"Know that my door is always open," Doris said kindly. "It's down the hall past this room," she said, pointing toward the entrance of the conference room. "I'll be happy to help you in any way I can." With those words, Doris flipped the small notebook closed.

"Well, folks," concluded Don, "that's a great place for us to end this meeting. Thanks again for your attention. I know you've had a lot of information to take in today. As Doris said, if you need anything, please let us know. You've got three more days to work in your classrooms. Friday, our boarding students will arrive and move in, and then we'll welcome our entire student body for a half-day of classes next Monday morning."

Don closed the meeting with a brief prayer. With the last "Amen," all at the table immediately began collecting their belongings to leave the conference room. Several new faculty members waved goodbye to Abbie from across the table. She sensed in her new colleagues the feeling of relief she herself was now experiencing. They had made it.

A new school year prepared by God lay around the corner. For the first time in many years, Abbie couldn't wait for it to begin.

CHAPTER
41

Don could hear the lively conversation in the second-floor conference room long before he reached it. Today had been much busier than expected, and he was running five minutes late to the Timothy House board meeting. From the sound of it, his absence had not been noticed. *Thankfully, Keith's got everything under control,* he thought, as he heard the voice of his director of operations. The purpose of today's meeting was momentous, as the board was putting the finishing touches on the Tentmaker's Project. As soon as he opened the door, all heads turned his way.

"Well, Don Fielding," said Portia Dockery, "all I've got to say is that you'd better have one whopper of an excuse for your tardy arrival or we're sending you to the principal's office." The self-proclaimed matriarch of the school's guiding committee beamed like a spelling bee winner.

Several other board members made a few more good-natured remarks. Don took them all in stride. As he took his seat between Keith and Chuck Hawthorne, he winked at his second-in-command. Today's meeting would be a decisive one regarding the future of Timothy House.

As board members and the other assembled guests pulled closer to the table, the sound of chairs scraping across the floor filled the room.

"Let me open our meeting with a word of prayer," said Don as he looked around the table. "Dear Lord, we thank You for all the men and women gathered today. Thank you for allowing us this opportunity to serve You as we seek to lead Timothy House on the path you have set for it. Give us Your wisdom and discernment, and help us to be doers of the Word, not merely hearers. Fill our hearts with your boundless love so that we may share that with the precious children entrusted to us. Forgive us when we fail You, and guide us in Your everlasting way. In Your Son's name, I pray, Amen."

A chorus of "Amens" filled the room as heads raised and every eye focused on Don Fielding.

"As you all know, today's a big day, as we will formalize our plans for the Tentmaker's Project." Glancing at the board member to his left, Don continued, "Chuck, thank you for all your hard work in putting together the proposal for this mentoring plan."

Hearty applause followed Don's remarks. Chuck smiled slightly but remained silent.

"Chuck," Don continued, "the floor's all yours."

"Thanks," said the board member from McHenry. "I am grateful to Don for his willingness to try this mentoring model with the Timothy House seniors. As I've shared before, a program similar to this one has been highly successful in the Hickory Ridge School in Virginia, where I've been a member of the project task force for the past seven years. If you'll remember, when we met at our June meeting, we voted to proceed with the Tentmaker's Project. You were also introduced to two of the program mentors, Summer and Elton Tidwell."

For a few moments, the attention centered on the young couple, potters from Craggy Bluff, a small community two hours southeast of Robbinsonville.

"There are several other mentors I'd like to introduce." Chuck turned to the two gentlemen seated to his left. "Please welcome Parker Goodwin and John Benson."

As before, quiet applause greeted the new mentoring program members.

"Parker lives here in Robbinsonville and owns and operates Landry's Grocery, a second-generation business. He has agreed to offer student internships and to allow several students to shadow him throughout this school year."

Murmurs of approval followed.

"To Parker's left is John Benson. Many of you may already know him, as his wife, Evelyn, is the chairman of our English department. John is an internist at Turner Memorial Hospital and, like Parker, has graciously agreed to allow two students to shadow him this year." Chuck grinned while looking over at Parker and John. "Welcome, both of you."

Once more, hands clapped.

"At this point, I'm going to turn the meeting over to Keith. Before I do, however," Chuck said, looking across the table to his right, "I'd like to say a special welcome to our newest board member, Lance Tate. Keith will tell you more about him, but I wanted to add my greeting."

Chuck and Lance nodded at one another.

"Thanks, Chuck," said Keith as he took over the reins of the meeting. "As some of you weren't here at our June board meeting when we announced Lance's addition to the board, I'll share with you a little about him. We grew up together in Richmond, Virginia, and were in the same high school graduating class. Lance went on to attend The Citadel, a military college in Charleston, South Carolina, and joined the Army Reserve Officers' Training Corps program. He is a Green Beret and attained the rank of major general during his twenty-nine years of service in the U.S. Army."

While Lance looked down at the papers arranged in front of him, the faces of some assembled bore witness to their admiration for this board member's service to his country.

"Over the years," Keith continued, "we've kept in touch, mainly with Christmas cards and the like. Three years ago, however, we reconnected right after Lance retired and he and his family moved to Maryville. Lance and his wife, Claire, have three grown children—two sons and a daughter—who have all followed in their father's footsteps as career Army officers.

"One of the things that always impressed me most about Lance is that regardless of where he was stationed, he always found a way to connect with organizations that ministered to at-risk youth, whether through a church he and his family attended or through a community organization. I'm especially excited about incorporating Lance's expertise and cutting-edge ideas into the Tentmaker's Project."

Turning to the old friend seated beside him, Keith extended his hand as the former Army officer clasped it. "Welcome to the Timothy House board, Lance."

A final round of applause ushered Lance Tate into the fold of the board of trustees. Once it lessoned, Chuck sat forward to share the overview of the program.

"Don is going to announce the Tentmaker's Project to the junior class tomorrow at a special meeting, where he'll explain the selection process. Students will have until October fifth to complete their applications. On October eighth, those selected to try out for the program will be notified. Throughout the next three days, a faculty committee of five will interview the applicants, and the inaugural class of Tentmaker's will be announced on October fifteenth. The program will begin the third week in November with a three-day, two-night orientation session."

Glancing over at Lance, he continued, "We're purposefully beginning this program with a small number of young men and women—four girls and four boys. This was Lance's suggestion, and he's seen new programs get off the ground successfully by starting small."

Lance nodded as Chuck smiled at his new colleague before continuing. "Students selected for the program will have the unique experience of building personal relationships with leaders in several areas—visual arts, retail grocery, medicine, and leadership development. There are only a handful of high school programs throughout the country that incorporate this type of personal development into a student's high school experience.

"Summer and Elton have been kind enough to invite the new student mentees to Craggy Bluff for their orientation during part of the Thanksgiving break. The Tidwells will introduce our students to apprenticeship skills. A local church is providing accommodations through families in their congregation. The other project mentors with us today—Parker, John, and Lance—will be accompanying us."

Chuck nodded toward the man seated directly across the table and continued, "Our fellow board member and program mentor, Eric, lives south of here in McHenry but has a place near Craggy Bluff. He and his wife, Lane, have graciously invited all in our group to spend the day on Sunday at their cabin, the Resting Place. We'll hold a lakeside vesper service that morning and then a cook-out for lunch. By mid-afternoon, we'll head back to Robbinsonville. Additional Timothy House staff will also be joining us—Keith, Don and Doris, Abbie Richardson, and me. We'll leave the Friday afternoon the week before Thanksgiving and return to Robbinsonville late Sunday afternoon, which will still allow all on the trip to share Thanksgiving with their own families."

Chuck looked over at Don and said, "That's all I've got for now."

"You can see why I am so enthusiastic about the Tentmaker's Project," said the director of Timothy House, admiration for Chuck's development of the program in his every word. "I can't wait to see how God will use this program to touch the hearts and minds of Timothy House seniors so they can in turn make a positive change in the world around them."

As he looked around the table, Don concluded the meeting. "Thank you again to each of you for your commitment to improving the lives of students through the ministry of this school and for your integrity in making sure that all we say and do brings honor and glory to the Lord's name."

———

Keith waited while several board members came over to welcome Lance. Soon, the two men were walking out the front doors of Sanctuary Hall and across to the parking lot. Keith was glad to see his old friend and catch up on old times. Lance had made plans to spend the weekend in Robbinsonville, as he had a few meetings scheduled with Don and Chuck and did not plan to head back to Maryville until Sunday morning.

As Lance opened the door of his car, he grinned over at Keith. "So I'm finally going to meet *the* Abbie Richardson?"

"Yes, you are," said Keith proudly. "I'm heading over to pick her up at her cottage right now, and then we'll meet you at Gravlee's."

"Well, all I can say," said Lance, "is I can't wait to meet the woman who's captured your heart."

CHAPTER
42

DeSean's senior year was underway, and the early days of September were already flying by. Coach Denning had called a meeting earlier in the week and told the team that practice would begin in two weeks. DeSean was still struggling academically, but the tutor Edna Smith had hired was helping him keep his nose above the water line, especially in math.

Tonight, DeSean was at the Crockett High School football game. The team was playing at home, but the game was supposed to be close. DeSean had ridden with Max to the game. Once they parked the car, DeSean told Max he was going to sit with a few guys who'd said they'd be there. In reality, no classmates had made such an offer, but the teen definitely did not want to be seen sitting alone with Max. Mr. Smith said he would meet DeSean at the car when the game was over. The two walked in through the ticket gate together as Max paid for them both. Once Max handed him his ticket, DeSean lost the older man in the crowded throng.

A quick glance at the scoreboard told him there were ten minutes left in the second quarter. Even though Edna had served a light dinner for Max and DeSean before they left, the teen was still hungry. Reaching into the pocket of his jeans, he felt the twenty-dollar bill Max gave him before they left home. He headed toward the stadium steps leading to the concession stand under the bleachers. DeSean figured he could grab a burger and drink before the half-time crowd arrived.

He hadn't been standing in line for more than five minutes before he felt a tap on his left shoulder and turned to find C.J. Dykes standing behind him. His friends, Ted and Nico, were next to him.

"Hey, boys," C.J. said, as he turned to his two compatriots. "Look who it is!"

"Oh, hey guys," said DeSean, a bit confused to see the three men there.

"We were standing along the fence enjoying the game when Nico spotted you," said C.J., sounding like a proud father extolling his son's accomplishments. "We wanted to come over and say hello."

DeSean smiled but did not speak, still a bit uncertain as to why C.J. was here.

"Look," continued C.J., "we're getting ready to go take a drive, maybe get something to drink." Nodding toward the concession counter, he added, "Something a little more substantial than they serve here at the game."

DeSean tried to act nonchalant as he moved forward in the concession line.

"We wanted to see if you'd come with us," said C.J., sounding like DeSean was one of his best friends. Turning to look at Ted and Nico, C.J. continued, "Isn't that right, guys?"

Both Ted and Nico nodded but didn't look like they were particularly interested in getting to know DeSean.

"What do you say?" pushed C.J.

"I don't know," stammered DeSean, feeling a bit trapped. "I came to the game with Mr. Smith, my foster parent. I'll need to go let him know where I'll be. Can you have me back here by the end of the game? I'm supposed to meet him at the car once the game is over."

"Sure, man," said C.J., slapping DeSean on the back once more. Nodding toward the fence line, he said, "Me and the guys will wait over here. Don't be long."

It didn't take DeSean long to find Max Smith. The teen squeezed onto the bleacher next to him.

"A few guys I know asked me to go get a burger with them," DeSean began, trying to make his voice heard over the crowd to sell a plausible storyline.

"Now?" asked Max, checking his watch.

"Yes, sir," replied DeSean. "Half-time's almost here. We'll be back by the end of the fourth quarter. I'll meet you at the car as soon as the game is over."

Although the man didn't look pleased to hear the boy's proposal about leaving the game with three guys Max had never met, he nevertheless gave his approval.

Eight minutes later, C.J., Ted, Nico, and DeSean were pulling out of the parking lot of the Crockett High School stadium.

C.J. drove and Ted rode shotgun. DeSean sat behind C.J. in the back seat. Across from him, Nico was as far on the right side of the back seat as possible, giving DeSean the impression that the older fellow wanted nothing to do with him. As DeSean buckled his seat belt, the thought crossed his mind that this ride might not be a good idea, but he shoved it away. As they drove down county roads, DeSean glanced at his watch as darkness descended like a blanket draped over the rolling hills surrounding Jonesborough. Seven forty-two.

The car windows were rolled down slightly, and the noise from the wind whipping past was loud. Several times since the four had left the high school stadium, Nico had reached down to either scratch an itch near his ankle or fix something in his boot that was uncomfortable. DeSean couldn't figure out which. He had tried to ask a few questions to the skinny, pale-faced guy across the seat from him, but the fellow only glared at him and then turned to look out the window.

While the car sped on into the night, C.J. asked DeSean a few questions. Ted asked one. Nico never uttered a word. Once the inquiries ended, DeSean listened as C.J. and Ted talked. He was only able to catch bits and pieces of conversation.

Suddenly, a siren sounded and flashing blue lights appeared in the car's rearview mirror.

C.J. uttered an expletive and slammed his fist on the steering wheel. As he slowed the car and pulled to the shoulder, he said aloud to the others, "Just be cool. We'll be back on the road in no time."

The blue lights were now directly behind C.J.'s car, making it almost impossible to see out the rear window through the glare. While a few cars whizzed by, DeSean and the others waited for the officer to arrive. C.J. rolled down the driver's side window further. A rush of cool air blew back onto DeSean as a shiver ran down his spine.

In the next instant, a blinding, bright light appeared outside C.J.'s window. Beyond it, the four occupants saw a tall, muscular police officer beside the car. "Sir," the officer said, his voice deep and commanding, "did you realize your right tail light is out?"

"No, sir, I did not," replied C.J. No one else said a word.

The officer held the flashlight steady in C.J.'s face as he continued, "I need to see your license, sir, and proof of registration. I also need to see your insurance card."

C.J. reached into his wallet and pulled out his license. Handing it through the window to the officer, he said, "I'll need to open the glove box to get the other papers."

Ted leaned forward and opened the small compartment, removing a jumbled wad of papers for C.J., who rifled through them as the officer waited.

C.J. turned to the open window. Sounding a bit sheepish, he said, "Officer, it looks like I forgot to put my registration and insurance cards in my car. I have them at home."

The bright light moved to shine directly into C.J.'s face. "Son," the officer said, "it seems you've forgotten more than your paperwork. This license expired four months ago."

C.J. did not say a word. Despite the cooler night air, the temp inside the car's interior seemed to get hotter. Ted and Nico pressed themselves further into their corners of the car.

The beam of the flashlight shifted as the officer stepped back from C.J.'s window and looked in the back seat, almost blinding DeSean and Nico. Soon, the officer illuminated the floor of the back seat and seemed to stop and stay in one spot. DeSean could feel Nico tense up.

DeSean's eyes followed the direction of the light until they settled upon what the officer must be seeing. A small plastic bag filled with several little pills. DeSean did not remember seeing it when all of them first got in the car and left the football game. Although he did not know what the pills in the bag were for, DeSean was instantly aware that something serious might be about to happen.

The policeman stepped back from the car and pressed a button on a radio mic attached to the shoulder of his uniform shirt. "Officer requesting back up," he said, and then named the road on which they were parked. The flashing blue lights of the patrol car were beginning to give DeSean a headache.

The four occupants waited for another officer to arrive. C.J. turned as inconspicuously as possible and said quietly to the others, "Stay cool. This guy doesn't have anything on us. I'll probably just get a ticket for the license snafu."

Soon the sound of tires rolling onto the graveled shoulder were heard as the blue flashes intensified. DeSean and the others could hear the heavy footfalls of the second officer's boots.

Returning to the driver's side window, the first officer shined the flashlight into C.J.'s face and said, "Sir, I need all of you to step out of the vehicle." At the same time he said this, a second officer appeared at Nico's window, and the man tapped on the glass. C.J. turned off the engine at the same time Nico opened his door.

"Sir, step out of the vehicle, and don't touch anything in the car before you do."

The officer placed his hand on Nico's door and opened it all the way.

In the intense glare, DeSean could see the small plastic bag of pills lying near the center of the floorboard. As soon as Nico stepped out of the car, the second officer reached into the back seat and retrieved the sack.

At the same time, DeSean jumped when the first officer opened his door and waited as he exited the vehicle. DeSean read the patch on the officer's sleeve—Robbinsonville Police Department.

Why are they stopping us? DeSean thought. *We've only been gone a short while from Jonesborough.*

Once the four guys were standing on the shoulder, the officer asked them to face the car, put both arms on the top of the vehicle, and spread their legs. DeSean was wide-eyed as he watched the officer on his side conduct a pat-down search of C.J. DeSean had never had someone search his person in this way. Now his turn, DeSean held his breath once the patrolman began his exploration. To say he was terrified was putting it mildly.

While the young men were still spread-eagled on each side of the car, the two officers walked to the back of the sedan. Although DeSean couldn't quite hear what they were saying, the first officer's words made his blood run cold: "You are all under arrest."

The officer closest to him pulled DeSean's arms roughly behind the teen's back. A series of words were repeated by each officer as he felt the circlet of steel handcuffs snap into place around his wrists. "You have the right" was a phrase said over and over as the officers repeated this same procedure on the other occupants of the car.

The manacles were cold and tight on DeSean's wrists. As a hand was placed on each of their heads to protect them from hitting the door frame, he and C.J. were loaded into the first officer's car. DeSean craned his head slightly to see the same happening to Ted and Nico. Suddenly, he realized he was supposed to meet Max Smith at the Crockett High stadium. Terror sent adrenaline coursing through his veins. Looking at the digital readout of the clock on the car's dashboard—nine thirty-five—DeSean knew that would never happen.

The processing of the four young men took a while before they were placed in cells at the Robbinsonville Police Department. Time seemed to slow to a crawl.

As he sat on the cold bench in the empty cell, DeSean wondered, *What must Max be thinking? How could I be so stupid to go riding with C.J. and his pals tonight?*

Finally, an officer appeared at the door.

"Son," the older man said, "you are allowed to make one telephone call. Do you have someone you'd like to talk to?"

DeSean sat stupefied for a moment. Max might be home by now, but then he might be out driving along the roads near Crockett High, looking for his foster child. *What an idiot I've been*, DeSean thought. Suddenly, Keith Haliday's face popped into his mind. DeSean remembered the Timothy House basketball coach from the skills clinic a few months ago. As scenes from the past few months flashed through his mind, the teen realized Keith had been perhaps the only adult, other than the Smiths, who had sincerely seemed interested in him. Keith had given him a card with his contact info on it and told DeSean he was welcome to call him if he ever needed anything. *Being arrested certainly fit the "need" category*, DeSean thought wryly.

The teen rose from the bench and stepped closer to the officer standing on the other side of the cell door. "There's a card in my wallet with a name and a number on it—Keith Haliday. Please call him."

"Will do," said the officer, eyeing DeSean suspiciously before turning away from the cell.

Please, oh please, be home, thought DeSean.

CHAPTER
43

Keith had gotten home from the Timothy House football game almost two hours ago. Not having Abbie beside him at the game tonight felt strange; she was in McHenry to see old friends for the weekend, leaving campus as soon as classes were over. Abbie would be staying with Lane and Eric but would also get together with the ladies of her quilting group, Loose Threads. He smiled as he thought about how excited she had been. The trip was all Abbie had talked about for the past week.

Once back at Stone's Throw, Keith made a roast beef sandwich and added a stack of sweet pickles and ruffled potato chips to complete the perfect late-night snack. Grabbing a cold canned soft drink before closing the refrigerator, he headed to the den. After getting settled in his armchair, Keith flipped through channels until finding one of his favorite Clint Eastwood movies. The sandwich hit the spot as he watched Eastwood take care of the bad guys.

Keith yawned as he tried to stay awake. He obviously lost the battle, as his cell phone ringing woke him up. Eleven fifty-five, his clock read. Who could be calling at this hour?

"Hello," Keith answered, trying to sound alert. However, when Trent Lockhart's voice greeted him, whatever sleepiness lingered within Keith was instantly gone.

"Hello, Keith," the police chief said, "sorry to call you at this late hour."

"No bother," said Keith. "What's up?"

"I've got a young man here that says he knows you. We arrested him and three other guys a little while ago. The kid is from Jonesborough but insisted we call you. Had a card in his wallet he said you gave him. His name is—"

"DeSean Matthews," said Keith, completing the chief's sentence.

"Do you know him?" asked Trent, sounding skeptical.

"Not really. We met in June at a skills clinic my basketball staff and I hosted at the Jonesborough Community Center. Something about him caught my attention. We ended up eating lunch together, and I gave him my card. Told him to call me if he ever needed anything."

"Well," said Trent soberly, "he needs you. My officers found drugs in the car—a bag of meth pills. This kid may be in serious trouble."

"Give me ten minutes, and I'll be there," Keith replied, already up and heading into the kitchen. Placing his plate in the sink, he grabbed a jacket from the kitchen table, where he had left it earlier. "Does this teen have any family? I think he's in foster care."

"Yes, I've already spoken with the police chief in Jonesborough. The kid lives with Max and Edna Smith. Jonesborough PD is getting in touch with them now."

"I'm on my way."

———

Upon arrival at the Robbinsonville Police Department, an officer escorted Keith to an interview room. The walls were an institutional gray, making the room feel cold and sterile with an air of uncertainty. A camera was mounted in one corner near the ceiling, the angle of which would record all conversations. A sizeable one-way mirror filled an ample space in the wall opposite the table, and Keith knew the arresting officers and perhaps a detective or two would be gathered on the other side to watch whatever happened in this room.

The door opened, and Keith turned around to find Trent coming through it. The two men shook hands and then sat down.

"How is he?" Keith asked.

"Terrified," replied Trent, "from the looks of it. The boy doesn't fit the profile of a druggie, and he sure doesn't look like he belongs with the others arrested with him."

"Who are they?"

Trent reached into his shirt pocket and withdrew a small piece of paper. "Let's see . . ." he began, trying to read his handwriting at this late hour. "Durrell Dykes, Ted Bond, and Nico Rodriguez. My officers found pills on the floor where Nico was seated. Once we got to the station, my officers found a larger stash stuffed into his boot. Don't think the Matthews fellow was in on this. My gut says he was in the wrong place at the wrong time."

A sick feeling swept over Keith. "Can I see DeSean?"

"My officer is bringing him here. I'll step out and give you the room when he arrives, but then I'll be back with the arresting officer. Unraveling all of this may take most of the night," Trent said, his eyes full of concern.

The sound of the door opening interrupted the two men. They looked up to see DeSean being led into the room, handcuffed and wearing an orange jumpsuit. The teen's eyes were red, and he looked like he was about to jump out of his skin. The officer pulled a chair out at the table opposite Keith and Trent, and DeSean sat down.

"Hi, DeSean," said Keith, speaking first.

"Hi," said DeSean, his voice faint and faltering. He did not meet Keith's gaze.

"I'm going to let you two visit," said Chief Lockhart as he rose. "I'll be back in a little while. DeSean," he said, looking over at the teen, "would you like anything to drink? A soda or a glass of water?"

DeSean looked up with a dazed expression, as if the chief had queried him in a foreign language. "A soda would be good," he said. "Thank you," DeSean added, his eyes filled with tears.

Trent nodded and left the interview room.

Keith uttered a silent prayer, asking the Lord to give him the words to say and the wisdom to know how to help this young man.

"DeSean, I'm glad you had Chief Lockhart call me." At the sound of his name, the teen looked up and locked eyes with Keith, who saw fear in them. "What were you doing hanging out with these guys?"

Before he could answer, Trent returned and placed an open soda can on the table.

"Thank you," DeSean said once more, this time looking directly at the chief.

"You're welcome," replied Trent. As he left the room, he glanced back, met Keith's gaze, and nodded as if to encourage his friend.

When the door closed, Keith asked again, "Tell me, DeSean. What were you doing?"

For the next twenty minutes, between sniffles and sobs, DeSean described how the night had started innocently. "When we got to the game, I guess I was acting too cool and didn't want to sit with Mr. Smith. I made up a story about sitting with some guys in my class."

Keith looked at him. "Had you made plans to meet any friends at the game?"

DeSean hung his head. "No, sir."

"How'd you end up in the car with C.J. and his pals?"

The teen looked up, regret filling his eyes, "It was near half-time, and I was in line at the concession stand. They found me in the crowd and invited me to go for a ride."

"And you didn't think that was strange?"

"I guess not at the time. I got Max's permission to leave with them. It's not like I disappeared or something."

"Oh, really?" Keith worked hard to keep his frustration in check. "And how do you even know these guys?"

"I . . ." stammered DeSean, struggling to find the words. "I met C.J. this past summer when I took the Smiths' car to the auto repair shop. C.J. works there, and we struck up a conversation."

Keith sat silently, trying his best to be patient.

Slowly, DeSean continued. "A few weeks later, C.J. drove past me on the street and stopped to say hi when he saw me. Told me he was in Jonesborough making some deliveries for the auto parts store. He had those two other guys with him. He invited me to dinner a few nights later, and I went. They seemed nice enough." The teen looked down at the table.

"Do you know anyone who knows these guys?" Keith asked. "Do you really know anything about them?" His tone was sharp, bordering on accusation.

DeSean sheepishly shook his head, still not looking up at Keith.

"Look," Keith said at last, as DeSean seemed spent with all he had to say. "You are in serious trouble. I will do all I can to get you out of it, but when Chief Lockhart and the officer that arrested you come in to interview you, you better be honest with them. Otherwise, you may be looking at jail time. Drugs aren't a laughing matter."

DeSean looked at Keith, his eyes wide with terror. "I swear I didn't know anything about the drugs." Despite his attempts to be brave, a tear slid down one side of his face.

When the interview room door opened again, Chief Lockhart and the arresting officer entered. As Keith exited, he asked Trent quietly, "Do you know when the Smiths will arrive?"

"Just got off the phone with Jonesborough PD. Max Smith is coming alone. He should be here within the hour," Trent replied. "My office is the second door down the hall on the right," he continued, pointing toward it. "Wait in my office until we've finished talking with DeSean. I'll have my staff bring Max to you once he arrives."

"Got it," replied Keith before closing the door.

———

By one forty-five, Max Smith had arrived at the Robbinsonville Police Department. The front desk clerk escorted him to Chief Lockhart's office, where Keith waited. The poor man, who seemed slightly older than Keith, was distraught. After the two introduced themselves, they sat in chairs before the chief's desk.

"We were at the high school football game," said Max, holding a weathered baseball cap by the brim and twisting it in his hands. "I panicked when he didn't show up at the car after the game. The school's security guard helped me search all over the stadium for him, but DeSean was not there. It was like he vanished into thin air."

Keith sat silently and listened.

"Finally, I went to the police department to see if he was there," continued Max, looking across the room, almost as if he was talking aloud to himself. "He wasn't, but an officer suggested DeSean may have left the game with friends. Told me to go home and wait for him. He also suggested I call area hospitals to see if the boy might be there." More turning the ball cap around and around. "When I got home, Edna had already made a few calls. I was about to make one more when the phone rang. One of the officers here in Robbinsonville was calling and told me DeSean had been arrested. What in the world?"

Max looked up, his eyes red and filled with apprehension.

"I honestly don't know," said Keith. "Trent Lockhart is the police chief and a good friend. He called me because DeSean had given him my name."

Max looked more confused than ever.

"I'm the head basketball coach at Timothy House. I met DeSean back in June." Keith could see that Max seemed a bit calmer with this explanation. "Before I left, I gave him my card and told him to call me if he ever needed anything. Strange, I know, but I had an uncanny feeling that DeSean might need a friend."

"So, you're the one he's been talking about?" said Max as a vague recollection washed over him. For the first time during this brief exchange, the older man seemed to relax a bit.

"Maybe," said Keith, shrugging his shoulders.

"I'm grateful to you," said Max quietly.

"You're welcome, although I'm not sure there's anything to thank me for," said Keith as he explained that although drugs were in the car, it looked like they belonged to the other three guys.

The office door opened, stopping the conversation. Both men looked up to see Trent enter. Keith introduced Max to the chief, and the three sat down.

"Well," began Trent, "even though the drug charges will stick with Nico, and possibly Ted and C.J., I'm inclined to believe DeSean's story." He then shared what he could about what he learned in the interview with the teen.

Max sat forward in his chair, the baseball cap clasped tightly in one hand. "Chief, although DeSean is a different sort of kid, he's never given us any indication that he was using drugs or even hanging around anyone who was. His story is sad, and he's been on his own for most of his seventeen years. Edna and I have tried hard these past two years to give him our love and provide him a home."

"I know you have, sir," said Trent, pausing to choose his words carefully. "While I'm not sure why DeSean called Keith rather than you and your wife, the law is clear regarding juveniles. I can only release DeSean to you, Mr. Smith, or if you would rather, I can call someone from the Department of Children's Services."

Max, never blinking, kept his gaze fixed on the police chief. "I want to take him home, sir."

Trent nodded and caught Keith's eye as he did so.

"Should I call anyone at DeSean's school," Max asked.

"No, sir," replied Trent. "Because DeSean is a minor, details of this arrest will remain confidential. Your son is the only one who could legally share that information with any of the school administrators or coaches."

Turning to look at Keith, the chief continued, "I understand DeSean is also on the basketball team."

Max nodded at Trent as the ball cap swirled in his hands.

After glancing down at his watch, Trent pushed back in his chair. "Let's see what we can do to release DeSean."

As Keith and Max waited for the teen, a plan began to form in Keith's mind. He sat forward to share it with the older man.

"Look, Mr. Smith," he said, hoping Max would agree to this plan, no matter how far-fetched it might sound. "The law says DeSean has to come home with you tonight, but how about allowing me to drive over later today, say around five o'clock this afternoon, and bring DeSean back to Stone's Throw, my cottage on the Timothy House campus? I want to introduce him to two boys who were at the basketball clinic with him this summer. I'd get them dinner and then we'd watch a movie. I could have him home by ten o'clock tonight. Though I don't have it all worked out, I've got a plan for DeSean. At least, I think I do," said Keith, as he felt some tension leave his body following the night's strange turn of events.

A look of wonder filled Max's face. "What kind of a plan?"

"Well, sir," continued Keith, "one where DeSean might be able to transfer to Timothy House to complete his senior year."

"Why would he want to do that?" Max's tone was matter-of-fact, as if he were merely trying to obtain more information about DeSean's future.

"For one," said Keith, turning in his chair to look more directly at Max, "DeSean is an incredibly talented basketball player. He's probably better than most players on my team."

Max eyed Keith suspiciously, grinning as he did so.

Keith lowered his voice and leaned close, "Don't ever repeat me on that, sir, or I'll have to refute it."

Max chuckled and seemed to relax at this.

"Though I'm not sure," Keith continued, "from what I remember of my visit with DeSean at the basketball clinic, Crockett High School doesn't seem to hold a special place in DeSean's heart. Am I wrong?"

"No," said Max quietly.

"The fact that he willingly went for that car ride with C.J. and his friends tells me how desperate DeSean is for attention. If he had friends at the school, at least ones that meant something to him, he would have declined C.J.'s invitation."

"You may be right there," agreed Max.

"I've got several phone calls to make later this morning, but I think there might be a place for DeSean at Timothy House."

"How much is tuition?" By the look on Max's face, it was evident he and Edna might not be able to pay the bill.

"Oh, there wouldn't be any tuition costs for DeSean. Thanks to a generous endowment established by the school's founder, Timothy House is amply provided for. While we charge admission, we also have an allowance when students like DeSean cross our path. We never want money to be the reason a child can't attend our school.

"The school is close to Jonesborough, and you and Mrs. Smith could be on campus often to visit DeSean and attend games or activities he's part of."

Keith knew that Trent would be walking through his office door any minute. "I'd also like to drop by to see you, Mrs. Smith, and DeSean about two o'clock tomorrow afternoon. With your permission, sir, I'd like to be with him for moral support if he decides to talk to Coach Denning. Although DeSean's the only one who can tell him what happened last night, I don't think your son needs to do that alone."

Perhaps it was the late hour or the worry from the night's bizarre events, but Max's eyes filled up with tears, and one or two of them slid down one cheek. He reached up and wiped them away with the back of his hand.

"Thank you," he said, his voice barely audible. "I don't know what to say."

"Well," said Keith with a chuckle, "don't thank me just yet. It seems to me that DeSean, Mrs. Smith, and you all need a break. This plan might be just the ticket."

Max smiled broadly, his unspoken gratitude reflected in the tears still filling his eyes.

Forty minutes later, a uniformed officer appeared at the door to Trent's office and asked Keith and Max Smith to accompany him to the reception area of the police station. Once there, the officer disappeared. The two waited in silence. When the metal doors to the waiting room clanked open, Keith and Max rose as a deflated DeSean Matthews joined them.

Keith gave the foster father and son space as they had a short conversation in the corner of the waiting room. Although he could not hear what was said, Keith knew Max Smith had spoken from a heart of love if DeSean's hugs and muffled apologies were any indication.

Trent entered the waiting room and followed Max, DeSean, and Keith to Max's car. As the teen climbed into the front seat, the police chief reached in and placed his hand on the boy's shoulder. "DeSean, you remember that two good men stood up for you tonight. Don't let them down."

"I won't, sir," replied the teen, his voice tired and flat. The chief closed the passenger door.

"Trent," said Keith, as they watched Max and DeSean drive away into the dark night, "I may have a plan to help DeSean."

"Really?" said Trent, his curiosity evident.

"I'll be in touch tomorrow, if not later today."

"Sounds good," said the chief, patting Keith on the shoulder. "Drive carefully."

Twenty minutes later, Keith was back in his den, thumbing through the contacts on his phone until he found the number he was looking for. Noticing it wasn't yet five in the morning, Keith knew this wasn't the best time to place a call. *He'll understand,* he thought as he dialed.

A groggy Don Fielding answered the phone on the fifth ring. "He-hello," he said.

"Hey, Don. It's Keith. Sorry to call you at such an awful hour." He told his boss about DeSean and the night's events as quickly as possible. "This kid may need a Plan B to finish high school," said Keith as he completed what he needed to say. When the call ended, the head of Timothy House promised to be at Stone's Throw by nine o'clock.

Keith headed into his bedroom, hoping to catch a few winks before this day got crazier.

CHAPTER
44

Even though the night had been short, Keith was surprised at how awake he felt. For the past forty minutes, he had been having his quiet time and talking to the Lord about this unlikely situation DeSean now found himself in, which Keith was now a part of.

A knock announced Don Fielding's arrival at Stone's Throw. Keith opened the door and welcomed his friend into the cottage, then led the way back to the den.

"Tell me what you have in mind," said Don once they were seated.

Keith sat forward, rested his elbows on his knees, and clasped his hands between them. "Don, this may sound crazy, but I want to make an offer for DeSean to finish his senior year here at Timothy House."

The head of school smiled.

"This young man is desperate for a home and an environment where he'll be accepted. It's like he's working so hard to keep the world at bay while silently screaming for attention. He reminds me of myself in those years when I struggled before I finally got my life on track with the Lord." As Keith heard himself talk, he was surprised at the strong emotions this young man elicited from deep within him.

"It's late September now," Keith continued. "He won't have missed that much of the school year. I know our senior faculty could help him with a plan to get him up to speed."

Don continued listening.

"This young man is an outstanding ball player. I think he could be a fit for our team. Andy and Davis were with me at the Jonesborough clinic. I think they would also do their best to welcome him."

"How do you think he would fare academically," Don ventured.

"I'm not sure, to be honest. That would certainly be a consideration."

Keith was silent for a few minutes, as if trying to determine his next step in DeSean's Plan B.

Soon, he continued. "Max Smith, DeSean's foster parent, appears to be a wonderful man, but he sure seems a bit old to keep up with a kid DeSean's age. I do, though, think that this man genuinely loves this boy and only wants what's best for him. An eight-month break might be just what the doctor ordered for all of them. What do you think?"

Keith looked expectantly at this trusted friend he'd come to love as a father.

"I like it," Don replied, his wide grin confirming his words. "Let me make a few phone calls and see what the school can do."

Keith's spirits soared. "The Smiths said they could be here for a nine o'clock meeting on Monday. Do you think you will know something by then?

"I'll make sure I do," said Don.

"I want you at this meeting," Keith said, inching forward near the edge of the sofa.

"I want to be there!"

The two friends stood and shook hands.

As Keith walked Don to the door, he silently prayed that all the pieces of this newly proposed, intricate academic puzzle would fall into place.

———

A much-needed nap was the gift Keith gave to himself after Don left the cottage. He couldn't remember being so tired as he lay down in his bedroom but knew it was more from emotional fatigue than physical. Three hours later, the alarm woke him from a deep sleep. Reaching over to turn off the digital clock beside his bed, Keith realized that without it, he would probably still be slumbering away. Swinging his feet onto the floor, he sat on the side of his bed. He still had a few hours before he headed to Jonesborough to pick up DeSean.

As he padded into the kitchen to scrounge a snack, he realized he had a few calls to make. Twenty minutes later, he completed his phone work.

As he changed clothes for the drive to Jonesborough, he hoped his Plan B for DeSean would work.

———

As promised, DeSean was ready when Keith arrived at the Smith home. When Max opened the front door of the small, tidy house, the teen stood just behind his foster father in the living room. Max welcomed Keith with a hearty handshake and invited him in. Keith followed DeSean and the older man through the living room and into the kitchen. Once there, he saw a woman at the stove, her back to the trio. At the sound of voices coming through the door, Edna Smith turned around.

"Hon," said Max, "this is Keith Haliday. He's the one I've been telling you about." Edna's gaze left her husband's face and found its way to Keith's. "He's also the one DeSean's been talking about."

As she stepped forward, Edna wiped her hands on her starched apron. "Nice to meet you, Mr. Haliday. Welcome to our home." Edna's tall, slender frame and firm handshake let Keith know she was in good physical form.

"Ma'am," Keith said, "the pleasure is mine. Please call me Keith." Smiling broadly, he continued, "Mr. Haliday was my daddy's name."

Edna smiled and said, "By all means, then, please call me Edna." She pointed to the breakfast table set with small plates, napkins, and a tray piled high with homemade chocolate chip cookies. "Would you like some cookies and lemonade?"

"That I would," said Keith, walking over to the table. Looking back at Edna, he asked, "Where would you like me to sit? Don't want to take your seat."

DeSean's foster mother pointed to the chair at the far end of the table. "Sit there, why don't you," she said.

Keith took his seat, and as soon as he did, DeSean slid into the chair to his left. Though he couldn't be entirely sure, DeSean looked somehow different this afternoon, like maybe he'd grown up a few years in less than a day. Keith met the young man's wide-eyed gaze and grinned. The boy smiled back ever so slightly.

The four made light conversation as they enjoyed sampling Edna's culinary skills.

"These are excellent . . . ," began Keith, and then stopped mid-sentence to catch a chunk of chocolate falling from the cookie headed for his mouth. He made a saving catch with his other hand.

Max, Edna, and DeSean laughed.

After a few more minutes of small talk, Keith decided it was time to move to the next part of Plan B.

"Thanks for letting DeSean come for a visit tonight," Keith began.

"Well," said Max, "I know he's looking forward to it." The older man turned his gaze to the teenager seated next to him. Love for and devotion to this foster child were written all over Max's face.

"I've asked a few boys on our basketball team to meet us for burgers at a malt shop near campus. We will take our food back to the lake and have a picnic."

Turning to DeSean, Keith continued, "Andy Beason and Davis Landrum are going to meet us at the restaurant." DeSean nodded slightly. "Once you see them, you'll recognize them from the basketball clinic in June. Thought you'd enjoy getting to know them."

"Yes, sir," was the teen's reply. Though the boy still looked withdrawn and distant, he met the coach's gaze head-on, perhaps for the first time, and his tone seemed steady and sincere.

Keith was flabbergasted. Though he wasn't sure what had transpired between Max and DeSean once they had left the police station, it was evident something life-changing had occurred within this young man's heart and mind in a very short time. *Thank you, Lord*, he thought. *I need all the help I can get.*

"After our burgers and fries, I thought we could go to Stone's Throw, my cottage, and watch *Rio Grande*, one of my favorite John Wayne movies," Keith continued. "A station out of Knoxville runs westerns on Saturday nights. I promised Max I'd have you home by ten tonight. Sound okay?"

Once again, the same steady, calm demeanor filled DeSean's face, "Yes, sir. Sounds great."

As today was a day to celebrate, Keith had a third cookie. *Abbie would love this recipe*, he thought as he washed down the last of the treat with a large gulp of lemonade.

Soon, the visit was over. The Smiths walked Keith and DeSean out to the front driveway. Edna's promise to send Keith the cookie recipe made him smile. He returned her kind gesture with his pledge to have DeSean home by the agreed-upon curfew.

Keith and DeSean climbed into his Explorer. As they drove away, Max and Edna stood on the front porch and waved goodbye.

Keith prayed all the way back to Robbinsonville that this evening's plans would go well.

CHAPTER
45

When Keith parked his Explorer in front of his cottage, the three guys piled out of the SUV and called, "We'll see you at the lake." He laughed to himself as he watched them disappear on the path. Before closing the door, he grabbed the bags of burgers and fries, threw a blanket from the back seat over his arm, and cradled the drink carrier containing the malts. As he headed to join them, he could hear their lively conversation.

As soon as Keith appeared, the boys gathered around like hungry birds. They sat down on the pile of large rocks near the shore. Keith took a few minutes to sort out the orders. Once each had his food, he said, "Let me bless our dinner."

He bowed his head, and Andy and Davis followed suit. DeSean, however, watched them all closely, his eyes wide open and his head held high.

"Dear Lord, thank you for good food, great fellowship, and the beauty of Your creation. In Your name, I pray. Amen."

As the blessing ended, DeSean looked at Keith quizzically.

"Want to ask me something?" Keith queried.

"Not really . . ." said the teen, and then he thought better of it. "Why do you thank God for your food? Aren't you the one who bought it?"

Andy and Davis looked at their new friend as if he'd spoken something in a foreign language.

"Well, DeSean," said Keith, trying not to take any tone that might sound judgmental or preachy, "I thank God because He is the One who gives all in my life to me—my job, my friends, my health, my money, the very air that I breathe. Thanking Him before each meal is one way that helps me remember from Whom all that I have comes."

DeSean shrugged and said, "Seems silly to me, that's all."

Andy and Davis still hadn't said a word.

"I respect your opinion," said Keith as he reached for his dinner. Turning to the other boys, he said, "Let's eat. Don't know about you guys, but I'm starving."

Andy and Davis dove into their meal. Soon, DeSean was unwrapping his hamburger. For a long while, the only sounds were that of the foil paper crinkling around the sandwiches and straws scratching against plastic drink cup lids.

"These burgers are great," said Davis, his mouth ringed with ketchup and a bit of mustard.

"Glad you like them," said Keith, motioning with his napkin that Davis needed to use his own to wipe his mouth.

"Never had a malt this good before," DeSean said as he slurped the last of his shake. His recent question about who had provided it seemed forgotten.

"The Main Street Malt Shop's one of my favorites," exclaimed Keith before putting a handful of fries in his mouth.

Though he'd not spoken, delight was written across Andy's face as he wolfed down his meal.

While the four ate, the sun began its descent over the lake. As he watched DeSean in the waning light, Keith hoped the teen might find the shelter and peacefulness at Timothy House that he desperately needed. He also prayed the Lord could find a crack in the boy's heart through which to slip in.

Once back at the cottage, Keith made a large bowl of popcorn for the boys as they gathered in his den for the evening's feature movie. Before the show started and during commercials, Andy and Davis kept the conversation going, and surprisingly, DeSean had joined in as if they'd been pals for a long while.

Keith could hardly keep his mind on the sermon in church for he was thinking about how well last night's get-together at Stone's Throw had gone. As he thought of how Andy and Davis stepped up to the plate, the sounds of the service faded. Though the two juniors were some of the most admirable young men in the Timothy House student body, Keith had never seen them so outgoing and accommodating toward another student close to their age.

The pastor's words brought Keith back to the Sunday morning service. "Love your enemies, and pray for those who persecute you." Smiling, Keith wondered what DeSean would do with those words where C.J. and his pals were concerned. However, if DeSean's heart wasn't filled with the love of God, this gospel paradox would not make much sense, and the boy would be hard-pressed to apply the commandment to Friday night's joy ride and subsequent arrest.

Once Keith had driven out of the Timothy House gates last night to take DeSean home, the teen had peppered him with questions.

"Tell me again why the information about my arrest is confidential?" DeSean began.

"Because you haven't yet reached the age of eighteen, in the eyes of the law, you're still a child. Any information about legal matters, such as an arrest, is confidential. You're the only one with legal authority to share that information with others."

"Uhm," was DeSean's only reply for the moment. Soon, though, he had thought of another question. "Why do you think they didn't charge me about the drugs?"

"To tell you the truth," said Keith carefully, "I'm not sure. I do, though, know that Chief Lockhart is a good man. I also think he realized C.J. and his pals were using you and that you weren't part of their group."

"Can you tell others about what happened Friday night since I had the police call you?"

"Nope," said Keith, hoping the questions would cease.

"That's good," was DeSean's only reply. He didn't say another word until Keith's truck pulled into the Smith's driveway.

Before Keith knew it, the service ended. Looking at his watch, he realized he had time for a quick lunch and a change of clothes before heading back to Jonesborough to visit with the Smiths. Besides thinking over the previous night's activities during this morning's church service, he prayed fervently that this afternoon's events would go equally well.

———

Settled on the couch in Max and Edna's living room, Keith waited for a break in the conversation to tell them what he was thinking. The couple was seated in tufted wing chairs across a small, oval coffee table from the sofa. DeSean was nearby in a wooden, spindle-backed chair, the cushion of which had long ago lost its stuffing. Although last night's Timothy House get-together had been a positive experience, DeSean seemed more distant today, like he'd crawled back into his shell. As Edna's story about the boy was winding down, Keith knew this was his time to jump in.

"There's something I wanted to run by the three of you," Keith began, making eye contact with Max, Edna, and DeSean. "Max and I briefly discussed it at the police station." At the mention of the arrest, DeSean's face turned a bright shade of red, and Keith caught a glimpse of the wounded teen he first met three months earlier.

"DeSean," continued Keith, looking the young man squarely in the eye, "God was watching out for you Friday night." Leaning forward in his chair, he placed his elbows on his knees and rubbed his hands together. "You do realize that no one held a gun to your head. You got into a car with three guys you knew practically nothing about. If those drugs had been on your side of the floorboard, we'd probably be having this conversation in a jail cell."

"What's God got to do with this?" DeSean popped forward momentarily, blurted out his anger, and then quickly returned to his sullen, silent state.

Keith sat a little straighter in his chair. "God has everything to do with this, DeSean," he said as he looked at the teen.

This young man might be the hardest to reach in all my years working with youth, he thought. *Help me, Lord, to say the right thing.*

"Whether you believe it or not, God loves you more than you could possibly imagine. One way He demonstrates that care is through the events in our lives. The fact that you're here in your home and not in a cold jail cell at the Robbinsonville Police Department is evidence of that love."

The boy stared at Keith with eyes filled with anger and hurt. Unfortunately, the coach had seen this look on many other faces before and was not bothered by it.

"Why would God love me?" DeSean asked suspiciously. "I'm not even sure I believe He's real."

"Oh, honey," Edna blurted out as she blinked back tears.

"It doesn't matter if you believe it or not," said Keith as he continued to look at DeSean. "What matters is His love is unchangeable and given to you freely. He created you, and He has a plan for your life. He is God, and nothing you nor I could say or believe will ever change that."

A defiant stare was DeSean's only answer.

Keith continued. "Max and I discussed the possibility of you transferring to Timothy House to complete the remainder of your senior year."

At this, DeSean's eyebrows raised slightly.

"You'd be living in the senior boys' cabin. The class is much smaller than the one you're in at Crockett. Plus, I'd like to offer you a position on our boys' basketball team. I was impressed with your skills and ball handling at the Jonesborough clinic."

Keith paused for a moment. "The thing is, DeSean, you'll need to make this decision now. As I explained to you last night, the details of that car ride are confidential because you're a minor. If you accept this offer, you must contact Coach Denning this afternoon and tell him you're leaving the school. You'll also have to tell him why."

"And why would that be exactly?" asked DeSean, surprising Keith with his inquisitive tone.

"Because," began Keith, working hard to keep his tone even keel and gentle, "you're the only one who can begin the process of freeing yourself from the consequences of what happened Friday night. Your coming clean with your coach will be a sign you're accepting responsibility for your actions.

"I also believe you're in a school environment where you've not received much of the support you need. I think you would find a warm welcome at our school." Keith glanced over at Max and Edna and then back at DeSean. "Timothy House is unique in many ways. It's a setting where I think you could develop strong friendships and grow in many ways, far beyond the classroom. Besides," he said with a grin, "we could use your skills on the basketball team."

For a few minutes, no one in the room said a word as Keith's words hung in the air between them.

Finally, DeSean said, "Would I have to talk to Coach in person, or could we call him?"

"I'm sure a phone call would be fine," said Keith reassuringly. "Max and I will sit with you while you make the call if you want us to."

The boy leaned back in his chair, his long legs sprawled before him. Looking down at his clasped hands, he seemed to wrestle within himself for a long while. Max, Edna, and Keith sat in silence with him.

Finally, the teen looked up and addressed Keith. "Why are you doing this for me?"

"Because I believe in you, DeSean," began Keith. "Timothy House is where I found a second chance, and I know what a positive difference the school can make in one's life. I believe God has something special He wants to do in your life, and Timothy House might be where that can occur."

Keith stopped and looked over at Max and Edna before continuing.

"I also believe the Smiths love you tremendously and believe the Timothy House environment can provide opportunities not available at Crockett High. Since Jonesborough is so close, Max and Edna can attend all your games and activities. They'll be able to cheer you on during your senior year."

DeSean nodded slightly.

"DeSean, the decision is yours, and I'll certainly respect which option you choose—stay at Crockett High School or transfer to Timothy House."

Though he could not be sure, Keith thought he caught a glimmer of hope in DeSean's eyes. Keith had said all he knew to say, and now the teen would have to decide which path to take. *Oh, Lord,* Keith thought, *please let this young man grab this lifeline.*

Suddenly sitting upright in his chair, DeSean said, "Let's make that call to Coach Denning."

CHAPTER
46

Two days later, Keith woke well before dawn. As he watched the sun rise over Shelter Lake, a great sense of excitement and expectancy dawned within his spirit. While getting dressed that Tuesday morning, Keith thought back over all that had transpired over the past five days. DeSean's poor choice. The joy ride with C.J. and his pals. God's provision for DeSean due to his age and his naivete concerning the drug gang. A new beginning in the relationship between DeSean and his foster parents. Don's acceptance of a Plan B for the teen here at Timothy House. DeSean's surprising willingness to leave Crockett High School. The sincere camaraderie forged between DeSean and Keith's players. The young man's maturity and courage when calling Coach Denning to quit the Crockett High basketball team.

God, you have certainly provided exceeding abundantly above during this weekend, Keith thought as he locked the front door of Stone's Throw. *I pray You're about to deliver the same at this morning's meeting.*

Keith headed for his office after grabbing a quick breakfast in the dining hall. Lance Tate was arriving for this morning's meeting with the Smiths and DeSean. Keith was looking forward to a short visit with his old friend before joining the others in Don Fielding's office. While making his way to the administration building, Keith thought of how fortunate DeSean was to have several key individuals, connected to both the school and the Robbinsonville community, who were stepping up to ensure the young man had every opportunity to succeed in this fresh start offered to him.

Keith had been deep in thought while working on some paperwork at his desk, so much so that Lance's voice startled him.

"Knock, knock," said the retired soldier as he stuck his head through the office doorway. True to form, Lance arrived at Keith's office precisely at eight forty as he promised.

A wide grin broke out across Keith's face. Jumping up from his desk, he crossed the space between and gave his pal a quick hug and a hearty slap on the back.

After the men sat down, Lance cut straight to the point. "How do you think the kid's going to react to this idea, this Plan B, as you call it?"

Keith looked across the desk and shrugged his shoulders. "To tell you the truth," he said, "I'm not quite sure, but I'm cautiously optimistic based on my interactions with him over the weekend."

Though Lance had agreed, on short notice, to be a part of DeSean's rescue plan, Keith hadn't told his friend many of the details of what had happened since DeSean's arrest. For the next few minutes, Keith filled Lance in on a pared-down version of the weekend's events, sharing only what he could without breaching confidentiality.

"I'm looking forward to getting to know Trent Lockhart," said Lance as he checked his watch. "If we don't get to Don's office, I may miss my introduction."

At this, both men rose and headed to what they prayed would be a life-changing event for DeSean Matthews.

———

After a round of brief introductions, the requested parties were seated in the office of the Head of School of Timothy House at nine o'clock sharp. While they waited, Don Fielding punched the number to his assistant's desk and waited for her to answer.

"Please hold all my calls until further notice. Only in an extreme emergency am I to be disturbed." Putting the phone down, Don looked across his desk at the faces of those who had gathered for this meeting. "Well," he said, "that should settle that. I should have taken care of that earlier, but it's been one of those days." Gazing over at Keith, Don continued, "This is your rodeo. I'm going to let you steer the wagon."

"Thanks, Don," said Keith, a bit uncomfortable in this role. He looked at the small group seated nearby. The expressions on the faces of Trent Lockhart, Lance Tate, Max and Edna Smith, and DeSean Matthews were hard to read. Keith silently prayed for the Lord's guidance and then plunged ahead.

Leaning forward in his chair, he looked directly at DeSean. The boy's steely eyes looked more frightened than anything.

"DeSean," Keith said, "we're here today to help you forge a plan that will allow you to complete your high school education at Timothy House. Before we talk about how that will happen, Chief Lockhart is going to share a little information about the guys you took a ride with last Friday night."

Looking straight at the teen, Trent began, "For the past four days, I've had my best detectives working around the clock to put together a solid case that would keep C.J., Ted, and Nico behind bars for a long, long time. Tony DiMarco, one of the sharpest arrows in my department, uncovered the missing link."

DeSean, Keith, Don, and Lance hung on the chief's every word.

"The Robbinsonville area has been plagued with drug trafficking for the past three years. Banking on a hunch that a lie is always easier to tell if based partially on the truth, Tony searched the database of the National Crime Information Center, keying in various combinations of Durrell 'C.J.' Dykes. After almost thirteen hours at the computer, he hit the jackpot. It turns out that those initials—CJD—belonged to the drug dealer, only under another name.

"C.J.'s real name, Cash Jones Durrell, had been repurposed to allow him to hide in plain sight in Robbinsonville. Although he used it as his first name in Tennessee, Durrell was a surname. Dykes, the surname used in Tennessee, was the name of a road on which C.J. formerly lived. Tony discovered that Mr. Durrell had quite a criminal history in the state of Illinois. Once we established C.J.'s real identity, it didn't take us long to determine the identities of his associates. Both of them also have criminal records."

Keith watched DeSean as the police chief detailed C.J. and his associates' possible prison sentences. The kid's face turned a ghostly shade of white when Trent described how the recent arrest of an auto body parts dealer from Jonesborough had made the case virtually airtight. Although he had no idea how DeSean was involved, Keith had now been around the teen long enough to believe this young man had dodged a huge bullet. As the chief continued to talk, Keith said a silent prayer of thanksgiving for God's watchful care of this wayward teen. Keith only hoped DeSean would accept the details of this proposed Plan B.

Once Trent finished summarizing his department's excellent detective work, he turned to Keith and said, "The floor's all yours, Coach."

"Thanks, Chief," replied Keith, then turned his attention to the young man. "As you know, DeSean, you're here today because everyone in this room believes in you. We have your best interests at heart."

Some color returned to the boy's face. On the other hand, Max Smith was now looking pale.

"Though Crockett High School has been a good school in many ways, we think Timothy House might offer you some unique experiences that would benefit you greatly."

DeSean's eyes locked on Keith's face, his attention focused on his every word.

"For starters, DeSean, you would live here on the school's campus. There's a bedroom waiting for you in Sequoia House, the senior boys' cottage. All your classes will be on campus. The senior class is small, with only twenty-one students—twelve guys and nine gals. You will find them eager to welcome you into their merry band."

Several around the room smiled at this last statement.

Keith continued, "Second, I'd also like you to consider joining the basketball team."

At this, DeSean's face grew red.

"You're a gifted player, DeSean, and I'd like to provide a venue through which you can hone those skills."

The boy nodded slightly.

"Third, I want to introduce you to a good friend of mine, retired Major General Lance Tate."

All eyes turned to Lance, and DeSean nodded toward him.

"Coach Haliday and I have known each other for many years," Lance continued. "You couldn't have a finer man willing to go to bat for you."

Once again, DeSean's face reddened.

"I am honored that Keith invited me to join him and Chief Lockhart to serve as mentors for you. Our plan," said the former military leader, glancing over at Keith and Trent, "is for the three of us to meet with you twice a month until you graduate. We want to use our visits to share much of what we learned when we were your age that helped us become better men."

"Thank you, sir," said DeSean.

Trent sat forward slightly in his chair. "DeSean, I want you to know that everyone in this room believes in you. I can assure you that if we didn't, none of us would be here. Although I don't know your life story, I know that life has dealt you some unfair cards. Never forget that you *always* have a choice regarding how you react to life circumstances. An opportunity like this doesn't come along often, young man. God has a plan and a purpose for your life. I pray that you will allow Him to prove that to you." Reaching into his shirt pocket, Trent withdrew a business card and handed it to DeSean. "Stick that somewhere you won't lose it, son, and if you ever need anything, you call me."

After DeSean pocketed the card, Keith again took charge of the meeting. "Don, would you mind sharing how DeSean will fulfill his graduation requirements?"

Don Fielding, who had gone largely unnoticed during the first part of this critical meeting, explained the strategy Timothy House faculty would use to help DeSean catch up on school work he'd missed since the beginning of the semester. Don also provided the Smiths with important information they would need to know as parents of a Timothy House senior.

"Do either of you have questions?" the head of school asked Max and Edna.

"I do," ventured Edna. "Certain subjects have sometimes been difficult for DeSean. Is academic tutoring available for him?"

"Great question, Edna," he replied. "Yes, we have tutoring offered by faculty and student peers."

The look of concern on her face was replaced with relief. "Thank you, Mr. Fielding."

Don leaned forward at his desk as he spoke again to the Smiths. "The main thing I want both of you to know is that we believe DeSean would be a wonderful addition to the Timothy House family. We'll take care of your son like he was ours."

At this, Max leaned over and took one of Edna's hands in his and gave it a gentle squeeze. Husband and wife looked reassured by what they had heard.

The attention of all turned back to DeSean with Don's following comment.

"DeSean, although it's been great to hear how everyone else feels about Plan B, as Coach Haliday has coined it, yours is the only opinion that matters, as you would be the person making this tremendous change in your life. What do you think about this plan?"

The office was suddenly quiet as the group waited to hear DeSean's response.

The teen sat for a minute as if trying to formulate his answer. When he finally spoke, all the adults in the room were moved by his courage and honesty. "Mr. Fielding, a lot has happened these last few days due to my bad choices. Though I'm not sure why all of you want to help me, I am grateful for this chance for a new start."

Turning to look at Max and Edna, he continued, "If it's okay, I'd like to transfer to Timothy House."

Looking back at Don, DeSean mumbled a faint "thank you" as tears glistened in his eyes.

With that pronouncement, broad smiles appeared on the faces of all gathered, none brighter than DeSean's.

Keith felt himself choking back tears as he knew he had just witnessed a miracle. Like saving Daniel's friends from the fiery furnace, God had plucked this teen out of a desperate situation and placed him on the path toward a positive future. He could hardly wait to talk with Lance and Trent to plan their first mentoring visit with DeSean.

CHAPTER
47

As Keith and Abbie drove toward Bays Mountain Lake, he tried to act as nonchalant as possible, hoping he was pulling off the charade. Across the front seat, Abbie chatted excitedly about the beautiful scenery. Though it was still a little early in the season, leaves on the trees were already beginning to signal fall's arrival with hints of scarlet, gold, burgundy, russet, mustard, and burnt umber. The mountains in this part of eastern Tennessee would soon look as if God himself had been out with His box of sharpened crayons and individually colored each leaf. Every few minutes, Keith would try to nod his head or add an "Uh huh" to the conversation. *Please keep her mind occupied*, he thought.

The sign they had just passed said eight more miles until the entrance to the state park. Keith's mind whirled as he mentally checked off the preparations made for tonight's picnic dinner. *Did I remember to bring the tiramisu? Did I add the extra napkins to the basket? Will she like the ham sandwiches I prepared? Should I have used sourdough bread instead?*

A question from Abbie interrupted Keith's self-interrogation. "How long before the trees lose their leaves?"

Lose their leaves? he thought. *I'm about to lose my mind.* "I'm not sure," he answered, trying to sound calm and collected.

Content with his answer, Abbie turned back to her window-gazing.

As they continued down the highway, Keith said a silent prayer of thanks for the kindness of Doris Fielding, who had agreed to spend the afternoon with the five girls living in Mistletoe Cottage, sit with them at dinner in Covenant Kitchen, and walk them back to the cottage and help with homework and bedtime preparations.

Lord, he thought, as they approached the park entrance, *I believe You have brought Abbie to me. You know how hard I have prayed about this decision. Please bless this special night.*

The main road took them on a circuitous route toward the parking lot near the lake. Glancing at the clock on his truck's dashboard, Keith was delighted to see they had arrived ahead of schedule. He had planned the timing of this evening picnic down to the minute—parking the car, walking the path to the picnic area, eating their dinner, proposing to Abbie while the sun set over the lake—all before the park closed at eight o'clock. As he turned his truck into the lot, he was pleased to see that very few cars were still here on a Thursday evening.

Abbie opened her door and stepped out. Before she could make her way to his side of the car, Keith quickly reached into the pocket on the back of the driver's seat and drew out a small shell-shaped box. The enameled paint gleamed softly in the early evening sun, the ridges of the shell's surface painted in alternating colors of blush and coral. A magnetized clasp kept the hinged lid closed from within. Keith hastily stuck it in his pocket. As he opened his door, Abbie appeared at his side.

"What can I carry?" she asked cheerfully.

Keith opened the passenger door behind his seat and pulled out a folded fleece blanket. "Here you go," he said as he placed it in her arms.

Reaching back into the vehicle, he took hold of a weathered, wicker picnic basket and a small beverage cooler. Once he closed the door behind him and made sure the truck was locked, he led her down the path to what he hoped would be one of the most special evenings of his life.

Twenty feet or so past the truck lay the footpath that would connect them to the Lakeside Trail, a walking path covering most of the lakefront in this area of the park. As they stepped onto it, Keith hoped they wouldn't encounter anyone. After a few minutes, they came to the main trail. Making every effort to appear as casual as possible, Keith suggested they head to the right. Far ahead, Keith could see that the picnic table he hoped would be empty was indeed waiting for them. As they neared their destination, his mind raced once again. *Does Abbie suspect anything? Will the weather hold out tonight? What if she says "No"?*

Keith had Abbie sit on the bench on the far side of the table, the one that faced the lake. He also told her not to turn around until he had set the table for their dinner. From the picnic basket, Keith pulled out a navy-checked tablecloth and shook it until it fell over the weathered surface of the picnic table. He also drew out two small glass votives and set them in the center. As quickly and quietly as he could, he set the table with paper plates, cutlery, napkins, and the meal he had made. Careful to make sure he did not reach into the wrong pocket and disturb the shell box he'd hidden, he pulled a small box of matches from within the other one.

Only after the candles were lit did Keith walk around in front of Abbie, bow slightly in front of her, and extend his arm, "Madame," he said in a mock European accent. "Your picnic is ready."

Giggling with delight, Abbie played along and, after taking Keith's arm, allowed herself to be led to the bench on the opposite side of the table.

If Abbie's "oohs" and "aahs" were any indication, Keith had hit a home run with his menu selection.

The main course for each was a carefully constructed Black Forest ham sandwich wrapped in waxed paper to appear as if it had come from a select deli. Each plate also held a small bag of potato chips and a plastic container of mixed fresh fruit. A small dish of spinach dip accompanied by cut vegetables in a zippered plastic bag sat on the table between each plate. Bottles of ice-cold sweet tea completed the feast.

While they ate, the reflection of the setting sun spread out before them like a golden carpet. The air was cool, but not too cold. The food was delicious. Thankfully, there was not much of a breeze, and the twin flames flickered cheerily before them in the small votives.

When it was time for dessert, Keith said, "Madame, please close your eyes."

Abbie giggled once again, covered her eyes with her hands, and played along with the ruse. As she did, Keith reached into the cooler, took out two servings of their favorite dessert—tiramisu—and set them on the table.

Touching her gently on the shoulder, he said, "You may open your eyes."

Seeing the treat before her, Abbie exclaimed, affecting a mock French accent of her own, "Oh, monsieur, this dessert is your pièce de résistance!"

Keith's heart swelled at her obvious delight. As they laughed and talked, the setting sun lent its last rays to the end of their memorable meal.

Afterward, Keith suggested they enjoy what was left of the sunset. Abbie helped him spread out the fleece blanket on the ground in front of the picnic table, and then settled down next to him on the soft coverlet. She nestled against him as he put an arm around her shoulder. They sat quietly as the setting sun commanded their full attention.

After a long while, Keith asked quietly, "Are you happy?"

"Decidedly," she answered, her voice soft and relaxed. "We've come so far, Keith—you and I. It's hard to believe how much has happened since we met." She turned to stare up into his eyes.

He held her close, giving her the chance to voice her thoughts.

Gazing once more out into the twilight, Abbie continued, "God has certainly been doing some heavy lifting, removing boulders I never thought could be rolled away from the entrance to my heart. He's cleansed the wounded place deep inside my soul and used your love as the salve to heal it."

Keith could hardly believe the words he heard. In planning this night, he knew where he wanted their conversation to end but wasn't sure how to lead Abbie to that place. However, her unexpected revelation had opened the door, creating the perfect segue to what would come next. He took a deep breath and prayed the Lord would supply what he needed.

"Abbie, ever since the night you told me you loved me, I've thought of nothing else."

Abbie leaned closer to him but said nothing.

Keith continued, choosing his words carefully. "The night you told me you loved me, you said that Mama Dee's shared advice gave you the courage to voice your feelings for me." He brought his hand up from where it rested on her arm and stroked the back of her head gently, feeling the silken strands of her dark hair play against his fingers. "Was there anything else that also gave you courage?"

Abbie sat up straighter and pulled away from him slightly. She shifted her body until she could look directly at Keith's face. "You are a very perceptive man, Mr. Haliday," she began, a shy smile playing at the corners of her mouth. "Yes, there was something else." She reached up and brushed strands of hair behind one ear.

He was thrilled to hear her speak his name.

"I've replayed the events of the day last April that we met in Peter's Chapel a thousand times in my mind. Days before, I spent an afternoon in the sanctuary of Oak Hills Church, crying and asking the Lord to give me another chance with you. How awful I was to you that night you came to see me at my house."

"You had every right to be on your guard," said Keith softly, turning slightly toward her.

"That afternoon at my church, I found a letter that stays tucked within the cover of my Bible, a letter my dad wrote me years ago before his death. Although I'd read his words countless times, it took my reading the letter one more time, with the memory of our argument fresh on my mind, to hear the truth of his words and accept it.

"A line from that letter helped me see what I couldn't before because of my fear and bitterness. 'I pray love—a real love—will find you.'"

There was still enough light from the last glimmer of the sun for Keith to see the tears glistening in Abbie's soft green eyes. "You are that real love, Keith," she said, her voice no louder than a whisper, her words a balm to his lonely heart.

For the longest time, their eyes conveyed feelings too grand for words.

At last, Keith broke the silence. "I have a surprise for you," he said with a twinkle in his eyes and huskiness in his voice. "Close your eyes."

He watched with delight as Abbie, expectant as a child at Christmas, shut her eyes, her dark lashes resting delicately against her creamy skin.

Keith then reached behind him and found the small enameled box where he had placed it earlier. Rising slightly, he knelt on one knee. For a moment longer, he savored the sight before him.

"You may open your eyes," he said.

Abbie opened them to find Keith kneeling in front of her, holding what looked like an opened sea shell in his hand. Inside, she saw a tiny bed of moss, and placed within it was a beautiful diamond ring. A ray of light, a parting gift from the setting sun, enveloped them both and sparkled across the top of the large oval-cut stone as if setting it ablaze with color.

"What is it?" she asked tentatively.

"It's yours," he said as he took the ring from the enameled case.

"What do I do with it?"

"Put it on," Keith said. As he slipped the delicate gold band onto her finger, Keith asked the question Abbie had hoped against hope to hear. "My dearest Abbie, will you marry me?"

"Yes," replied Abbie softly, looking first at the ring now adorning her left hand and then back up at his adoring eyes. "Oh, yes, I will, Keith." She rose to her knees and wrapped her arms around his neck.

Pulling her down to sit beside him on the blanket, he took her face in his hands. "I love you, Abigail Richardson, with all my being, and I'm going to do all in my power to make you the happiest woman on earth." Then he gently kissed her, sweet and tender and full of promise.

———

They only had a few more minutes until it would be time to leave. Keith and Abbie savored the end of this momentous day as they sat, arms wrapped around each other. This little corner of the world seemed to be all theirs as the first evening star twinkled above.

"I want you to know," said Keith, "that the events of this special evening are Drew-approved."

Startled by his comment, Abbie moved back and turned to look at Keith in astonishment. "Drew knew about this?"

"He certainly did," Keith said proudly, drawing her close once more. "In fact, he helped me pick out your ring."

"What am I going to do with you?" exclaimed Abbie as she jabbed him in the ribs. Pure joy enveloped her like a soft blanket.

"'Grow old along with me,'" he said playfully, quoting a line from one of her favorite English poets.

He could feel, rather than see, her smile.

"Abbie," he continued, as they sat in the waning darkness, "there are no guarantees in this life, but I promise that I will love you faithfully until my last dying breath. These past years we've endured have been long and terrible, but God has seen us safely through our dark valleys. No matter what lies ahead, God will be there. We will make it through each day God gives us . . ."

Abbie finished the sentence for him. "With God's help."

A holy hush settled over the couple as they now knew with certainty that no matter the future, they would tackle it together.

Because . . . God would be with them.

ACKNOWLEDGMENTS

Initial ideas for *The Timothy House Chronicles* trilogy came to me twenty-one years ago.

Abbie Richardson, the main character, appeared one day in my imagination and has been there ever since. If you've read Book One, *Abandon Not My Soul,* then you know about the heartbreaking tragedies that upended her life and that of Keith Haliday. You also know some of the reasons that led Abbie to accept a position on the faculty of the residential school, Timothy House.

Book Two, *Through a Dark Valley,* introduces readers to several new characters—DeSean Matthews and C.J. Dykes—and offers greater insight into two of my favorites from Book One—Chloe Minton and Teencie Curtis. Many of the plot lines in this second book posed a challenge as I would now be stepping beyond the bounds of the proverbial writing convention, which says, "Write what you know."

Book Three, *Higher Ground,* is soon to follow and will bring full circle the lessons of love and forgiveness and the belief in the promise of hope that Abbie, Keith, and many others struggled with learning throughout the series.

My deepest gratitude goes to Tami Hutson and the Honorable Staci O'Neal, whose invaluable insights concerning the foster care and juvenile court systems allowed me to create believable plot scenarios. My admiration for your tireless efforts on behalf of at-risk children and youth knows no bounds.

I am especially appreciative to William Lindley and Luke Thompson for your willingness to impart your expertise and professional knowledge regarding the intricacies of law enforcement, which ensured the credibility of specific parts of this story. Thank you for all you have done and continue to do as you stand up for the right in this dark world.

My heartfelt thanks go to Frank Janotta, Hollie Jeffery, Kristy Timmerman, and Nancy Walton for your assistance as I searched for deeper understanding of the intricacies related to the topics of foster care and military life. The examples of integrity and excellence set in your professional careers inspire me.

Though Timothy House is fictional, I have had the pleasure of discovering that schools and family support organizations like it do exist. Sincere appreciation goes to Lance Ragsdale and Jim Wood for helping me build believable and factual accounts regarding the responsibilities of and relationships between faculty and staff at a residential school. Special thanks go to the following for your commitment to creating loving, supportive environments based on biblical models where children can reach their God-given potential: F. Stewart Edwards, Jr., and Lance Ragsdale of French Camp Academy; Jim Wood of Wears Valley Ranch; Myrle Grate and Ron Veazey of Sunnybrook Children's Home; and Shea and Philip Carter of Sunnybrook Cares. Readers will find within the pages of this story a facsimile of each of these special programs.

I am thankful to my dear friend, Martha Stockstill, for your copy edit of the manuscript and for always cheering me on in my writing endeavors.

The prayers of my sweet friends in the Hallowed Hearts Bible study group have energized my pen and kept me connected to the true Source of all imagination. Thank you for your petitions offered on my behalf.

My sincerest thanks go to my publisher and friend, Lawrence Knorr, for having faith in the worth of this story and the value of this book series. Special appreciation goes to my editor, Sarah Peachey, for challenging me to make this story the best it could be. Working with you has been a delight, as you have been an excellent literary guide. A huge debt of gratitude goes to Crystal Devine, Book Designer, for your superb work on the interior components of the book. How grateful I am for the exemplary efforts of all on the Sunbury Press team in bringing *Through a Dark Valley* to life.

As always, my deepest appreciation goes to my better half, Mark. Your belief in my writing abilities, encouragement to employ those skills, and the space you've given me in our marriage to pursue this passion for writing are priceless, treasured gifts.

A special thanks go to my extended family, my greatest supporters.

Most of all, my heart abounds with thanksgiving to my Lord, from whom all blessings flow.

MAKE A DIFFERENCE

Through a Dark Valley welled up from deep within my heart, and although many of these characters and settings may resemble real people and places, they are fictional, mere figments of my imagination. However, the plot lines involving DeSean Matthews and Chloe Minton illustrate the grim reality of unfortunate circumstances that far too many children face. If this story has touched your heart and you would like to make a positive difference in a child's life, here are three schools and/or organizations I can heartily recommend, through which your sincere desire to help another can become a life-changing reality.

French Camp Academy
1 Fine Place
French Camp, MS 39745
(662) 547-6482
https://frenchcamp.org

Sunnybrook Cares
Sunnybrook Children's Home
222 Sunnybrook Road
Ridgeland, MS 39157
(601) 856-6555
https://sunnybrookms.org

Wears Valley Ranch
100 One Fine Place
Sevierville, TN 37862
(865) 429-5437
https://wvr.org

ABOUT THE AUTHOR

The writings of **Sherye S. Green** reflect her journey of faith and explore the heart's inner landscapes. An author, singer, and speaker, she has long been intrigued by the power of words to influence and shape thought and action. A former Miss Mississippi, Sherye has enjoyed two careers—one in business, the other in education. She is the award-winning author of an inspirational novel, *Abandon Not My Soul*; a devotional collection, *Tending the Garden*  *of My Heart: Reflections on Cultivating a Life of Faith*; a World War II survivor memoir, *Surviving Hitler, Evading Stalin: One Woman's Remarkable Escape from Nazi Germany*; and the suicide survivor memoir, *Mission Vigilant: A Mother's Crusade to Stem the Tide of Veteran Suicide*. Sherye and her husband make their home in Mississippi.

For more information, please visit:
www.sheryesimmonsgreen.com

——— ◆ ———

Follow her on Facebook at
Sherye Simmons Green

If this story has moved you and you would recommend it to others, please consider writing a review for *Through a Dark Valley* on Amazon.

Made in the USA
Columbia, SC
25 September 2024

43041394R00155